SWEETLY CURSED

CHAPTER ONE

She rolled over while in a dream. Her lip brushed against his bare shoulder. She awoke thinking her lip had split open causing gushing blood, hit against a stone boulder as she tumbled down rapids. She pulled on her lower lip. It tingled, but no blood. She remembered where she was and smiled blissfully. She lay next to her fiancé Steve. They were both naked. They lay in a hay loft in a barn after the wedding of Steve's college friend Chad.

Shit we fell asleep Julie thought. *How'd we fall asleep? That wasn't supposed to happen.* Her mind questioned but her body knew the answer. After euphoric explosions and sweet sexual release that Niagara Falls powerful, the overwhelmed body has to shut down and reload in order to recalibrate what the usual reality of things feels like. Loose itchy hay stuck to her damp back; before sleep the hay had looked like gold and felt like the burning pink cloud pinned to the sunset she had seen as she had run, hand in hand, with Steve towards the barn; a playful spontaneous champagne buzzed escape from the dwindling party to satisfy carnal lust. He slowly opened his sleepy, heavy eyes and peered into her eyes. The full moon out the barn window love, distant one sided romances and sad and embarrassing infatuations; only pretty sandcastles washed away and melted into the tide. Steve was a steel tower one hundred stories high, a Casino in one story (there's always a gamble in every relationship, but gambling can be fun and worth it, especially when you feel a winner). She had thought she had an orgasm before Steve but he made her realize she hadn't really; or not the *glitter from exploded stars rushing through your bloodstream* way his touch could make her feel. While musing over him she sometimes stopped herself, ashamed that she allowed herself to indulge in too many romance-novel type clichés; putting people on pedestals is unfair after all; she knew this from personal past experiences dealing with some cute, mostly creepy boys basically *worshiping* her. Yet other times she allowed herself to indulge in the possibility that more truth than fantasy was contained in Steve's near perfectness. Handsome, funny, bold, young at twenty four, already with a good solid job at a bank doing noble work mostly in loans and fraud; in school, pursuing an MBA in finance. (Some of her friends who were attracted to rebel types thought he was a little boring but she found him thrilling. Those same friends would agree that he was also handsome, charming, and *perfect* [there's that word again] for her; quick to qualify their opinion that they didn't think *she* was dull or anything).

Julie Goodwin and Steve Williams had met at a swanky New Years Eve party at the EMP museum in downtown Seattle, while she was home from Stanford over Christmas break. She had caught his eye; she and her friends had noticed him checking her out and she felt flattered and intrigued. They instantly clicked; he said she looked like Arielle in her sparkling sea-foam green dress, she said he looked like Prince Eric. He had asked *are we both Disney dorks* and she had replied *don't tell anyone, I'm trying to keep my edgy-cool vibe;* both later would admit that, through the pulsating pumping electronic beats the *Little*

Mermaid ballad *Kiss the Girl* had swam through their heads at that moment. They had their first kiss at midnight. They got together physically nearly every weekend, him visiting her at Stanford, her trekking up to Seattle. After Julie graduated with a B.A. in English literature she moved back to the Puget Sound area and begun a promising job at a top interior design firm. Their relationship accelerated. He purposed during a stroll along the sand at Golden Gardens Park; he had arranged for her to find a large pink clam; she picked it up, opened it and gasped at the sight of the diamond ring. She spun and looked down and saw him on one knee, beaming up at her. Perfect. A sensation of gratitude towards the universe welled up in here. She felt as sure as she had ever felt anything before: this was meant to be.

Chad and Jessie's wedding was the first wedding they had attended together as an engaged couple. The barn sex had been mind blowing.

"Once more?" Steve suggested.

"Do that thing you do," she playfully recommended.

"What thing?"

"Where you turn fluffy pillow talk into the dirtiest smut."

He laughed again. "I'm a hummingbird heart racing a billion beats a minute, in desperate want of the nectar from your pussy flower."

Julie laughed. "Now *that's* fucking poetry."

"Stand up," Steve said. "I want to see the moonlight caress your curves."

She obeyed. She posed. He ogled her, the silver moonlight spilled over her generous and taut feminine shapes. *I want to live in this moment forever* Steve thought. *Freeze this image. Is it possible for her to look any sexier than now? She is a goddess. God I'm so lucky.*

"Flutter over here hummingbird," she cooed.

He obeyed. She clutched his hair in tight fists to keep her quivering legs from giving out as he worked on her. They then switched positions and she returned the favor. He held off and spun her around and climaxed inside her. They lay back over the hay, panting, uttering gibberish exaltations and snuggled together.

"It's funny," Julie said. "Night, dark, in a barn, surrounded by nature; I'd normally be afraid in a setting like this. This is horror movie set stuff here. But I feel so safe, so protected, so warm, so happy."

"What do you fear?" he asked.

She smirked, unsure if he were being playfully frivolous, tossing out a cliché pillow talk type *deep* question or making fun of pillow talk deep questions. But she decided to take his query more seriously than maybe he intended.

"That it's all too perfect," she answered. "That it can't be so good. This good. Forever."

He thought this over. She *had* given a more serious answer than he had intended. Sometimes she shocked him with her blunt honesty and her ability to say so much, give him so much to think about, with so few words. In contrast, some of his past girlfriends could natter on for hours with phrases and thoughts so vapidly light they'd float away before even having the chance to enter his brain. Julie had just uttered a valid and troubling fear. What if we're at a peak and it's all downhill from here?

"Pledge to always stay in the moment," Steve suggested.

"I solemnly vow," Julie answered teasingly through a smile, riffing off of the wedding ceremony they had witnessed earlier. "What do you fear?" she asked.

"Nothing," he said, wanting to sound brash and brave. Yet a list ran through his mind. *Fear of not making enough money. That you'll leave me for someone rich, better looking. You could probably have anyone; athlete, actor, celebrity. Yes, I know it's an irrational fear, you're not that superficial, but I saw you reading that romance novel about the alpha male billionaire. I can't shake the feeling that that's what all women, including you, really want. Fear of not being good enough, and even that I have this fear may be proof that I'm not good enough. Yet I can't, I won't pretend with you or the world; I can't live that way.* "I love you," he said.

It was just the twelfth time in their three year relationship she had heard him say this out loud. She had kept a tally. They weren't the type to use the phrase as abundantly and cheaply as saying *hello* and *good-by.*

"I love you too," she answered.

"We should probably go," he said.

They stood up and exchanged shy glances over their glistening naked bodies again, still shockingly exposed in the dim light. They then searched in the darkness for their cloths. His black slacks, tan jacket, white shirt and purple Italian silk tie lay crumpled next to her red backless lace crochet dress and pink panties. As Julie reached for her dress she felt cold little paws scurry over her hand. She shrieked and snapped her hand back.

"A mouse," Steve said. He reached into his jacket pocket. "Thank god, my phone's still there." He turned on his phone and tapped on the flashlight app. They both winced at the sudden brightness. They used the light to finish dressing and search for Julie's gold earrings and necklace.

They climbed down the rickety ladder to the main floor of the barn. The wood below them creaked as they stepped. Julie spit away a spider-web strand which had somehow gotten in her mouth.

"Funny how something so Amish quaint and cute can turn so Halloween-y creepy," Julie said, surveying the rusty farm tools leaning against the wood wall.

"You no longer feel protected?" Steve teased, squeezing her with his left arm as his right hand held the phone light.

"I'm still floating," Julie said breathily back. Although truthfully it did jolt her how quickly the warm ooze of after sex comfort seeped out of her as she had descended down the hay loft. She had never been the jittery type, yet the nagging urge to leave the barn grew more urgent, like the feeling of wanting to flee a dark room where you suspect a killer is lurking. She brushed off her fright as irrational; of course it's irrational; the only factor which transforms an old Amish barn from being cute and quaint to sinisterly scary is mood lighting and imagination.

Steve also felt a strange unexplainable and irrational fright which he tried to dismiss. He didn't believe in ghosts. The ugly, heavy nauseous feeling which seized him, robbing him of the tingling after sex glow, must have some non paranormal explanation; maybe some nearby rat carcass or spider egg nest.

A demonic sounding hiss screeched loudly. Julie shrieked and tensed, her fingernails clawing Steve's biceps. He jolted and swung the light towards the sound. Two green tinged quarter sized eyes shined back. The orange bob tailed calico cat hissed again, showing fangs, then ran off, knocking over a pitchfork. The iPhone light struck a glossy surface leaning against the wall next to the pitchfork. Julie and Steve looked at it, curious, immobilized by the competing forces of wanting to leave and wanting to move towards the object. Steve stepped back while Julie stepped forward, then Julie turned towards the exit while Steve moved towards the object. They exhaled awkward giggles like two strangers twice blocking each other as they pass along a sidewalk.

"Just see what it is, quickly," Julie suggested.

"Curiosity killed the cat," Steve said.

"The cat ran away—just go, we can try and exchange witty banter in the car later," Julie said, slapping Steve's shoulder.

Steve walked briskly towards the object. He picked it up with his left hand.

"What is it?" Julie asked.

"A book," Steve answered. He wiped his thumb across the glossy cover. "A paperback. Thin. There's no dust on it."

"What's it called?"

"If you read this you will die," Steve read.

Julie let out a cackle.

"What?" Steve asked through a smile. He loved her laugh, especially when it burst out with the suddenness of a popped balloon.

"I just find that really funny. Like that *Ring* movie right? *If you watch this you will die.*"

"Anyways, that's weird," Steve said. He leaned down to place the black book back where he had picked it up. Then he stopped. "Do you want it?"

"Um… not really?"

"Me either," Steve said. He couldn't release his grasp as if the slick cover were flypaper glue. *Maybe this thing is valuable* he thought, and then wondered *why would it be; why'd I even think that; this isn't like some buried pirate treasure or anything.* He decided he'd toss it at Julie. If she caught it, maybe she'd keep it for a day; if she let it drop, they'd leave it. "Heads up."

She saw the book float through the air towards her. Although not a total frilly girly girl, she never developed expert catching reflexes. She flinched and turned her shoulder towards the hurled object. It hit her chest, landed in her arm, and slid in her hand. She looked at the cover and read the title. It didn't seem quite so funny, reading the title compared with hearing it said out loud. *If you read this you will die.* Steve was right; no dust on it. The cover felt cool. She flipped through the pages; they felt warm like they've been freshly xeroxed. She held it to her nose and sniffed. She liked the smell; fresh glue and ink. Strange. Very strange. Steve placed his hand on the small of her back, startling her.

"Let's get out of here," he said.

recognized the girl as Zelda, Chad's raven haired little sister. Zelda; great name, cute name for a precocious child and an elegant adult; underused due to the only famous Zelda, the jazz age writer's wife, being most famous for going crazy. Still, both Steve and Julie had it on their *future baby names* lists. Her cheeks were smeared with once damp now dry heavy mascara, giving the impression of war paint.

"Well if it isn't the cute wittle barf bunnies back from a screw," Zelda spit with slurred speech. "Everyone hates you, you know. *Everyone!*"

"Excuse me?" Julie challenged.

"She's drunk," Steve observed.

"Just drunk enough to tell the truth. I heard you grunting up their like pigs. Screwing like banshees. Then it was quiet. We thought you'd fucked yourself dead." She then burped out a laugh.

Julie looked at her feet in embarrassment. Had they been loud? She hadn't thought so, but they both had been wrapped up in the moment. She thought the barn distant enough from the main thinning out gathering that they'd be secluded, safe from potential eavesdroppers. Yet also, the quasi-public outdoor setting had also been part of the appeal and thrill; the fear of getting caught.

"Rich little plastic Ken and Malibu Barbie. Dull perfect little dolls. Hump buddies," Zelda barked, then added in a slurred mumble more to herself: *everybody hates you.*

"Okay, you know what?" Julie began, tensing and stepping forward. She hated blonde resentment and stereotypes; a major pet peeve being called *Barbie* and *plastic*. Guess what, you *can* have more fun, *and* be smart. Her hair grew naturally thick and gold. Not like she had some *little princess* upbringing, despite being blessed with a monetarily successful father; her parents divorced when she was twelve, she's had a disproportionately large number of pet dogs and fish die on her in unnatural freak accidents, she dealt with jealous *mean girls* drama, and her older sister Candice had spent time in a mental institution for, among other things, thinking she had magical powers and could talk to crows. Stressful stuff!

Steve held her back. "It's not worth it," he said. He turned towards Zelda. "You don't have your keys do you?" he asked, implying that she should not drive while drunk.

"Why do you think I'm still here?" Zelda said snidely. "Have you told your dumb blonde doll about us yet?"

Shit Steve thought.

"We made out at a frat party when I was underage. I thought I love you, you know. You broke my heart."

"She's drunk," Steve said.

"Let's just go," Julie said.

They walked past Zelda quickly yet gingerly, like passing a homeless person on a sidewalk who you fear might spit on you. Steve opened the door for Julie then walked to the drives side and got in. He started the car. "Go Outside," by the Cults played. He drove over the gravel road and merged onto the main paved street.

"It was a beautiful evening," Julie said. "Chad and Jessie were great. The cake and DJ were good. The flower children were cute. Romance, laughs, good food, such a *our own killing. We'll hire people for that.* Ha-ha, munch, munch.

Although Steve and Julie had decided not to move in together until after they married, they had, however, managed to live on the same street, called Fortune Lane, up the hill a few miles from the wharf. They each rented a house they shared with three roommates; Julie's roommates were named Sarah, Melissa and Alice. There was a doughnut, sandwich and coffee shop called 'Sweetly Cursed' on the corner of their street open twenty four hours. Steve parked by her house.

"What some coffee?" he asked.

"It's nearly 5:00am," she said.

"Time to make the doughnuts," Steve joked.

"I could sleep for days," Julie declared. She had nearly slept during the ride but pesky troubling thoughts had kept her awake. She desperately wanted a shower. Not a sexy shower with Steve, but a solitary long hot shower, where one allows the spray to also posses symbolic properties of washing away the past; let her creeping jealous thoughts of Zelda and the strange prick of unexplainable fear she felt in the barn be scrubbed and fall down the drain along with the sudsy water and shampoo. And then sleep to dream only pleasant things.

Steve wanted to hear her laugh before she left. Her laugh delighted him and reassured him everything was fine and would be well; she's not annoyed or agitated at him, she still loved him. He adopted the voice of the *boorish sexists wedding comedy guy,* a character he loosely developed a few days before Chad's wedding: "After a fight, a wife says to her husband, 'I was a fool when I married you'. And then the husband goes, 'yeah I know, but I was blinded by love so didn't notice. Ba-da-bing, here's to Chad and Jessie."

Julie faked a laugh. She had pretended to find this character funnier than she actually had. He was so handsome.

"Have you heard about the guy who sent a telegram out asking for a wife? He got back a hundred letters the next day from guys saying 'here, take mine'."

"Ugh. Groan. Booo," Julie uttered teasingly.

"It's a work in progress. Fine tuning it for my *Saturday Night Live* audition," Steve teased back.

Julie leaned over the seat and kissed him. "Tomorrow?"

"Tomorrow," Steve echoed. He almost said *I love you* again but held off, not wanting to be cheesy and believing that overuse of the phrase cheapens it. If he were to say something completely honest to her in that moment it would be something like: thank you for being so gorgeous, with your soft chin, big eyes, generous lips and staying so fit and getting so naked in front of me and letting me plunge my gross lance of a dick up your vaginal canal so forcibly repeatedly; you really have no idea how great all that is; how good it feels; tonight, one of the best ever.

She opened the door and stepped out. She stepped quickly towards her front door. Steve would usually walk her to her door, old fashioned gentleman like, but he too felt tired. She turned to wave good-by then entered. She left her Gucci handbag on her car seat.

Steve didn't go back into his car until the next day, Sunday evening, to head to the gym. He saw the book resting on top of Julie's bag. *Weird,* he thought. *Why would she take out that book and place it there? Does that mean she wants me to have it? Wants me to read it? Maybe she did it as a joke. I don't remember hearing her unzip her purse before she got out of the car.* He hadn't seen her yet that day; both slept in until late afternoon. If she had her phone in her bag, that'd explain why she didn't answer any texts though, he reasoned. He decided he'd return her purse to her after his workout. He worked on his core, his quads, and his biceps, grunting, sweating, feeling the burn. Since his relationship with Julie bloomed, he kept a hard body more for her than for his own vanity, or so he told himself. She was hot, he had to keep up, in order to remain a synched up attractive couple, whom others envied. Although, nabbing and keeping a hot girlfriend turned fiancé can also be vanity and ego boosters as well.

Steve showered at the gym. He couldn't help to notice when attractive female gym members checked him out. It flattered him. He didn't have too bulky of a body; not like professional body builders; more the lean six pack abs male model physic; it took work to maintain and he took some pride in the work (always mindful to never appear vain or meat-headed or superficial, which meant flexing and checking himself in the mirror only discretely when no one he cared about was watching).

Steve walked to Julie's front door, holding her purse. The book still lay on his seat. He hadn't wanted to touch it. He had a key but due to her having roommates he usually knocked. Julie's roommate Sarah opened the door; a small bottled blonde girl who he suspected had a crush on him. She smiled brightly and let him in. "Julie!" she called.

Julie bounced down the stairs. "You have my purse?"

Steve handed her the bag. They exchanged a light kiss while Sarah looked. Julie zipped open her purse and dug out her iPhone. "Thank god," she said. "Living without this thing is like waking up without hands."

"You left the other thing in the car," Steve said.

"What other thing?"

"You know… the book from the barn. *You will die if you read this.*"

"What are you guys talking about?" Sarah asked.

"Oh. I totally forgot about that," Julie said.

"Do you want me to get it?" Steve asked hopefully.

"Um… no, that's okay. You read it and tell me if it's any good or not first."

"You guys are so weird. You have the strangest inside jokes of any couple I know," Sarah said.

Steve and Julie smiled at each other.

"I'll microwave some Quesada's," Julie said.

"Sounds good," Steve replied. "You guys still have that salsa?"

"I bought some more of the kind you like," Julie said.

"It is really good; glad you guys turned me on to that stuff," Sarah interjected.

"Game night or TV?" Julie asked.

"I feel like just chilling," Steve answered. "Although if you feel like playing Rook or Gin-Rummy. There's nothing pressing I really want to watch."

"I feel like just chilling too," Julie said. "*Mad Men* is over, unfortunately, but I think maybe the new *Walking Dead* spinoff starts tonight."

"Zombies totally freak me out," Sarah said. "Mind if I chill with you guys?"

Steve reluctantly went back to his bed in his own house after *Jon Oliver* on HBO. Not that he had an unsuitable urge for sex again; just cuddling with Julie into sleep offered its own welcoming pleasantness. Leaving her at night did give him the pang of longing to be married already, which, he figured, was a good thing to feel.

He got back in his car the next morning wearing his suit and tie to start the work week. There it was, still sitting on the passenger seat next to him like a severed head, the black book. *If you read this you will die.* Such a silly title; dumb even, Steve thought. A stupid reverse psychology attempt: a dare, in order to try and lure any potential readers in. Are you brave enough? Aren't you curious? No? In the afternoon while at his desk he typed into his work computer, quickly with trepidation, the title of the book into Google. He paused before clicking the search button. There are about 643,000,000 results to this search, Google told him. The top of the list was a wiki how article titled: "How not to get creeped out by a chain letter." He felt a bit silly; there was nothing more cryptic about the title that any other silly, trying to be spooky 'chain letter warning' thing, which were once kind of a fad way back when MySpace still ruled, he recalled; blog messages warning of horrible things to happen unless some task or dare is accomplished and the blog post is passed on to five other people. Kids are always trying to conjure silly and dumb ways to spook and creep each other out; the latest fad using the phenomenon of gravity and pencil stacking to suggest you're communicating with a demon child named Charlie. Other search results were a series of blog and Facebook posts beginning with: "Carry on reading! Or you will die". Apparently there's some ghost Clarissa, (a little girl, obviously, because kid ghosts are the creepiest kinds, just as premature child deaths are the saddest) or something who just hates it when people don't finish something they begin reading and then haunts them and kills them. Maybe Clarissa was a self published author, like Chad's friend Trevor, who killed herself because nobody liked her books? *You don't understand,* her spirit screams at lazy readers as they cower under covers, *this is fucking poetry man!* Steve felt silly that he had let some book with a kid's game title creep him out, even just a little bit. How absurd. Near the bottom of the first page of the search results was a Paul Krugman blog from January 7th 2011, nearly five years ago, titled "If you Read this Blog Post, You Will Die." Steve clicked on it and read the blurb sized blog entry: Paul attacking absurdist accusations against the ACA, the first line after the headline being, 'of course, if you don't read this, you'll eventually die too'. It offered another indictment against the title of the book lying in his car: read or not, you'll eventually die anyways. The thing could just as well be called *if you don't read this you will die.* Everyone will die. He went on to Amazon and typed in the title. No books with that title appeared. There was no author name on the cover.

He got back in his Bentley after work, around 6. He looked down at the book, his little traveling companion. *You're more little frog than severed head, aren't you* he thought. He drove home. He reached and put his hand on the book. It felt hot. Not so strange; it was summer after all, sun heat intensifying through windows turns cars into ovens. It also felt sticky: again, heat can change texture. But should it feel this hot and this sticky, Steve wondered. It seemed to cling to his hand not by being sticky but by electricity. He had had a large lunch, eating a steak and shrimp combo platter at Sizzler with a client (the client's choice) and didn't feel particularly hungry. He greeted his roommates playing *Call of Duty* in the living room and then went upstairs. He flopped on his bed, opened the book and began to read.

CHAPTER THREE

(Contents of the slim black book and some of Steve's thoughts while reading.)

Prelude

Your eyes have laid on the words on this page and so it is all ready too late. You will die in fourteen days; the oath is made, it is sealed in bloods fate.

Let me reiterate: your eyes are locked on these words and so you have opened a door and so in fourteen days from this day on you will be no more. Fourteen days of hell will pass to end in gore, and at last you will be no more.

The spell has been cast, you cannot turn away, and just as you are compelled to read till the last page, in fourteen days you will have lived your last day. There is now nothing you can do. Dark sorcery is real and here is the proof.

A bit redundant, Steve thought. Rather silly; or, a lot silly actually. Stupid book, I don't have to read you. In fact, I won't read you; I don't like your style or your premise. He smirked at his thoughts: having an imagined conversation with this bossy book. Are you really trying to rhyme? Not very well; not a very skilled poet behind these words. Was it trying to open with some type of hook? Compel you to read further to find out just what the hell this is? Is it going for some reverse psychology dare trick, the way some children's books do, such as warning *don't you dare read this,* to which the juvenile reader is supposed to react *oh yeah, you can't tell me what to do, I'm brave, I'm going to continue reading you, you dumb book.* He flipped ahead. After about the first twenty pages dribbled with ink followed a hundred or so completely blank sheets of paper. He had to guess; the pages weren't numbered. How weird. He continued to read the prelude starting where he left off:

Seven afflictions will inhabit and inflict your soul; seven diseases will corrode your soul to the point that you wish to live no more. Seven trials will now commence and after the seventh your breath will cease hence. You cannot fight it; there is no defense. It has begun and so it is already done and so you are done.

Two days each for two weeks, the first affliction will be jealousy, followed by two days of lust, then two days of disgust will lead to two days of rage; it cannot be stopped, you are engaged. Followed by rage will come two days of stupidity, how far the mind sinks now that you've begun to read. Two days of stupidity followed by two days of self-pity, then soon will come final rest. The last two days of life will be filled with depression and then finally death.

People come to believe many a strange thing, but in this trust me, it will come to pass, because you have begun to read, beginning tomorrow on the fourteenth day you will live your last. You think you can change it, think again; the spell cannot be undone, it has begun and so it will end.

Rare is the book that brags about making you stupider after you've read it, thought Steve, somewhat bemused, somewhat, against his better judgment, intrigued.   He turned the page and continued to read

.

CHAPTER ONE

FIRST TRIAL: JEALOUSY

The monster with green eyes loves to spy, it is never satisfied, it thirsts with greed, it burns with envy, it is very petty. The green eyed monster is what you will be.

Here is a story: a man wants what he does not deserve; he sees what others have and he is lured; he is unsatisfied, unhappy with his lot; he sees their happiness in their riches and he wants what they got. He wants her but she is gold and he is muddy slush; his soul stirs and aches in the want; his soul becomes destroyed and crushed.

The green eyed monster lurks in you and he is let out; now you know how it feels to feel you are constantly without. The green eyed monster always asks why not me, he cannot see truth, he twists reality, he thinks he deserves what cannot be, he thinks he alone should be the one to be lucky. He is full of resentment; he wonders where his life went wrong; he laments; his soul screams, it should be me; he thinks there is a personal injustice done; the green eyed monsters smile is always forced and faked; he never has fun; he always wants to take, he never feels he has won.

You are smitten by this monster of jealousy because you have read what is written, so now in you dwells the spell seed, you have been bitten indeed.

Jealousy is not only the desperate want of what personally cannot be, brought by delusions of belief, but allowing this lacking to make one feel angry. Yet true rage will be delayed until the seventh day, the spell at halfway, and it will be followed by stupidity.

Here is another story, take heed and read carefully; a girl will also read this whose name ends with 'e'; for two days she too will also be afflicted by extreme jealousy. She will be clingy, needy and belittling. Both your souls, you young lovers, are wilting.

Steve stopped reading. How did the 'green eyed monster' become symbolic of jealousy, he wondered. He vaguely recalled seeing something on TV long ago which provided the answer; Persians or Pagans put some green emerald on their door, which looked like an eye, to ward against some evil spirit of envy or something. He made a mental note to maybe Google that if he were still curious about it later; he guessed he wouldn't be; he really didn't care. He realized that the constant 'e' refrain in the loose and sloppy rhyming attempts, could also work with 'Steve' and 'Julie'. The writing was dense. Reading it made him feel woozy. He decided that he wouldn't put much thought or effort into trying to understand it. He'd just gloss over the words. Julie, an English major, once tried to show him how to read and appreciate poetry. Don't get frustrated trying to decipher it. It's meant to provoke your emotions more than your mind, like an abstract painting means to illicit a mood rather than convey reality. The goal of this book was obviously to try and disturb him. Was it working? He wasn't sure; he wanted to read until the end to determine. He felt compelled to read further.

Chapter Two

Trial Two: Lust

Lust wants, lust takes, lust is hungry, lust is ready, lust sweats, it demands satisfaction, it is greedy. Lust is all in and for the body and mind, the soul too can partake if it helps to make it great, a debauchery three way; fantasy is a lubricant to get there, climax after climax. The body tingles with it, it shakes, lust turns men into animals, feathered snakes, wanting to partake. All else fades away but physical want, to look, to lick, to taste. Lust is full of shame but it ignores shame and blame it drives men insane. It is a drug, it is not love, it makes the body quake and shake in want and pleasure, to get to the hit those in the rush of lust will go to any measure. Lust corrodes all worthy goals; Lust is a lack of self control.

Lust is good but make no mistake, it can be a disease, just like anything, when it is indulged too great; it is like the high of a drug and like a drug, the abuse of it takes away parts of you, parts of your soul, your reason, your clarity, your pure goals, your sanity, among many other things. Lust is base. It is desire untamed. When it overflows uncontrolled it changes you; you are not the same. You are a monster willing to debase. Do anything, everything gross and good and damned just for the taste; if lust doesn't go away, it is a curse, make no mistake; soon you will be in the hearse after everything you've really loved is taken away, ruined by lust, you wish not to, but pricked, there is no stopping, you simply must.

Lust drowns and sinks in seas of gluttony; lust is never satisfied, always hungry. Lust can be fun, is usually fun, at first, but it is dumb, does not use the brain, and the wreckage it causes brings eternal pains and eternal flames making change for the worse; soon you will be in a hearse with a body no more, a ghost unable to feel flesh or bleed or cause gore, so take your fill now, feel all for soon you will be gone, to hell for your lack of self control, body over soul, you must pay for all your wrongs and abuses; you have read this and been warned, you have no excuses.

Lust puts you in a cage, you want, you want, you want, you can't escape. Make no mistake, it is a curse to be this way, to live life so low you always want to escape, to feel so bad you always want to scrape away the dull and the pain, seeking physical pleasure always; you are a monster, a lust monster, that is an ugliness, make no mistake. You cannot be truly healthy this way.

Quite preachy, Steve thought, dismissively, about the weird text he just read. He felt pretty sure the loopy text contradicted itself, sometimes in the same sentence, claiming that lust is brainless and soulless, yet also claims that the brain and soul can be used in a *debauchery three-way*. Lust is good and fun, the text claims, but also horrible and ruinous, bad and painful. He thought of the saying: what's the difference between a sex addict and someone who enjoys sex? Guilt. That wasn't exact; it was something like that. The idea behind it being, if no one is hurt by it, than lust and sex shouldn't be guilt inducing; it doesn't have to be life ruining or something needing to be overcome through group therapy, necessarily. He once had a friend who argued that much of guilt is delivered from ancient religious constructs designed to extract money from the weak willed made to be frightened of hell, in order to make priests rich. Self manufactured guilt, this college friend claimed, can be more damaging and soul crushing than the actual *sin,* which supposedly is the sole culprit to earthly and eternal ruin. The dejected feelings of crippling worthlessness and the life stymied self torture comes from self manufactured inner guilt, not from some outside supernatural godly punishment. His thoughts on lust and sex were complicated, entangled in the conservative religiosity imbedded in him since a child. Pausing to consider it for too long would just wrap him up in tangled restricting weeds, wasting time without any real enlightening conclusion emerging. The gibberish on the page scrambled his thoughts, causing them to also be incoherent. He had cheated on past girlfriends before, but his guilt for doing so didn't last too long because none of his past romantic relationships had been as serious as was his with Julie. Also some of the girls he cheated with had, in retrospect, been worth the heartache. He continued reading:

Lust is an addiction, it enslaves, lust is an affliction, it misbehaves. Lust is a disease, it overpowers all other needs, it brings you to your knees, it saps your self control, it erodes your soul. Lust is a fire, unquenchable desire, it blazes bright, yet blackens what's right, scorching earth so nothing can grow, lust shrinks the soul, it shatters worthy goals. Lust is selfish and sad; it will drive you mad, although in the moment you feel glad.

The text continued on like that for a few more pages. The prose got even worse when it ventured towards "women's lust": *Women's lust erodes trust, it's emotionally fed, it gushes red, it bleeds out when bled, it lurks in the bed.* After reading the chapter Steve's initial reaction was that it made him want to masturbate. Not because there was any 'sexy' imagery or action artfully, carefully and seductively detailed and laid out. Self-pleasuring is a temporary escape from boredom, a release from stress, pressure and frustration, and that lust "chapter" had made him feel pretty frustrated, trying to make sense of it. It'd be nice, he thought, to take a break, relax, and release some of the tension and frustration that this book caused him so far. Basic premise: lust is bad, because you just read this now you'll be cursed by insatiable lust for two days, and oh yeah, did I mention that after fourteen days you'll be dead? I did? Well I'll mention it again.

Steve recalled an uncomfortable church talk he was once forced to sit through. The topic was the sin of lust, specifically masturbation. The preacher claimed that it is bad because it ignores the soul and only concentrates on the flesh. Even as an eleven year old boy Steve had not completely bought that argument. He had loved and lusted a Victoria Secret model, and it wasn't just her beauty which excited him; he watched videos of her and read her interviews. Her ebullient and bright personality made him like her more, caused the lusting and loving to feel better to him. Was this preacher trying to argue that it's okay if you masturbate to someone's 'soul'? (You get glimpses of a soul through voice, personality, talents, movements, thoughts, smell, a glint in the eye and other non-physical yet capable of being sexy attributes.) The preacher then made the case that lust is not a victimless crime, because it hurts your wives or girlfriends. Steve didn't have a girlfriend at the time. He just rolled his eyes at the whole thing. Despite the preachers hell-fire admonishing Steve hadn't really thought that he committed 'lust sin' an abnormal unhealthy amount. Sure, it causes problems for some, the claim that it ruins some people's lives and relationships are valid for some, but not for him.

The next chapter was about the trial of disgust which he'd be afflicted with after lust, because he was reading the stupid thing. *Why am I still reading this,* Steve thought multiple times, yet he continued to peruse. He enjoyed some of it; the weirdness of it. He usually found weird things distasteful. Partially enjoying this thing, enough to continue with it, betrayed his usual nature. The purpose of the 'Disgust' chapter, other than hammering the 'you'll die' refrain to death, seemed to be to make the reader want to barf; a lot of mentions of maggots and rotting flesh and types of slime, gross odors and fecal matter, still presented in twisted and tortured random rhyming schemes. *Vomiting over maggot squirming in bloody rancid flesh/ Disgust is this test/ Disgusted over the way of the earth/ Disgusted even by her/Bones and saggy flesh/ Standing in shit wearing a urine soaked dress/ It is hard to get through this test...* that kind of thing, for pages. *A world full of hate, war, insanity, stupidity, and no love is one of disgust/ and so you will see you must leave it, you must... Everywhere there is no one and nothing you can trust, and so in disgust you leave everything, you must... What if your lover next to you in bed woke up with a cockroach head, could you still love such a hideous and disgusting thing, although all else in body and mind it were a human being, of course you would not, and so true love falls apart, disgust can ruin everything...* The disgust chapter did tamper down his gurgling horny itches from reading the 'lust' chapter. But not completely. He decided after he read the book he'd reward himself by allowing himself to view online porn, some cute Playboy Playmate shower strip video, nothing nasty, no big cocks or squirts. He hadn't looked at online porn in months. He hadn't really needed to. Wasn't the purpose of some of the romance novels Julie read basically to titillate the straight female brain the same way images of hot and supple wet nude girls titillated the straight male's brain? Don't they both contain about the same amount of fantasy?

While reading through the next chapter, about the 'rage trial' an epiphany struck him: this was trying to be like beatnik stream-of-conscious poetry stuff, right? With a more firm context for this manuscript, he eased into it better, going with the flow of the words rather than against.

Rage boils, it wants, stirs, and creates trouble, it sees red, it wants to kill dead, it breaks beyond the rational of the head. It wants revenge, right or wrong be damned, it is insanity, it damns a man. It goes beyond perceived injustices, for there is no room for clear thinking involved, rage is lizard brained, it is the opposite of evolved, like lust it sees only red, you will have it for this thing you have read and soon you will be dead.

Rage grits teeth, it stomps over beliefs, it finds no relief till destruction is had, rage is beyond anger, it is a form of stupidity, it is always bad. Rage does not think, it only sinks. Rage is written on this page and it will bleed out you, and you are doomed, you will come to believe, there is no reprieve.

Rage makes the blood flow and heart rate increase, just like lust, you think rage makes you strong but it really makes you weak and the least for you can't think clearly, you slide into stupidity, and this begins the end of all of us.

Rage is very scary.

Steve began to see the humor in the prose and no longer felt it as menacing or disturbing. There is absurdity in exaggerations, empty threats (from a book! What can a book do?) in trying so hard and failing, to creep him out. This whole book is a failure, he thought, mid way through the text. You've not worked on me; I've won. You don't creep me out; you're stupid. He no longer felt quite as horny. Maybe I won't watch porn after I'm done with this after all, he thought. He hypocritically thought it morally better to view videos of high quality nude shoots without paying. Paying meant that you financially supported pron. There were plenty of places to see the Playboy videos, with the prettiest best paid nude models (by company reputation anyways) stripping, posing, stretching, strutting, spinning and gallivanting in sometimes scenic locations to sometimes slick fitting songs, for free, although one wasn't 'supposed' to be able to. He felt too tired for the needed shower a good porn watch requires after. The desire to jack off was like a butterfly he watched float away on a warm wind, no longer wanting to rev up the energy to chase it. He knew that Julie didn't like him watching porn. The book made for good bedtime reading; it was making him sleepy. At least the 'chapters' were getting even shorter, as if the author also grew tired, drained by the effort, as he scrawled along.

Stupidity is silly and can delight, but to realize stupidity will be the cause of mankind's fall, creates quite the fright. Stupidity is ignoring facts because they irritate, stupidity is reading the warning sign yet still walking through the gate, and now doom awaits, it is too late. How could we be so stupid, we collectively yell; we were stupid, so we fail. You are stupid, will be afflicted with the dumb disease, for two days, and you will beg for this all to end, your life, while on your knees. Stupidity is not just being wrong, stupidity is being wrong yet still shouting your stupid song with delirious glee; we were all so stupid, you most of all, so very, very, very.

Verily, stupidity makes you trip, there you sit, fallen, you stupid idiot, look at what you've done, you were wrong you didn't care, you were wrong you didn't want to become aware, now all is doomed, you are doomed, and there is nowhere to run; the end is soon, it's already begun. Stupidity is in your head, so now soon you will be dead. It will be in pain, enough so that even you'll feel it and know it in your stupid brain.

Stupidity is seething into complacency when complacency is the disease which will cause you to cease being, yet still you agree.

Again, funny, Steve thought. Not in the laugh out loud way, of course. Not directly. The more he read the 'funnier' and less menacing this book appeared. The longer it went the more ridiculous it became.

He finished the book, the last sentence (a semicolon heavy run-on of course) just a reiteration of everything it was saying before: *Jealousy, lust, disgust, rage, stupidity, self-pity, then depression and finally death, this is what comes next; Seven trials each one to last two days will now on you inflict, and after fourteen days death you will wish, and you will get your wish, you will be dead, because of this book which has just been read; and so as this book comes to an end, it is also your end.* He placed it down on the bedside table. *What the hell did I just read,* he wondered. He heard his roommates scream in celebration, like they just witnessed Russell Wilson throw the game winning touchdown in the Superbowl. Maybe they just won *Call of Duty.* Sometimes he envied their bachelorhood status (technically he was still a bachelor, but being engaged is like being in bachelor limbo, where the definition sill fits, without any of the perks; although, being engaged was its own hazy wonderful world). He wondered if he were leaving the bachelorhood world too soon. Still as a college student. Was he missing out? He suddenly fell asleep with the thought of standing outside the door of a raging house party, not being let it, burning into his subconscious.

CHAPTER FOUR

Julie woke up early, 5:30am. She had a nightmare where she was forced to strip while in an old timey Western brothel in front of half-men half-pig creatures, and then a severed hand leaped up and choked her. She rolled over and turned on the lamp on her bedside table. She had placed her romance novel *Betty washes her hair,* by the lamp last night. She only wanted to read happy type books for awhile, save the deep literary crime and murder disturbing stuff for after she felt comfortably submerged and safe in her wedded bliss, maybe with a few kids running around; inject a little shadow and intrigue in her life to counter all the simple brightness in kids entertainment which toddler parents must be blasted with in efforts to keep their child entertained. On top of *Betty* was the thin glossy black book first found in the barn. It startled her, almost like catching a glimpse of a ghost. She stared at it. It took her too long, due to the delay of dreamland fog burning away by the reality of wakefulness, to settle on the only rational conclusion: Steve had used his key to come into her house, snuck into her room, and placed the book next to her. Some practical joke. He *was* genuinely funny, or so she thought anyways, which is all that really mattered within this world they were creating just for themselves, yet perhaps this joke was an instance of him trying a bit too hard. She didn't laugh.

She called him. This is how he knew he loved her: in instances when she'd wake him up way too early he was never

annoyed or angry. He hoped this would always last but knew it
probably wouldn't. When younger, although not that long ago,
he had the habit of becoming infatuated with certain starlets,
even while having girlfriends, nothing nearly as serious as Julie.
He'd become certain that he'd be a dedicated fan forever, no
matter what, buy all their movies and magazine covers and
albums, defend their honor against internet trolls. Yet inevitably,
although still remaining a fan and supporter, the infatuations died
out, just as all bon fires eventually do. Would it be the same
with Julie?

"Very funny," she said. As soon as she said it she
realized her tone was too hostile, like the cliché of a nagging
housewife. Her mind was too fogged by her sleepiness to think
of some clever and quick correction.

"What?" Steve responded.

"Trying to scare me with the barn book."

"I genuinely have no idea what you're talking about,"
Steve said. He looked over at his own nightstand where he had
placed the book after he had read it. He had planned to burn the
thing, or throw it in the dumpster at least, that morning. It was
missing.

"Well… that's weird," Julie stated, not sure what to
think. Was he lying? Trying to prolong this *prank*?

"I think I know what's going on," Steve said.

"What?" Julie asked.

"One of our roommates is messing with us. Placing
multiple copies of that book around for us to find."

"Heh. Yeah, you're probably right. Did you read it?"

"It's the dumbest thing ever," Steve answered.

"What is it?"

"Do you remember those chain letter things that were popular in MySpace blog messages, or whatever they were called, back when MySpace was a thing?"

Julie laughed. Thinking of *MySpace* made her laugh; she was in Middle School when that social network site was huge; thinking of it brought back memories of all the high stakes histrionics and hysteria of the time: literally crying over changing lineups of people's *top eight friends*. "Yeah," she said. "Dumb but funny."

"Yeah, but it's not even funny," Steve said. "It takes itself real seriously, trying to be scary or something. And it's sort of unintentionally funny I guess, except that it's sort of impossible for bad books to be unintentionally funny the way movies can, for some reason. Maybe because reading demands more effort and brain power than just watching something, so when things aren't what they intended to be there's less ability to delight in the badness."

"It's not scary?" Julie asked.

"It's just twenty pages of gibberish and then like, a hundred blank pages."

"Weird," Julie said. "I do find the weirdest stuff to be the creepiest stuff though. You know, unexplainable. Strange. We fear what we don't know, right? Like that's the only reason why darkness scares people; you can't see what might be there lurking."

"I don't think you should read it," Steve said. His bluntness surprised her. Why had he stated this so adamantly?

If it's just this dumb little nonsense thing, why would he care if she skimmed it over or not? He didn't want her mind tainted by the book. As soon as the suggestion of controlling her mind struck him he realized its wrongness. He curled his nose and lip, a bit disgusted with himself for having conjured up the idea of controlling her mind. Of course he can't control her mind. Yet still he couldn't stop thinking of the proposition. I want to know what's in her mind and contour her mind so that it will only have good thoughts of me, never stray from me, always love me, he thought sleepily. No matter what she says, I can't really know if she loves me and plans to stay with me forever or not; not knowing drives me crazy, I want to know, to be reassured, put at ease. An anxiety suddenly grew in him. He recognized the feeling as foreign to his usual demeanor yet still unmistakable, like someone who isn't usually prone to nausea suddenly becoming nauseous and wanting to vomit. I've seen Julie ogle other men, Steve thought. She doesn't really find me attractive. I've seen her read novels of young hunky commanding billionaires; I wish I could be like them, be like the people she really wanted and really loved. He recalled a line from the first "chapter" in the book: *Jealousy is the ugly bitter fruit bled from insecurity, and jealous is what you will be, during the first two days, after you read.* Strange, how being aware you have an outlandish and unwelcome thought, bred from emotion, still does not allow one to dismiss the thought, just as becoming aware of a purple bruise on the back will not cause the pain from the bruise to go away. He felt budding tinges of both sadness and anger, the aroma of bereavement wafting from them, percolate from his knowingly absurd lament that he couldn't be a young hunky alpha male tech billionaire, who also played piano and flew planes, like the protagonists in the romance novels Julie read. All these thoughts and emotions struck him fast, like hitting a wall, making him dizzy; Julie was in the midst of some humorous monologue, he guessed, judging by the pleasant chime in her voice.

"I'm sorry, what was that?" Steve asked interrupting her.

Julie laughed. "You didn't catch any of it? My story was so boring you slept through it?"

"No, you were saying…" He really hadn't any idea.

"Do you feel alright?" she asked with concern.

"I'm fine. I have to go, get ready, I have to go to work early," he said. He worked full time during the summer; his classes at Seattle Pacific University started up again in the fall, when his Wells Fargo work hours would go back to part time.

"Well… okay," Julie said.

Steve hung up on her. She picked up the book and thumbed through it. Sarah leaned in her doorway. "Do you know anything about this?" Julie asked, showing the book to Sarah.

"Looks weird. Is there an author's name on it?"

"No," Julie answered. "It *is* weird." She looked at the time, thumbed through the book again, and decided to just read the dumb thing before heading for work. She lay back in bed and begun to read.

Steve immediately regretted having hung up on Julie. He had been afraid that he might say something crazy to her; he felt rattled and so the possibility that he might say something disdainful to her was high, which is why he ended the conversation so quickly. He might say something crazy to her and not even realize it was crazy. Self diagnosis is a tricky endeavor; the demented don't know they're demented. But with her off the phone now, she was free to gossip about him with Sarah or her other roommates; say how she wishes he were richer, had more personality (he knew some of her friends found him dull) wishes he were more manly, not so afraid of heights (he had teased he was afraid of heights once while on top of a Ferris Wheel; maybe she hadn't realized he was only joking). *She hates me,* he thought, *she's laughing at me, she'll leave me.* He didn't play the piano; she wants and deserves someone who plays the piano. Not showy about it; someone who could surprise her with his skill at a grand piano in the Paris Marriott lobby one morning, giving an impromptu concert, playing Vivaldi's Four Seasons. *Will you ever cease surprising me,* she'd say in wonder, to her lover. He couldn't do that for her, be that guy for her, the guy she deserved. (To really fulfill the fantasy he supposed he'd have some vulnerable sexy quirk which made him both dangerous and vulnerable that only her love could cure, thus rescuing him, making him whole and perfect).

He looked at where the book had been and then looked at the floor, maybe it had fallen. No, he could not find it. The book had predicted, claimed really, that'd I feel jealous the next day, and I do… I am. Jealous of whoever it is Julie truly loves. Some imaginary guy. I know it's crazy, yet I am. He went downstairs and woke up his roommate Ron who had passed out on the couch.

"Did anything strange happen last night?" he asked.

"Dude. You have no idea," Ron said groggily.

"What?" Steve asked urgently.

"Josh and I got hammered. Girls. You warbled out."

"I what? I was singing?"

"No man, I meant wobbled. Tipsy, like a drunk zombie. We thought you were drunk too. But you were like sleep-walking, like a zombie."

Steve was stunned. He had never slept walked before.

"They say don't wake up sleep-walkers right? It's traumatic for them or some shit; that's what I heard anyways."

"Where'd… or… what?" Steve stammered, not quite believing it. He tried to recall what he had dreamed last night. He couldn't remember.

"I've just seen you like that one time before. Dude, if you're keeping some sweet stash of hash to yourself…"

"No," Steve said, taken aback. "You know me. What exactly did I do?"

"You just walked right out the door. I think you were holding something. In retrospect I guess we shouldn't have let you; you know, you could crawl out in the street or something, like a baby. But you came back pretty quick. We assumed you just, uh… were with Julie for a quick…"

"Have you imagined Julie and I having sex? Do you imagine her naked?" Steve accused in angry agitation, appalled at the idea.

"No man, not at all dude," Ron said defensively. "Anyways, that was just one of a many weird things that happened last night. Seattle summer nights, am I right?"

"What other weird things?" Steve asked.

"Nothing else involving you dude."

I always miss the party, Steve thought. *They all have their best fun when I'm gone.*

You've read this so now you'll be dead, did you hear what I said, the words are in your head, so now it's begun, soon you'll be dead. Huh… that's… interesting, Julie thought, mulling over the sentence she just read. But what else to expect from a book with a title such as *If you read this you will die* other than weirdness which, being kind, one could call *interesting*. Well, maybe a reader should expect something other than just 'you will die' repeated for twenty or so pages and then one hundred blank pages in anything they read, no matter what the title. This is… different anyways, Julie thought. That's something. Her mother would say when pilfering through the slush piles of submissions to the small publication house that the hope was to find manuscripts that fit in the sweet spot of being original and different enough to stand out, yet conventional enough as to not chase potential readers away. Even champions of the avant-garde need to make money occasionally. This thing was obviously self- published. The next question which came to her as her eyes continued to scroll over the words was: is this the only copy? Was it created just for Steve and I to read? Who placed it in the barn? Who placed it next to my bed? A ghost or something?

The first trial will be jealousy; do you really wish to be married? What is it that you said; if you can't have him than you'd wish to be dead?

Julie froze. Holy shit, she thought. I never said that out loud before, even to Steve. How did the book know? It was like it had read her thoughts. A tingle danced down her spine like a tickling long legged spider. She wanted to throw the book across the room but instead she gripped it tighter as her heart race increased. It stuck to her hands. She didn't want to keep reading but she was compelled to. She couldn't physically keep her eyes closed for longer than two seconds. An alien force were controlling her, refusing to allow her to keep her eyes shut for longer than a few seconds. She had to keep reading.

If you can survive jealousy you can survive anything; if jealousy destroys your marriage you don't want anything; isn't that what you thought? You've been caught.

And what of lust? What if either of you are inflicted by lust, then there is no room for trust, and your love will dissolve, and if that can't be solved you wished to be dead instead of living, so this is what I'm giving; these curses to inflict you for fourteen days, at which at the end with your life you pay. Stupid one, you can't overcome these spells, after your trials under earth your dead body will dwell.

She read nearly as fast as pouring water only marginally understanding the words yet still feeling the full force of the threats.

Through these seven trials no love can survive, and so your wish will be granted, you will die.

Last will be unspeakable depression; you will no longer be happy, your love is gone, and so too will your body fall, slashed by the end note of this sad song. No love can survive these seven trials, and so you will die, you will take your own life, it is not up to your will, you cannot fight it, you simply will. If you can't keep him you'd rather be dead, that's what you said, and so you will die, you can't fight it or hide, there is no other way, you can't look away, in fourteen days your last day awaits.

Julie flipped through the blank pages ahead frantically; there must be more, it can't end that way; there must be some clue to what this is, how to undo it. What had she done? What just happened? She hadn't thought she had ever said anything out loud about rather being dead than having her love, her marriage with Steve fail; she had felt certain she had never written anything like that down in her journal. She had thought it before however. Many times. Especially after their last fight; the details were so hazy; were they drunk? Yes, they must have been drunk; that's why she can't remember. As she flipped words formed on the bottom of the pages; words that she hadn't thought were there before. *Steve & Julie, Steve & Julie, Steve & Julie, dead, Dead,* **perfect** *dEad dEAd, dIE DIE DIE DIE DIE DIE DIE DIE DIE DIE DIE...* she threw the book across the room as if a giant cockroach had just crawled over her hand.

CHAPTER FIVE

The book banged against the wall. Julie thought that she hadn't thrown it hard enough to cause a black smeared indent where the books spine struck, but she apparently had. She stared at the lifeless object, limp on the ground. It assumed the posture of innocence. Like a doll. But Julie knew better. The thing was wicked. Like a doll possessed by a demon. Evil hides in dull daylight by assuming ordinary forms. It wanted to do her harm. Maybe it had already done her harm. It claimed it had. *The spell is cast, there is nothing you can do, the fourteenth day will be your last, your life is through.*

But that's insane, Julie thought. Maybe I just haven't fully woken up yet. The illusion of dreams soaked into my perceived wakefulness, causing me to see things, *"Die Steve and Julie"* that aren't really there. Or this is the beginning of some brain disease which causes hallucinations. I'd recently read of a newly diagnosed brain disease which strikes females in their early 20's. It's suspected that past cases of demonic possession were really just victims suffering through neurologic brain seizures. Is it hereditary, Julie wondered fearfully. Her older sister went through a psychotic break; doctors still aren't sure how much of the cause is biological.

Sarah entered her room. "I heard you scream? Are you okay?"

Julie hadn't recalled screaming. She must have shrieked while she threw the book. Sarah followed Julie's wide and frightened eyes towards the tossed paperback leaning against the wall. She gave Julie an expression suggesting, *are you kidding me? You let a book freak you out?* Sarah walked towards the book. She couldn't help but to smirk dismissively at Julie tightening in a ball in her bed. She approached the object against the wall. She picked it up.

"Look inside," Julie said with a trembling voice.

Sarah thumbed through the thing. "What's this?" she asked. "Looks stupid."

"Look at the bottom of the blank pages in the back," Julie said.

"I don't see anything. Just blank pages. Where'd you get this and why'd it freak you out?" she scoffed.

She could be lying, Julie thought. *I was sure… no I was positive those pages were blank before. Then the words just appeared…*

"Do you… want me to throw this away for you?" Sarah asked. She held it by the corner, as if it were a tissue picked out from the waste basket.

"Yes… no wait, can you… okay this sounds really strange, but you can you put it in a zip-lock bag for me? I think we have the big kind." She wanted to show it to her sister Candice. But she didn't want to touch it.

"Yeah, okay, I guess," Sarah said, looking at Julie strangely. She walked out of the room.

Julie steadied her breathing. *If the curse in the book is real then Steve should already be feeling jealous,* she thought. *And then I'd start to feel jealous tomorrow; always be one day behind him. No, this is stupid,* she decided. Curses aren't real.

Sarah and Julie drank coffee together at the small table in the breakfast nook. Even in the sealed plastic bag the strange tome resting on the table next to Sarah still menaced Julie. She tried to dismiss the creepy feelings the book gave her; to put on a façade and act normally. Sarah had steered the conversation towards the topic of whether love is more selfish or selfless.

"But if you really loved someone, wouldn't you always want what's best for them? And how do you know *you're* what's best, that he can't do better; that he wouldn't be happier with someone else?"

"There's always chance involved with love and relationships," Julie answered nonchalantly, refusing to exert the mental strain over the question which Sarah had wished her to.

"Yeah, I know, but what if you, like, actually knew the person? Knew the person that he'd be better with, knew she liked him back, knew they'd make a better couple... would you sacrifice their happiness for your own? And if you were willing to do that does that mean you don't truly love the person? You love yourself more? Is that true love then?"

"That's an interesting question, I guess," Julie shrugged, still rattled by the black object in plastic on the table; in no mood or condition for philosophy.

"You're the only close friend I have who I can have these types of deep conversations with," Sarah said.

"So early in the morning too," Julie said then sipped her coffee.

Sarah laughed. "But seriously though?"

"Well alright," Julie said. "I'll take a swing at your pitch. First off, there's a lot of assumptions in the hypothetical you threw out. But I'll go with it... okay, well, I guess I wouldn't see it as loving yourself more than him, but, having confidence in yourself... and not only in yourself but in each other, as a pair. Maybe he'd be happier with someone else, but maybe not; you don't really know for sure. But you should have confidence that he makes you happy, and that you can make him happy."

"Smart answer," Sarah said, a hint of disappointment in her tone. She had either wanted to stump Julie or make her agree with her that it is selfish and against pure love to keep a boyfriend you know would be better with someone else.

Julie continued: "I mean, yeah, being unsure about some things is part of any relationship, just as it is with life. That's natural. But if everyone had to cross this threshold of uncertainty that you're talking about, then no one would ever get married, you know? So, yeah, I mean, there definitely is some selfishness in love, I'll give you that. But… so what? If there wasn't then maybe love wouldn't be worth it, ever."

"Can I be frank with you?" Sarah asked.

"Please," Julie responded.

"You and Steve… kind of annoy some people sometimes. I mean, that thing you do, calling each other *nickname,* I mean, how corny. Like, gag."

Sarah's directness could be both her most appealing and appalling attribute.

"You think you and Steve would make a better couple than Steve and I?" Julie asked. She took another calm sip of her coffee, keeping her eyes on Sarah. Sarah: cute, hair dyed blonde in the shade of Julie's, sort of little-sister-like in both her admiration and resentments of Julie.

"Oh no, not at all," Sarah said after a beat, in a fake way that let Julie know that's exactly what Sarah believed.

"Steve is texting me again," Julie said. "Fifth time already this morning."

"What's he say?"

"He wants to know what I'm doing." Julie texted back: *Coffee, work soon, (I hate Mondays) love you, see you tonight.* She added a few heart and kissy face emoticons.

Steve had a bad day at work. It was his co-workers 63rd birthday. There was cake in one of the manager's offices. Steve complained that the cake was dry. He stole one of the birthday balloons and put it by his desk and thanked costumers with fake sincerity when they told him *Happy Birthday.* He disconnected the phone and modem of his friend, a co-worker three years older. The IT guy had correctly pinpointed the cause of the disruptions as sabotage. Steve confided in his boss, silently, that he didn't think his co-worker was very smart. Which he knew was a lie, but didn't care. A few of his co-workers asked if he was okay, asked if he was sick. They stated the obvious: you're not like yourself today. He took multiple trips to the bathroom to splash his face with water and use the towel dispenser to dry his armpits. In the bathroom stall he'd take off his tie, unbutton his shirt, take off his shirt and flap it, as if there had been ants crawling inside of it. He avoided his reflection in the mirror; he hated his face. He usually had thought of himself as handsome. He constantly texted and called Julie, around twenty times each hour, demanding to know what she were doing right that second. *She'll leave me if she finds out she's better than me,* he thought, so began to add little random and weird passive aggressive smears against her, like, *you'll never be a rock star you know.*

In the first two hours or so Julie liked the text attention. Just as they didn't say *I love you* to each other much, they weren't big texters either. But she correctly recognized the texts and calls for what they were: signs of jealousy. She recalled a line from the book, sealed in the zip-lock bag, sitting in her car seat: *On the first day, jealousy will be your way; Jealousy will be your first trial and sin, and so the horror will begin.* It wasn't just her paranoia from being freaked out by the book, allowing it to make her see things that aren't really there. No question: Steve was acting strangely. Not only the frequency of texts but their bi-polar tones as well, as if multiple personalities had possessed him, all of them alien to his true self. Their flowery worshipful gushiness swinging to direct questioning, then to sarcastic hints of anger and then even put downs; verbal abuse in efforts to damage self esteem is part of controlling, to cage the partner into believing she is unworthy of leaving or seeking a better partner. 'Controlling' is an aspect of jealousy. She had looked up traits of jealousy online after the third hour of Steve's text barrage: clinginess, wanting to control, pettiness, an inability to be happy for others success, minimizing others while making grand statements about the self; what a horrible way to live. She couldn't help but to wonder if one of his friends had stolen his phone and were playing a mean prank on her. If not for that book she had read that morning the 'steal and prank' scenario would have been her strong assumption. She had to turn off her phone. She couldn't work with Steve's distractions. Her boss had begun to be irritated by her constant fussiness with her phone, she had noticed.

Julie ignoring his texts made Steve paranoid. She doesn't love me, she's cheating on me, she's off with some other guy, some guy she truly loves, who is more charming, has more money, is better looking, maybe owns a helicopter and works at Google; maybe the guy who invented the driverless car and has other marvels yet to unveil. She just puts up with me to amuse her mother, Steve worried. He so badly wished he could be the guy who invented the driverless car, or the guy who'd invent the solar powered car that has enough power as diesel cars, and cheaper to produce; the guy who'd be able to grow meat through cell regeneration, therefore creating meat in a humane way, no animals killed (imagine the money from India such an invention would bring; Hindus finally to be able to enjoy the deliciousness of barbecue pork). Maybe the man Julie is cheating on me with will be President one day; he'll make her the First Lady, and Julie will be the most beautiful and glamorous universally loved first lady in American history, more than even Jackie Kennedy. It depressed Steve that he wasn't smart enough to make meat steaks without death, create solar powered cars, win Wimbledon and the U.S. Open, and be President. It felt unfair to him that other people could accomplish these things and he couldn't. He knew, of course, his thoughts were ridiculous, yet he couldn't dismiss them or blow away the negative feelings they brought to him any easier than someone can blow away blanketing black thunderclouds.

Julie decided to be proactive concerning the curses that the book promised to inflict. To entertain the insane and accept the possible that the curses the book promised could come. The only person she knew who had dabbled in witchcraft and who claimed to have personal manifestations verifying the truth of supernatural powers, voodoo, ghosts and miracles and things, was her older sister Candice. During her lunch break she called Candice and asked if she could come over after work to discuss strange things with her, and show her an odd object. Ask her opinion. Candice said sure. Julie did worry that brining up the topic of curses could trigger bad memories for Candice, of her time in the mental institution and when she fuzzed the line which separates fantasy and reality. Candice thought that she had been foolishly enticed by darkness, had dabbled in it, intoxicated by its power, and only god's light and forgiveness had cured her. While driving to Candice's apartment complex in Bellevue, Bruno Bars *Locked out of Heaven* blaring, Julie reminisced about a conversation she had with her older sister at a Starbucks a month after Candice was released from Fairfax Psychological hospital. Candice still held strict religious strictures over marriage and celibacy, passed on by her mother, and had correctly suspected that, like 97% of all other Americans, her younger sister and Steve hadn't waited until marriage to bang like horny bunnies.

"I know why in those old slasher horror movies why the teens who just had sex are the first to get murdered," Julie recalled Candice saying. *"It's not a moral statement or anything; it's just all about fear. When you commit sin you expect something bad to happen to you. Your senses are attuned to it, you wonder about it; what punishment will be inflicted because of this thing I did which had felt good but that I know to be bad. The universe must be in balance. So, the audience, because we all have god's light in us, after witnessing the fornication are expecting something bad to happen to the fornicators. We sense it, expect it, but don't know when it will come, thus, creating suspense which is the fuel for fear. Wondering when disaster will strike."*

Honestly, Julie didn't like talking with her sister or her mother sometimes. 'God talk' so quickly and easily slipped into what sounded like esoteric gibberish to Julie, non pertinent or useful to anything in her life (although she did consider herself a Christian and sought to be a good, empathetic, moral and caring person). Yet she decided she must talk to Candice about this book. She parked in the guest parking, got out, picked up the plastic bag carrying the black book and climbed the stairs to Candice's door, number 22B. Candice opened the door. Julie, with quick reflexes, grabbed Candice's calico bounding out the door. The cat purred. She looked up at her older sister and strained a smile. Candice had the same pretty face as Julie but was less petite, had broader shoulders and auburn hair. She took less care with her appearance and maintenance than Julie; wearing minimum makeup if any at all, not into fashion or vigorous exercise (although she had added color to her closet after she relaxed her grip on the Wicca world, after being cured from her mental breakdown).

She placed the book on the kitchen table.

Candice shuddered. "What's that?"

"The 'odd thing' I was telling you about," Julie answered.

"It's giving me a bad vibe," Candice said.

"You… sense that?"

Candice rubbed her palms on her pants then paced to the fridge. She opened and then closed the door.

"If you don't want to talk about this, I mean…" Julie stammered, already feeling guilty she had shown her sister this object.

Candice walked to the coffee maker.

"No thanks," Julie said.

Candice opened her cupboard, took out two clear glasses, filled them with water from her sink and sat down at the table where the book was placed. Julie joined her. She took a drink.

"It hasn't left me," Candice said in a low audible mumble. "I still know things I wished I didn't; seen things I wish I could forget… it still entices me…"

"Do you… or would you mind… looking at that?" Julie asked hopefully, gesturing down at the book in the plastic bag.

Candice took it out. She held it and grimaced. She put it to her nose and inhaled and grimaced again. "Where did you get this?"

"We found it… in a barn."

"What were you doing in the barn?"

"It was at Chad and Jessie's wedding."

"Yes, but what were you doing *in* the barn," Candice asked again.

Julie rolled her eyes. "That's irrelevant," she said.

"Nothing is irrelevant," Candice snapped back. Julie wondered if Candice were really a virgin. Julie remembered that when Candice was deep into her Wicca coven, her and this pale and skinny red-headed girl seemed intensely close, beyond mere friends. Although Julie knew that Candice would deny being a lesbian so it was pointless to ask. As far as Julie knew Candice, despite being near thirty yet with the demeanor, Julie thought, of a broken down middle aged lady, had never had a boyfriend or a girlfriend; never even kissed anyone. Candice opened the book, cracking its spine, and flipped through it. "Blank pages," she said.

"Look in the front."

Julie saw Candice's skin whiten and her jaw drop. Candice clutched the book tighter and then carefully placed it down. She used one finger to scoot it further away from her.

"What?" Julie eagerly asked.

"Where did you get this?" Candice said again, in a disturbed whisper.

"I told you, in a barn. It was... what was the place called... the ranch outside town that caters weddings and family reunions ... or maybe it was private property, someone Jessie knew..." Her mind was going blank on those details; it perturbed her, she usually had a keen memory of places.

"What did the book... tell you?" Candice asked.

A weird question, Julie thought. "Why...what did it tell *you?*" she asked back, cocking her head. She placed the nail of her index finger against her teeth.

Candice gulped then took a drink of water. "It said it wasn't for me. It was for you."

Julie looked at her blankly. She looked back at the book and read the cover again: *If you read this you will die.* "What do you mean?"

"*This is not for your eyes, but for Steve and Julie, who read it and now will die,*" Candice said, quoting.

Julie took a drink. Candice wouldn't kid about this kind of stuff. Would she? Was she in on the prank? No... that doesn't fit, doesn't make sense. Still it seemed so unbelievable.

"What did the book tell you?" Candice asked again.

"It... said because I was reading it, that I'd be cursed. I didn't want to read it, but... I was compelled to; it was short, I thought, harmless. Just gibberish. Bad poetry smashed all together, line after line."

"What did the gibberish say, more specifically?" Candice asked.

"Do you know what it is?"

"What did it say," Candice said again with a more demanding tone.

"It said whoever read the book... which was just Steve and I, I guess... would be cursed with seven trials, two days each, for fourteen days: First jealousy, then lust, then disgust, then rage, then stupidity, then self pity, and then depression. And then we'd... die."

"The *write your own story* spell," Candice mumbled in a whisper. She stood up and shuffled her feet, aimlessly pacing.

"I'm sorry, what's that?" Julie asked.

"But that doesn't make sense... but that's all I can think of which might..." Candice mumbled to herself.

"What are you talking about, talk straight to me," Julie demanded urgently. She wanted to also stand, but felt frozen, drained of the needed energy to lift herself up from the chair.

"It's very rare, very powerful, more of a rumor... even when I believed in... crazy things, I was unsure about this rumor. Only the most powerful of witches would be able to cast is successfully."

"What is it?" Julie asked.

"The *story* spell... would require your blood. It can either be used for a curse or blessing."

A bang thundered against the door. Candice and Julie flinched.

"I know you're in there you bitch!" they heard the voice of Steve yelling on the other side. "You can't hide from me! Open up! I know he's in there with you!"

"The first curse is jealousy," Julie said with intense softness, wide eyed. Steve continued to bang on the door and yell. Then he began kicking the door.

"This is proof the curse is real," Candice said. "It is unlike Steve to act this way is it not?"

Julie nodded her head yes, eyes wide with worry and concern.

"Bitch!" Steve screamed, slapping the door. "Cheating bitch!"

"You're out of your mind! There's no one here!" Julie yelled through the door. "It's the book, it's cursed you!"

"Stop lying to me!" Steve yelled. "I know you're cheating! I've always known! Open the door or I'll bust it down!"

Candice cautiously walked towards her door. She placed her hand over the knob and undid the lock. Steve busted through the door, knocking Candice down. He tore towards the bedroom and flung off the mattress, then opened the closet. He stormed into the bathroom. He punched the bathroom mirror, shattering it. Blood dripped from his knuckles.

"You're not being yourself; this isn't you, calm down!" Julie screamed. If this was jealousy she feared what beast rage would transform him into. And herself. Shaken she threw herself against the wall, darting his lunge at her as he whisked past still in his furious search for this imaginary man he was certain she was cheating on him with. She slide down the wall, shut her eyes and balled, shaken by shock. She had never been seriously frightened of Steve until that moment.

Steve stopped and stood still, his heart racing. He looked down on his fiancé. She was so pretty. Even when she 'ugly cried' she was still so soft, delicate, stunningly pretty. She could have anyone. There were a billion men on earth better than him who she could have. He lifted his head and looked at Candice. Her eyes were wild, her jaw clenched. She pointed a kitchen knife at him. He wondered if she had ever killed before, during her crazy days; doing some sacrificial ritual to appease some demon. He looked at his bloody hand; the sting first making itself known. His anger from jealousy emptied, replaced by sadness from jealousy. An irrational jealousy, he knew. *What's the matter with me?*

"Are you calm now?" Candice asked with tight lips.

Steve looked at her and nodded. She lowered her knife.

"It's the book," Julie said softly, regaining her breath between her sobs.

Steve slumped next to her. She leaned against him. "I'm sorry," he said softly. "It's like… all day; it was like, an out of body experience. Looking at myself from afar, not recognizing myself. Being aware of how crazy I was being but helpless to stop it. I just love you so much, I didn't… don't want to lose you."

"It's the book," Julie whispered again.

Steve stood. He sensed the book was near. He saw it on the table. He reached and grabbed it. "We'll burn it."

"No!" Candice yelled.

"What do you know of this?" Steve demanded.

"She called it a… what was it… *write your own story spell?*" Julie said.

Steve wrinkled his nose as he tossed the book down. "That almost sounds cute," he scoffed.

"Like all powerful spells it has many names," Candice explained.

'Strange, I am already shamed with guilt over an act I have not yet done, because I know I will do it. If she lets me but I know she will let me; it's why I came to her, under other guises (to confront her about the possibility of her placing the book in the barn. She was the only one around). I want more than anything to be in a happy and strong eternal marriage with Julie, full of trust and stability, but 'eternal' and 'happiness' are such esoteric things; the desire of the moment is solid, literal, comprehensible and here; it overpowers everything else; I am so weak, so pathetically so, so helpless, a twig blow over by the power of a hurricane.'

His thoughts weren't quite as lucid or long as all that; they came in a flash and were gone. Mostly he was mindless, except for the panting exalting in praise of Zelda's petite raven haired beauty, her svelte frame; the word *sassy* even sprung to him as a turn-on adjective used on her; he so badly wanted her perky little breasts free and soft and hanging to be cupped and smashed by his pressing sweaty palms; he wanted to lick the upslope curves and then let his lips travel up to her collar bone and shoulder and then to catch her beautiful blue feline like eyes slinking a dagger sassy look at him, and he'd kiss her and then concentrate back down to her breasts and lick her nipples like a cat lapping from a saucer of milk. He wanted to turn her nipples as hard as diamonds. He wanted to see her pull down her panties for him. Little teasing tugs, a little cling, a tear, a snap, and there she is, there it is, that tight space where her legs lead up to, bare, exposed, cute, wanting to be filled by him, dripping with want. The vivid visions excited him; strange how real they felt, like they were happening now already rather than about to happen.

Zelda took a step back, shaken, physically, literally, by the power of this thrusting arousal of lust emanating from Steve's essence, blasted at her. She blushed, partly from flattery, partly from the shyness brought on by the startling realization that she never felt as strongly before, that she had the power within her to make a man such as Steve, handsome, ambitions, charming and strong, tremble like he was. She wasn't a virgin, yet never before had she seen a man look at her with such desperate, on the verge of sad, desire. It frightened her. Part of what attracted her to him was his goodness; he was such a gentleman, almost old-fashioned goofily so; really, how many boys regularly open car doors for girls? His pulling away from her during their make-out at the frat party was also a gentlemanly act; how he handled it. It frustrated her yet also endeared her to him, maybe even made her fall in love with him a little bit. Which kind of messed up the high-school romance craze thing just a bit, but all that juvenile junk is dumb anyways, she concluded after graduation. She had the power, she realized, to turn good boys bad. Cheating on his fiancé, the perfect and poised blonde little smarty-pants Julie, would make him *bad*. Julie probably bored him, in conversation and in bed, she surmised. Maybe I'd be bad too if I let him cheat on her with me, Zelda thought, but she didn't care much about that. This realization (the power to turn good boys bad) startled her, frightened her, yet also titillated and thrilled her. She had recently decided to adopt a life philosophy that anything worth doing was probably frightening. *Run towards fear, not away, if you really want anything really good to happen. For dreams to come true.*

She brushed her hair behind her ear and bit her lip. He tensed, like a cheetah, ears perked, ready to sprint while he looked at her, waiting for her to give him the signal. She smirked, her fingers caressing down her neck to her collarbone. She gave a nod.

He literally ripped her blouse off of her. Blouse shredded, ruined. It was one of those types of things she'd wanted to happen at least once in her life (experience sex so passionately cloths literally get ripped) but never really expected to happen, because stuff like that only happens in movies.

'I bet he never ripped the cloths of Julie off like that' she couldn't help but to think proudly. It tickled her that a man wanted to get at her breasts so badly. Although they had recently grown a half-size she had always had smaller breasts then other girls, which she had been teased about by both girls and boys in her class. She looked down, his face buried in her cleavage, which looked ample, pushed up by the force of his caressing hands. Then he looked up at her; it disarmed her how much like a sweet little boy he appeared; cute in his vulnerability while in the throes of his passion, working to quench his unquenchable desire. How serious yet thankful he looked; almost lost in wonder of his good fortune; a hint of sadness and confusion (also sweet) in his look as well, as to suggest his helpless wonder over what was happening to him, why couldn't he control himself.

She slit her eyes and smirked at him (just as he had foreseen in his vision). *Don't worry little boy* she thought. *I will satisfy you.* She reached back and unhooked her bra. He kissed her mouth, a long delicious kiss; gentle; even overcome with lust he knew not to kiss too hard right away. She opened her mouth and felt his tongue swipe inside and tickle inside her. Then he dove back down and tickled her nipple with his tongue. It shocked her how good it felt.

Steve, esthetically, usually preferred girls with bigger boobs than Zelda, although, at his disgustingly base physically objectifying preferences, he'd rather ogle and feel an athletic and taut flat chest girl more than a chubby large breasted girl. In his lust state he was like a boy first pricked by puberty's first startling self realization of the sexual allure and sexual signifiers of girls breasts; highly alerted towards them. Zelda's perky breasts fully fascinated and aroused him; the softness of them, of their shape, how well they complemented her frame, how remarkable that they were there at all, sloping happily towards him, two curved mounds, wanting to be frolicked over and slid on. His fingers and tongue would be the sled free falling and climbing all over them; how fascinating how her skin there felt both warm and cool; he wanted to explore further how could this be; how warm could he cause them to become, and how cool, in the shadows. The softness of her, all of her, and her feminine shape; her tautness, and athleticism, all thrilled him to look at and think of and feel up. The she had breasts at all titillated and thrilled him; it meant she was a woman, which meant she had a soft slit in her crotch, a tight and snug inversion in the place where he had a gross protrusion; a crease which he'd get to after her breasts were teased to extreme (and whatever else) like a climatic dessert after the satisfying main course. She was so cute; she seemed perfectly cute to him, any change in her, including her breast size, would make her slightly less perfect; what a tight shiny cute little body she had, what a pretty face, intoxicatingly black and long thick hair which made her blue eyes pop so vibrantly. While he admired her body, nude now and open to his grouping attacks, he imagined her in myriads of cute little outfits, tight cotton panties, red tight Volleyball bottoms, tight white dress, blue bows in her pony tailed hair, a yellow summer dress, twirling; and he imagined ripping them all off, to get at the perfectness of her all natural nudeness; he clawed at her; she was taken aback but liked it.

The sex hadn't lasted long but that didn't matter. Both had entered the rare bliss where time becomes obliterated for a moment and there is no time, and in this timelessness an hour is no more or less than a minute. One of her past lovers prided himself on maintaining his sexual stamina for over an hour before climaxing, and although good, he had not made her explode the way Steve just had.

Steve felt awful while still deliriously sexually satisfied. Only for a moment; his boner popped back up as quickly as a magician blowing up a balloon. Clearly only some spell could make it do that; make it feel so excited it was like it wanted to rocket away from his body. He couldn't help but to glance down at it, and not recognize it, never before had it been so large, curved and purple—and so soon, seconds, after it had released all its pent up energy inside Zelda. She was still humming and panting heavily. He thrust it back in her, pounding, causing her rhythmic happy yelps of glorious astonishments. Even as he pounded her he felt guilty; shame that it felt so good, as good, maybe even better, than any moment with Julie, despite Julie being superior in every way; smarter, classier, prettier, fuller breasts. So he rationally told himself while pounding Zelda, although all the senses in his body were telling him Zelda was perfect because nobody else had ever made him react like this (but it's false, he told himself, it's just the curse, the curse is messing with my mind and body like a drug, altering perceptions and reality). Zelda's pussy felt tighter than Julie's though, and it got naturally wetter, making the friction from the pounding slide easier, not needing lube; what vulgar things to think, he scolded himself; think and now know. *I'm a cheater, I'm a monster, I'm disgusting.*

It scared him how the sex (third time now, right in a row) felt so good that he wanted to thank her for it, thank Zelda, say *I love you for giving that to me, making me feel that way, thank you.* How awful; what an awful thing to think; awful thing to feel, even while his body pulsed with pleasures. Jet streams of his semen gushed up her so strongly he worried he made her pregnant even if it wasn't her time; what a nightmare that would be.

Then there was the matter of the brand new birth of a springing boner, yet again, sitting spryly in his lap, so soon after the orgasmic death of his last erection; the life and death and rebirth sequence of sexual urge replenishing at unnatural science-fiction speeds. "Wow," Zelda said, nearly out of breath. She moved towards the bed, she needed a break. She pulled out a cigarette and lighter from a drawer, lit it, and hopped on her bed, and took a deep drag. She could not believe his massive erection. He stood in front of her with it out, pointed up towards the planet Jupiter, wanting to reach the furthest reaches of the solar system. She guffawed and shook her head in amazement at that *thing,* and what had just happened, and what, once again, after she finished her cigarette and caught her breath, would happen again. She took another drag, her fingers twitching, her trying to look poised and elegant while feeling a bit deliciously wrecked. He was attractive, beyond just that *thing* on him, overpowering, refusing to be ignored. She took her eyes off of it to admire his six pack abs, this firm pectorals, his biceps, his flushed handsome face, his mused up thick hair on his head; that wild expression he still gave her, totally animalistic, so unlike him, or how she had thought him to be. Even in her most vivid and bizarre fantasies of him, she never imagined him making an expression like that. He looked at her, he wanted her. He wasn't a fan of smoking, hated the smell and ill health of it, but god, she looked so sexy smoking, he was so glad she was smoking in her bed because of how perfectly sexy, and bad, you bad little girl, it made her look to him in that moment.

The metaphor of a male orgasm to a geyser works on multiple levels: the direct obviousness but also the natural process of underground built up pressure and then the release of the pressure. After the 'pressure' is released in the eruption it takes time for the pressure to build up again. Steve's new boner, locked, loaded, ready to fire, after seconds after such a powerful release was like a law against nature. He felt disgusted with himself. Sex is strange; how even bad sex is good and even great sex is sort of disgusting. Especially, he imagined, for women; a type of disgust he often felt shame for. He sometimes felt he could empathize with asexual women; those who become nauseated by the thought of sex. The ability to fantasize, to mentally smother a Vaseline smear over some of the crudeness of sex, help's to make it better, or tolerable for those that usually don't like it.

"The rare male multiple orgasm," Zelda said, trying to sound cool as she arched an eyebrow. "Are you even human?" She smirked. She gingerly placed the comforter between her legs and rubbed. The sex pleasure still kicked in her. She felt like she had had a dozen multiple orgasms all at once, that last time.

"I didn't know male multiple orgasms existed," she said. "Are you like Bigfoot or something?"

"You witch. You Bitch," he said. "What have you done to me?"

Zelda beamed. *I have you* she thought confidently. *Julie can't give you what I just gave you; she can't make you quake like I made you quake. And you* need *this, I can tell, like a heroin addict needs the next hit; after experiencing that pure taste of heaven you now can't live without it.* She felt triumphant and empowered. "I wrecked you good," Zelda said flippantly, cocking her head back.

She's right Steve thought. "What do you know about the book?" he demanded. It felt really strange and wrong to confront her still with his raging boner, making it hard to concentrate on anything other than how much he wanted to kill the thing, his boner, limp, which required marveling at her beauty, her nakedness, her shine. The witch. The bitch.

"You were the only one by the barn that night. You placed it there."

She laughed. "I have no idea what you're talking about."

He slipped his red boxers back on. His boxers did a comically abysmal job concealing his humongous pants tower. Zelda couldn't help but to guffaw again. God, he was still panting! Her heart beat quickened. The poor boy. He was flabbergasted. He thinks he can walk away.

"Yeah right," she said. She shrugged. "Okay. Not like I need any more." She slipped out of bed, picked up her panties and slipped them back on while he watched.

"You bitch," he said, panting.

"Ouch," she said. "The material hurts against my raw pussy." She pouted. Then she slipped off her panties again and flung them at him. He caught them. He looked at her. He couldn't stand it. She crawled back in bed and crawled under the comforter concealing herself.

God, you're sexy, like a sleek cat; you're a witch, what is this spell curse you put on me; god it looks like I'm seeing you for the first time again, not seeing you, you hiding under the covers, wanting to see you, all of you again—oh wow you're all naked under there, how dare you teased me, putting on your panties before taking them off again, and then crawling in bed, covering yourself when I so badly want to see you, feel all of you again, outside, inside, everywhere, have you rock me all over again; I need it, you bitch.

He slipped off his boxers.

"That a boy," Zelda said coyly.

He eagerly joined her in bed.

CHAPTER SEVEN

(Interlude)

Steve and Julie sat in a downtown sports bar, Spitfire, last mid-September afternoon, with another couple, Danny and Lisa, who they sometimes double dated with, watching the University of Washington football team play BYU. BYU's freshman quarterback squirmed free in a mad scramble then chucked the ball from near midfield towards the end-zone. His receiver caught the hail marry for a touchdown. The ESPN camera's panned across the front rows of the student section capturing the gaggles of young Mormon's, a group of blond girls maybe all sisters, and shirtless dudes with 'BYU GO' painted across their bares chests, going wild in jubilant celebration, mugging for the camera's, flashing the 'number one' sign.

"Look at *alllll* those virgins," Steve deadpanned.

Danny snorted a laugh. "Dude, I dare you to shout that out."

Steve shook his head and stuffed a chili rubbed lamb skewer in his mouth.

"Are we playing Truth and Dare now?" Julie asked. She hadn't seen the play; she was admiring some of the new local art on display against the brick wall. She liked the charcoal drawings of this guy named Ian, who also fronted a local indie band named Mayberry.

"Double dare," Danny said.

Steve shouted out *Look at all those virgins.* The joke didn't land as hard among the crowded bar as it had at the table. Julie didn't feel embarrassed though; she thought it was funny. She winked at Steve while smiling at him. He smiled back. Julie knew some others thought of them as a boring couple. Maybe a debauched juvenile drunken game of *Truth or Dare* would begin to change some people's opinions. Streak around the block naked, call up some middle school kids and go tee-peeing with them, or something dumb like that.

"Dare me to say it too," Julie teased.

"It's a lame joke; besides the camera's not panning on the crowd anymore, it wouldn't make sense," Steve said.

"Look at all those virgins!" Julie yelled, louder than Steve had. Some surrounding patrons trying to watch the game glared at her. Steve, Danny and Lisa laughed heartedly. They went back to slowing munching and watching the game.

"It's funny how they allow boys squeezed into tight shiny pants affect their moods for the day," Julie said to Lisa.

Lisa laughed. "Totally," she agreed. "Like they have anything to do with the win or loss."

"I have a high school friend who just graduated from BYU," Julie said. The boys were strange conversationalist while intensely watching intense sporting events; one couldn't really count on them to pay attention or to illicit responses other than surface level jokey or irrationally irritated. Part of her envied Steve's ability to derive so much excitement from something she usually found mostly boring, watching sports. She did however come close to matching his competiveness when they played mixed couple doubles tennis. They were both good and rarely lost. She mostly directed her speech towards Lisa.

"I heard the dating scene is like, 1950's era hokey there," Lisa said.

"Totally," Julie said. "On campus water-gun fights. Board games like Trivial Pursuit and Scrabble. Although, it would be nice, don't you think, sometimes, to date knowing that the guy isn't always thinking about sex the whole time, because it's not allowed or whatever."

Lisa arched an eyebrow at her.

"I mean, not *all* the time, like when you're horny, but sometimes. No drunken frat boys either."

Lisa took a drink of her cocktail. "That would be nice. You were with Steve during most of your time at Stanford, right?"

"Seeing what my roommates and friends go through, I really don't think I missed anything, having a steady through college."

"Well, when you found the one," Lisa said and raised her glass.

Julie beamed at her. Steve and Danny moaned and grunted over something on the screen. An interception. *The pain lets me know I'm alive and the love is real* Steve muttered to himself. It was his sports fandom mantra after devastating losses, mostly said in jest, it being a tad humorously melodramatic, especially placed over something as ultimately trivial as sports. Sometimes he meant it with greater soul barring truth.

Just then an old plump lady with unruly wild gray hair and a raggedy red dress barged through the bar doors. She screeched, barreling towards Steve and Julie's table. She grabbed a pitcher of beer from a nearby table and threw it at Steve and Julie. Despite their flinching they still got drenched.

"You took my sister away!" the old lady screeched. "Candice is not crazy! You are! Damn you to hell! I curse you! I curse you!"

The bar security doorman rushed at her and picked her up and carried her flailing, screeching, out of the bar. The patrons murmured, their eyes off the game. The manger approached Steve and Julie's table and apologized. He offered to pay for their meal. Steve politely bartered with him and in addition received vouchers for four more free meals.

"Any day you get free food is a good day," Steve joked.

"She's *my* sister," Julie angrily grumbled, her pretty peach Prada blouse ruined.

CHAPTER EIGHT

Julie Curse: Day Three

Julie woke up with a tingle racing and kicking pleasingly through her pulse; a pulsating vibration, wanting to be petted and then released. Oh wow, she thought. So this is lust. It's a gushy wanting, needing thing. She had thought she had been horny before, she had been horny before, but not like this. If this is what boys and men feel constantly… poor them, no wonder they're idiots, she thought. Not to excuse their piggish behaviors, when they're piggish. Yet still. Oh wow, oh god. She's heard females libidos reach their peak later than men's. Women mature faster, body wise, physical growth, but it takes them longer than boys to reach sexual peak, as far as the itching want, the desire, the thirst, the hunger. She wasn't supposed to feel this way, feel this full of lust, for another ten or twenty years, she guessed. Yet, here it was. Because of the curse. Her heart began to beat heavier, thinking about sex, wanting sex, to feed the hunger; please the demanding begging in her head, for the touch, to ogle, to marvel, to feel it, the heaven of sex, of being fed, being filled.

She got up and ripped off her pajamas and stood naked in her room and stretched. The breeze tickled her body. Her sensations were heightened, every skin pour. She knew she looked sexy; she wished someone could see her and appreciate her looking so nice. She sauntered confidently into the bathroom. She looked at herself in the mirror, admiring. She rubbed her ribs which her skin stretched tightly over. Her skin, so soft. Her hand cupped her breast, brushed passed her nipple; ecstasy. She now saw, or understood, how men are so attracted to the feminine shape.

The feminine shape is divine. That's a nice word; divinity; spiritual in the power of the beauty of its soft curves; the protruding breasts and hips and cinched waist, the slopes, the legs. The light of life is in the shape; the triangle of the crotch. She slowly slid her hand down to her crotch. It was bare; Steve liked it bare; she realized she did too; nothing between the touch of skin to skin, hand to pussy muscle, wanting to be touched, explored, stretched, fed. She wasn't a lesbian, never before had lesbian tendencies. Still, a pretty women, to her, was always more pleasant to look at than a handsome man. They were more interesting, more complex, more mysterious; the reasons and wonders of how they're so beautiful.

The attractiveness of men is in their brut display. To really appreciate their handsomeness is to give in to their grossness. Let their grossness overpower; submit to their grossness. Willingly; that is key, of course, willingly submit to the dumb obvious brut appeal; let imagination and fantasy transform their grossness and engorged aurora, literally and metaphysically, into attractive rather than repulsive adjectives. Little girls get infatuated by feminine soft faced pop stars because they are less scary than the big and harry monsters men become. But being a women means becoming able to enjoy the scary thrill of a big brute of a man. Being a straight women anyways. Admiring herself, for the first time, she thought she understood the appeal of lesbianism. No, that's absurd, she scolded herself. Yet still, wow. I am glorious. I am like a supermodel. She looked at herself with brand new eyes. She saw herself how Steve (and other men) saw her. And she was a goddess.

Women always find things to hate and be disgusted about their bodies; the tiniest little things; a perceived flab at the waist, a mole, a mark, a sag, anything. Too much intimacy, too much knowledge of one thing can sometimes work to dull it, make it less admirable. A little mystery can work wonders; she knew this, she used it, to attract men, before she and Steve became inclusive, and then with Steve as well; during sexy time, in the bedroom, making him wait until she peeled everything off. He loved that; he hated it, but he loved it. Her own body wasn't enough of a mystery to herself. She grew up with it, went through the horrors of puberty with it, the transitioning, than dealing with the new world of male harassment; a less safe, sadder world; a loss of innocence, sadly, party attributed to the maturing of her body. But all her past knowledge of her body, all her insecurities and personal disgust and negative connotations melted away; she saw herself brand new, brand naked, and she was glorious.

Oh god, that's horrible, she thought. A friend had once remarked to her, innocently or ignorantly, a homophobic, or so she perceived, thought: can homosexuals fall in love with themselves, physically? How stupid, what a homophobic question, Julie had thought. They're not all narcissus, they're just like normal people, not magical creatures (except in a playful-pretend way when they want to be), full of the same body issues as everyone else. Love is more mental than physical anyways; everyone should love themselves, but *falling in love with yourself,* the way you would with a romantic partner is impossible; it takes two to truly create love; real love with all the physical, mental and emotional ingredients. But... I do look amazing, she thought. My breasts (she cupped them, pushed them up, squeezed them together, they were so soft, the touch tickled her, made her giggle, and then she gasped; her hands, cupping her breasts way up high, so far from her crotch where they wanted to plunge and rub, to feed the hunger, made her body twitch) are so glorious; they nourish babies, they are miracles, they make me a woman, a full woman. She desperately wanted someone to come admire her, so that she would stop admiring herself; what a crazy thing to be doing; it's the spell, the lust spell, the horrible, glorious, oh wow this is making me delirious, this is so great, is this really so horrible, well yes, if this continues, you won't be able to function or get through the day, let alone life, lust spell.

Sarah opened the bathroom door, caught Julie's full nude body, her head back, her hand rubbing her crotch, the other hand around her neck, her shifting her shoulders rhythmically back and forth. "Oh!" Sarah yelped and immediately blushed. Julie glanced at her and she didn't stop rubbing herself. Sarah diverted her gaze to the ground, shut the door half way and then paused. She was intrigued, curious. She hadn't ever seen Julie fully nude like that before. And seemingly glowing. And so bold; strangely bold. And just in that fraction of a second her gaze hit her, she shot at her a… it was like a laser beam which communicated a message to her, the message being, come in and play. Look at me and let me look at you. I showed you all of me; I'll show you more, now you must do the same. It was totally sexual; totally full of lust; the laser Julie shot at her was like transferring some of her own lust into her, causing it to stir and kick in her in new ways. Being naked with other girls, in dressing rooms and things, had always been kind of strange and uncomfortable, mostly because of the inner self consciousness it brought, but never sexual, to Sarah. She thought it strange that suddenly, so suddenly she should be… what's the word, and was it true… turned on, sexually, by Julie's nude body. Julie was obviously enviously gorgeous; Sarah thought so the first time she laid eyes on her. She was jealous of her looks. That someone as attractive as that could look at her that way, with so much want, so much lustful want, no, need, flattered her. Her heart began to race at the thought. The racy thought: I want to enter the room and explore, see what happens; should I dare? Am I that daring? It would be totally weird experimenting sexually with Julie; we know each other too well, are too friendly; what do you do afterwards; wouldn't the awkwardness kill us both? But that person, nude and glowing in the bathroom, Sarah could tell just by glancing, was not the normal Julie. She was a creature transformed. Another thought struck her: this could be my way into Steve. If I am ever to get with Steve, like I want to so badly, wanted to since I first saw him nearly, it would, I have to admit at this point, probably be through a three-way. At first. And here, I see it, Julie wanting me. If she wants me, then she'd be open to a three way with me and Steve. She'd probably even suggest it. And not just to satisfy him, but to satisfy her as well. And me. They're such a boring couple; I've heard them fret over being a boring couple before; they'd entertain the three-way, go through with it, to spice things up, their love life and everything else, Sarah told herself.

Sarah creaked the door open wider and peaked in. There she still was, standing, writhing, rubbing her hands over her ribs, her breasts, down the side of her hips. Where before there was playful mirth in the glint in her eye in that gaze Julie flashed at her, an oops, you caught me, you naughty spy, I don't care, don't you like what you see, come on in and play, type of thing, now she looked at her with something closer to wrath; a slit eyed teeth baring anger that she wasn't there all ready, nude and satisfying her physical needs. Julie looked almost demonic, possessed by lust, no longer in control of it, letting it control her. Like a dog in heat. Sarah was attractive, had a short bobbed haircut currently she dyed blonde, and blue eyes, and had turned plenty of boys mad with want in her time, yet she had never seen anything like what nude Julie was showing her; the anger in lust, demanding in the want; a human so transformed into something other human. It scared her, titillated her, perplexed her, enticed her. She took a step in. Julie growled; but it was a sexy growl; so weird. Sarah gulped and then struck a sexy type pose, leaning on one leg. She looked down shyly. Her heart beat faster. She smiled. She pulled down on her white cotton shirt she slept in, making the cotton tight against her breasts. Julie growled again. Sarah couldn't help but to giggle in response.

"Take it off... take it off," Julie demanded through measured panted breaths. Her eyes slit her teeth grit through deep gasps, her writhing in rhythmic timing to her heavy breaths, doing strange, yet wonderful things to her body; it quaking from within. Julie had moved herself against the wall to keep her balance, to keep standing. Her hands were like claws. "God, take it off, all of it, show me your tits, show me them, all of them, take off your shirt!" she shrieked.

Sarah smiled. This was so wild. She had to obey, just to satisfy poor Julie. Sarah pitied her for the first time ever, Julie's body so violently inflicted by these throes of lust. Bitch Julie, Sarah had always thought Julie was sort of bitchy, despite being her friend, so perfect, the new degree from Stanford, the great interior design job, the rich daddy, the perfect fiancé. And now, here she was, begging for her. Julie's hand thrust down to her crotch and rubbed so hard and violent it startled Sarah. Julie threw her head back, moaned, and then lowered her chin again, giving Sarah that wild look. Through Julie's pants she gave a wild smile. Sarah smirked back. 'I think I could literally make her explode if I tease her too much,' Sarah thought. 'I could seriously hurt her. Give her a heart attack or something'. Sarah pulled up on her shirt. Julie growled a grunt through a smile. More, her eyes said. More. Sarah pulled up more, just under her breasts. And then over her head. She had happened to go to sleep in a pink lace bra that night.

Julie gasped, ogled, in disbelief over the beauty Sarah showed her; the beauty of her body, her tight stomach, supple skin, the skin tone, the whiteness. How the light and shadow bounced off her near nakedness. God, and her legs, in those tube socks, and there, her pink panties and bra, oh god. Such a petite thing, I thought I was petite, but she's a minx, she's a magical creature, with that short bob pixie haircut, oh god. Her breasts are bigger than I thought; more than I noticed, what a damning amazing combination, the petite feminine body with the ample bosom, I wished they were freed from the cotton bra, no wait, this is nice, to be teased, to wonder, to see the material push up on them, causing the shape, the blub shape, the upslope curve, the definition of the circles there; I want them let lose, I want to see them all, I want to see her nipples too, and marvel over all of her, all the skin exposed, no cover to block the color of her skin into different shapes, but to make all one shape. "Take it off," Julie said, wild eyed, panting.

"Come take if off," Sarah teased.

Oh god. Such sweet music. Such sweet words. Go. She unleashed the beast. She let the beast loose. Come here and take me, she said. I will come and take her. Oh god so bad, I want it so bad, to see her, to feel her, so bad.

Julie stepped towards her. Sarah instinctively took a flinching step back. Then she firmed, threw back her shoulders and lifted her chin, to brace for the impact. The impact came. Startling hard. Julie swung her around and pushed her towards the shower, her hands clawed over her shoulders. Sarah shirked. Her bra ripped off and then her panties, all at once, in a whirlwind. Her nipples tingled as if struck by a cold breeze; she wasn't sure where or why that sensation had come. She looked down and saw slobber over her naked and exposed breasts. Then she yelped again, and flinched, then laughed. A nibble occurred, a small bite, right on the inside of her pussy; how had she gotten her teeth in there? So quickly? It made her laugh and then burst in giggling. Owe ,owe, not so hard, Sarah said, in response to Julie pressing so hard against her breasts, her back smashed against the cold tile of the shower wall. It was too rough, just a bit, but Julie's hands were also smaller and softer than a mans and in some ways it wasn't too hard but just right. The shower turned on, cold; Sarah yelped again from the sudden touch and then giggled, spontaneously, involuntarily. "God Julie, oh my god, what got into you, what's happening?"

"You fucking angel, you devil minx, you perfect damn angle," Julie yelped, looking at her up and down, then licking her lips, almost feeling like she wanted to cry from disbelief, her good luck and fortune to be in the presence of this sex goddess creature she saw, through her insatiable lust, Sarah had become. Julie kissed her on the mouth. Sarah hummed. It felt good. She opened her mouth and they engaged in open mouth kissing. Aggressive but pleasing. Sarah kissed back, she touched Julie's skin, on her side boob and then down her ribs, in a rubbing stroke, in mirror response to Julie's touch. White light flooded her brain. Julie's skin was soft, sensitive, raised by bumps. She sensed, and felt, through even the slightest of touches, Julie's pulse racing, all through her veins. Sarah laughed again: Julie was grinding her pelvis against her leg, humping. It felt good. Really good. She touched and took Julie's hand and placed it over her pussy. Then she thrust her hand over Julie's pussy and rubbed, slow. Julie unleashed the loudest orgasmic moan. She burst in climax, another one, multiple after multiple, like an exploding extending fireworks show, even from the slightest touch seemingly; oh god Sarah's hands were like the hand of a golden god of light, especially when they tickled near and over her gentiles and the ticklish spot between her rib. It was bliss. Not even Steve had ever been able to make her explode that way. Which she sort of felt strange and guilty about, but in the throes of passion everything but the bliss of the orgasm melt away. She knew, in the deep reserves of her rational mind under the flood of exploding endorphins and pleasure sensors in her brain lighting up like Christmas lights, that this wasn't real; these feelings, this attraction, this blissful pleasure; it was the curse. In the moment, the word "curse" needing to be in quotation marks; this was amazing.

As Julie rubbed Sarah's crotch she also moaned and panted and came to orgasm, as the shower water ran off her body. She had suspected at some point she might go further with a girl than just the drunken dance kiss at a rave thing, which she had done a couple of times already, but she had never suspected that another women would ever actually bring her to orgasm. What this might mean, if anything, she decided she may have to mull over later. Would it be possible for her to fall in love with Julie? Her mind boggled over the thought, as she lay in the bath, panting, exhausted, overcome.

Julie had fully appreciated the female form, as she never had before. Enjoyed the sight and feel of it. Marveled over it. Her multiple orgasms were in dedication to and in honor of the divinity of the female form, the female body. Yet still she was unfulfilled. Even during the throes of passion, being the aggressor so assuming the traditional male energy of intercourse, she had wished that she could either turn into a man, in order to fully devour Sarah, penetrate her, thrust into her, take her, or that Sarah could turn into a man, so that she could feel a full missile of a high powered engorged cock repeatedly ram her, fully feeding her, taking her, again and again through the desperate and clumsy eager thrusts. She wanted to pound but more so to be pounded in a way that Sarah could not give her (but the absence of space in her groin was the source of power and mystery as well, that so titled and thrilled her, to fill that space with her hand and mouth, to love the feel of the slopes which led to the pinpoint of absence of space there, in that special place that so delighted her in that moment; delighted, tickled and thrilled; her little space there and her own little space there, so like hers but so unlike hers as well; how fun, how funny, how tickling and silly and great and everything, how orgasmic, that thing they need, come about so naturally and spontaneously, where they looked at each other's pussies, both shaved raw bare like their boyfriends liked them, a pain and chore made for the boyfriends sake, but now for our sakes because we like this bareness in each other, they both communicated with their eyes as they locked eyes after looking down at each other's pussies, then looked back down at each other pussies, eyes allowed to linger longer, to compare them; both were cute tight little things, everything tucked in tight and well inside the little crease, and then, seemingly accidently, seemingly perfectly nature wanting, like two magnets finding each other, their bare pussy muscles bumped each other, brushing each other, and both felt the tingle chill of it run from their crotch up their spines to spark off pleasure sensors in their brain, causing them both to giggle, Julie, even in her heated aggression still unleashing the girlishly sweet giggle to match Sarah's, and then, oops, they bumped into each other again, a little more head on and direct, and then again, harder, and then again, as if their pussy lips were kissing the same way their mouth lips had kissed; they laughed and delighted in it; the feeling, the silliness, the wild wonder and *I can't believe this is happening, I can't believe we're doing this,* thrill.

It was so great, yet still, after the thing, Sarah done, convulsing in the bath, Julie wasn't done, she wanted more, she wanted dick. Her lust, happy yet wanting even more, still insatiable. She stood and climbed out of the bath, leaving Sarah, naked and wet lying in it, like a victim of her murder. She wrapped a towel around her; oh god the softness of it, the skin of her body could hardly take it, it was so sensitive. How cute it felt, to be covered again, how badly her body wanted to be uncovered again, for how greatly the softness of the towel felt, still the breeze over the nothingness covering her was even more pleasant. She smiled wickedly knowing soon she'd unleash the towel and be free of cloth soon again, in order to surprise who she suspected sat on the living room couch. Won't he be surprised to see her and what she would do to him; what she would show him. Bad, bad girl Julie, she thought in delight, still delirious by lust. Her roommate Rebecca's boyfriend was attractive, she had always thought. Athletic and black. She always wanted to be with a black man, at least once. How great her white skin would look contrasting against that delicious dark color. She envisioned it often; her playing a young prostitute to a young and muscular Denzel Washington, laying in bed with him, her arm draped over his bare brown chest; what a nice picture that would make. Paulo was his name; he was Brazilian actually. That'd have to do. That'd be even better maybe. She had held, or her rational non 'cursed' self, had held, a slight lament that she had become engaged so young, therefore meaning she'd never be with a black man (was it slightly racist to be enticed by the perceived 'danger' in it; was it permissible to allow it to be 'taboo' and 'dangerous' within the fantasy, when in reality it was no such thing; are all things permissible within fantasy because it's just fantasy; it would raise the eyebrows of her perhaps slightly racist parents anyways, perhaps) for she of course imagined she'd be with Steve forever, either that or die, she had always believed, but now, overwhelmed by lust, she had no choice but to obey the needs of her body, feed its hunger, nothing, not morals, not love, not fear of future regret, could block the fire of lust raging any more than a forest can block a fire from raging; she will have him. And there he was, Paulo, sitting stiff on the couch. She didn't care where Rebecca was, out just for a second to the grocery store perhaps. He tried not to look at her but he couldn't help it, he glanced at her, wrapped in her towel, wet, and then cocked his head straight, nervously. Poor boy. He was helpless. Like a rabbit with its foot stuck in a clamped bear trap. She knew she was a goddess. She knew he wanted her if she made the temptation impossible to resist. Which would be easy, she could tell, she could sense, by his tenseness. His knees knocking tightly uncomfortably together, his hands in his lap, couldn't conceal his raging boner poking up from his silk long basketball shorts. He had heard her and Sarah in the bathroom. He had heard everything. She giggled. She sauntered in front of him, in front of the open living room window. Poor silly boy, maybe he thought placing himself in front of an open window would protect him. It won't. Don't you know how insane I am with want. How insane I'll make you with want for me. How god damn lucky you are.

She stood in front of him, posing. Playing shy and a bit demure, swiveling her bear toe over the carpet. Giving him the same teasing, 'play with me' look she had given Sarah, now wrecked, bewildered in the tub. She raised her eyebrows and reached to play with the end strand of her hair, letting her towel slip just a bit. Her raised eyebrow look said, *yeah? You like?* She knew it was dead sexy; she knew she had him. He gulped. She loved it; seeing him sweat. *Oops.* She dropped her towel. She stood, posed, shoulders back, chest thrust out, head cocked back in confidence, completely nude. She tried not to smile but then couldn't hold the *cold smolder fake innocent* look any longer; she smiled, sweetly.

"Fuck," Paulo said. "I'm fucked."

She skipped towards him and bounced onto his lap. It wasn't two minutes later he was bare assed drilling her from behind, giving it to her hard like she wanted. She panted and moaned, begging him to give it to her even harder, more, more, more, yes, yes, yes, oh god yes. 'Like this, how's this, you bitch' he chanted back, his arm tight around her waist, his other around her neck. 'You wrecked me you bitch, you know that, you like it like this huh, how about this, uh, uh, uh, uh, he grunted; harder, harder, harder,' she yelled back, then matched his grunts, louder than him, partly in a mocking way, a 'I got you, you sucker' way. A mother out with a boy, early teens it looked like, walked by and then peaked into the window. The old lady screamed and covered her sons face and forced him to run. Julie burst out in a maniacal demonic laugh. She wanted to chase after the boy, rip his pants off, grab his hard cock and thrust it up her snatch. She gasped in her laugh and then began to cry at the sheer evil of it. She had never had such a criminal evil thought before. It scared her, shocked her that it had flashed to her as it had; that evil, evil, want. That act of statutory rape which flashed through her mind.

"Fuck, you crying, you cry laughing, you crazy bitch" Paulo said and he seemed to soften a bit.

"Harder, harder, harder!" Julie screamed. She looked behind, gave his a desperate look, reached behind her and grabbed his cock and squeezed it. He climaxed, groaned and yelled in strange ecstasy. Then he pulled out. He slumped on the floor, panting, defeated, bewildered. She turned, enraged. "That's it!" She wasn't satisfied. More orgasms had exploded in her, but like a drug addict becoming gradually immune to heroine, thus needing greater and greater dosages to reach the highs that are so craved, the orgasms already (already!) were beginning to lose some of their bright and toxic potency. Higher dosages were needed.

A crash struck the glass of the living room window, creating a crack. She looked out the window and saw Rebecca, mascara smeared on her wet cheeks throwing rocks at the window, yelling obscenities in incoherence.

"You bitch, you fucking bitch, you crazy fucking bitch," Paulo said, lying on the ground, eyes closed. "I was going to propose to her."

Julie felt partly bad but mostly she wanted to feed her body. She was like a monster; I'm like a monster, she thought. Like a mindless zombie with an insatiable thrust for brains, or a vampire in desperate deathly want for blood, in order simply to survive. Yet I want sex. Still, it is not enough. This lust, this cursed, (yes, cursed, no more parentheses around the word, surly a curse) lust spell.

A police car, sirens blaring, raced and screeched to a halt against the curb in front of the window. A policeman leaped out of the car and raced towards the front door, oddly ignoring Rachel throwing rocks at the window. He pounded on the door. "We have a case of indecent exposure here!" he yelled. "Open up, you are in violation of the law!"

"Oh Shiiiittt," Paulo said.

Still uncovered Julie went and opened the door.

"Mamn, I'm going to ask you to please cover up," the officer said.

He wasn't particularly handsome or young or fit, but Julie found his uniform sexy. She right then decided that she has always wanted to do a cop. She lunged at him and bit his lip, then pulled him into the living room by dragging him in, her bite over the bottom of his lip. Her lust gave her a jolt of strength. The cop fell over and held out his hands instinctively to keep balance and not smash his nose into the ground. His hands groped her breasts as they thumped on the ground. She was so soft, her skin was electric, he never felt anything like that. Startled, confused, he reached for his gun and pulled it out of the holster. She reached for his hand. He burst in sweat, his heart racing, nervous at the thought that he'd shoot her. Afraid of and excited by the thought, his finger tickling the trigger. He loved shooting his gun. He withheld from squeezing, just barely. He knew he should have, his training would advise him if an aggressive assailant reached for his gun, to fire away; your life is in danger at that point. But god, she was so pretty and so naked; the most beautiful naked girl he'd ever seen, even through the tough tussle of this thing happening, so suddenly, my god, he thought, she's beautiful; hookers aren't like this, crack whores aren't like this; no one is like this; she must be on drugs, poor girl, someone as young and so soul destroying angelically beautiful as that destroyed by drugs is the saddest thing; but she didn't look wrecked; no blemishes on her skin, no stink; she smelled clean, her skin glistened with sweet smelling sweat; the dampness made her flesh look even more plush and squeezable; I'd so much like to squeeze her rather than squeeze the trigger; wait until the boys down at the station get a load of this story; laughs and slaps on the back for days, months, maybe the rest of my career; of all the crazy things that happen on the job this may take the cake; wrestling on the ground with a gun with someone as stunningly pretty, like a supermodel, as this broad. To shoot her dead would ruin the story. Maybe that's why he didn't pull the trigger; he didn't want to ruin the story. She pulled his gun attached to his hand towards her pussy and then stuffed the barrel in. She fiddled with it, playing with it, ticking her innerness with the metal, taking control of the gun, the cop's sweaty hand, in shock, letting go of it, letting her take it. The cop found this highly, highly, arousing. A fantasy of his actually. His dick rocketed into a boner. He looked over at the young muscular black man, who had slipped his shorts back on, lying on the ground, like a dead man; this weirdly added to his arousal. He saw Sarah slip, with her pink underwear back on, from the bathroom back into her room, feeling shamed.

Sarah had enjoyed, immensely, disarmingly, her encounter with Julie, so much so that she immediately thought afterwards that it could be a life altering event. Maybe a polymorphous relationship with her, Julie, and Steve was in the cards? Could she accept that? Could she be in love with both of them; would that work? Why not? But then she heard Julie and Paulo. And she felt disgusted with herself; like she were somehow partly to blame for the crime which was taking place. Shame that she hadn't satisfied Julie, shame that Julie hadn't really cared about her at all, just wanted to satisfy lust, used her as a flesh object she discarded, literally mere seconds after she were through with her, used like a rag, on to more flesh. And then, to slink out and see a cop and whatever the fuck was happening; Julie masturbating with a gun as a dildo while the cop and Paulo watched, sweaty, gross, with wide lusty eyes, was just…. Sick. Bizarre enough to stop and gawk at, yet she was so disgusted, with that scene, with herself, somehow feeling responsible, she didn't want to linger to watch; she wanted to escape, to barf, and run far, far away, from her shame. She crawled in her bed and buried her head in her pillow, trying to muffle the sound of Julie's orgasmic moans, sounding nothing like herself; a sound which so recently yet seemingly so long ago also, had delighted her and made her laugh.

The cop couldn't stand it. Still on the floor, he scooted to where Julie was rubbing the gun and licked the tip of his gun which also so happened to tickle the inside of her pussy. His heart raced by the possibility that at any moment the gun could go off and explode.

Paulo cackled, softly then louder. This pervert cop was coming to arrest us for indecent exposure, and look what he's doing now, just a second later. The window is still open! You're a part of this dude, cop! Paulo thought; his thoughts telegraphed clearly through his cackling. Rebecca still threw rocks at the window, yet with lesser force, her arm tired, her body weak from her crying. Sometimes during disasters all you can do is laugh at the craziness.

The cop decided he went this far, the damage already done, so might as well go all in. She wanted it, he could tell, god he'd never seen a pussy so pretty; so clean and bare and tight; everything snug and comfortable where they should be inside; nothing weird. What a delightful pussy belonging to this golden skinned golden haired wild young girl. He pulled off his pants and she let him in, and it was the best he'd ever had in twenty five years at least, maybe in his life, although it was over so quick and it was a bit of a nervous thing; wanted to get it over quick because of the danger and wrongness of it; yet still, never in his life did he think he'd have something like that, something that good, oh god, what luck, the boys at the station will never believe this. I can't tell them, damn it, he thought; only the few I can really trust, only the old school cops, not any of the new Boy-scout types. He got done, she was still panting, still needing, still wanting, the weird girl, but he had given her all he could give, had tried his best, and felt a bit ashamed that she was still obviously wanting more. The black boy still sitting on the ground shrugged, as if to say, *what can you do?* The cop cleared his throat, took his gun, wiped it against his pants he just put back on, walked over to the window, found the string which closed the blinds and closed the window. He cleared his throat again, wiped sweat off his brow with his forearm and then walked out of the house. He felt it his duty to ask the young rock throwing woman now lying on the grass in front of the window if she were alright. She didn't answer but she was breathing so he assumed she'd survive. He could only hope she wouldn't... say anything about what she saw. Damn it, he thought, why was I so sloppy, but god, oh my god, thank you god, that was... strange. But amazing. He decided to not say anything to the poor girl, let her be. She was probably just heartbroken, he reasoned; the black guy in there was probably her boyfriend, he correctly surmised, using his detective skills.

For a few glorious seconds (was that all?) Julie felt relieved and satisfied, emptied, as she lay panting naked on the ground. Finally. But then like flood water filling a room, the lust returned. And she dreaded it, feared it but was helpless to resist it and so quickly gladly welcomed it again; her lust reserves returning to full power, overflowing power, once more. The spasm kicking in her, literally causing her leg to twitch and kick involuntarily. The tingling so acute, the want again so hard, it hurt; pain in the residue pleasure working through her and the insatiable want for more, again, as if nothing near satisfaction had come. She stood. I was too quick, too rough with Sarah, she thought. I didn't appreciate her beauty as hard or as well as I should have. I want her again, I want, no, need, to try her again. Poor girl, I think she too is crying. I long for her. Just as each person's skin has its own tone, its shades of whiteness or tan or brown or gold, so too does each person's skin have its own feel, Julie learned that morning, in her hyper-sensitive super horny state. Sarah's skin had its own mix of slippery slickness and friction different than Paulo's and the cops. And the feel of the hand as the slope where the waist juts out at the hip on Sarah was a much more fun a feel than the boys, she thought, in that moment, wanting again. Julie sauntered towards Sarah's room. She stood in the doorway.

Sarah saw her silhouette standing in the doorway, dark, framed by the light pouring outside. Julie did have a wonderful womanly shape; the classic hourglass figure, in that sexy pose, weight on one leg, one hip thrust out a bit more. She looked at the silhouette and thought 'demon, she's a demon'. It scared her. But strange, in her disgust with herself, in her soft crying, she longed to be comforted. And already disgusted with herself, a part of her thought, why not go ahead and further degrade myself; the damage is already done. Would I be able to stop her anyways? A part of her was titillated all over again, by the power of this evil sex demon Julie had transformed into. Maybe giving in to it would be a form of emotional, maybe physical, self-abuse, but Sarah sort of felt so ashamed and disgusted with herself that she sort of wanted to go through with it again; find physical comfort in this beautiful monster. Escape, once more, fly away, briefly, in the throes of ecstasy which this creature had brought her; feelings she had never before experienced; a new awareness and appreciation of the beauty of the female form, Julie's specifically, and disgust and shame at herself, to indulge this creatures lust, and let it pull out her own lust, causing strange and otherwise unwelcome things to happen, ugly things in the glare un-gauzed by the intoxicating influence of lust.

"You're crying," Julie said softly. "I was too rough on you. I'll be softer. Slower. Let me make it right."

Sarah let out a whimper. The sound highly aroused Julie. But in her state, everything did; Sarah, laying there, so soft and vulnerable, unleashing a new pheromone which so allured her and turned her on. In the darkness of the room, under her covers, looking so soft and fragile; I broke her, I want to hold her and fix her and smash her delicate parts all together again, squeeze her, glue her together, Julie thought. I want to lick all her creases, make her smooth everywhere all over, put her back together. Sarah shifted in her bed, sat up, scared, nervous, her heart again beginning to beat faster. This is so ridiculous, she thought, in wonderment, fascinated by it all in a way; the strangest morning of her life. Part of her sadness was in the realization that she could never compete with Julie for Steve. Julie somehow was able to transform herself into some super-human lust monster. How silly of me, stupid, vain, to think I could ever compete with her, now that I'm more aware of her allure, am able to see her a little bit how Steve sees her; the overpowering lust aurora of her, the strength of her super powered sexuality. Maybe if she takes me again some of her power will soak into me, Sarah thought, ridiculously, she knew;

but she felt ridiculous and in her state she thought, why not indulge it, indulge everything which made me feel so confused, strange, shamed, just to… why… she didn't know why, just because that's what, at the moment, felt could maybe make her feel better again. Even if just for a moment. Accept the grossness, allow it in, by the power of touch, thought, imagination, turn it into bliss, once more.

"I see you put on your bra and panties again," Julie said. "Take them off. They're so restricting against you. You'll breathe better without them." Julie slinked into the room. "Get out of bed, stand before me, let me look at you," Julie demanded. Sarah obeyed. "Turn around. Let me look at your ass. I didn't get a good look, a good appreciation of it before." Sarah obeyed. She flexed. "Now slink those panties off." Sarah obeyed. They fell to her ankles. She was still soft and wet from the shower; it had turned from cold to hot. She sensed Julie approach closer and she tensed up. Then she felt the cool touch and hot breath of Julie on the back of her neck. She turned. Julie kissed her lips slowly, softly, carefully. "Get your vibrator from your closet," Julie demanded. Sarah obeyed. She then walked towards the edge of the bed. Julie hugged her. The warm embrace felt pleasing. Sarah began to cry again, in shame, or, she didn't know exactly why. A soft cry. "It's alright baby," Julie said. She turned on the vibrator and placed it on Julie's neck. She tipped her over causing her to fall and land gently on top of the bed. This is too much, this is too indulgent, Sarah thought. This is ridiculous. But it felt good. The vibrator tickling over her breasts then down her ribs then on her hip bone. Julie kissing her face and neck, softly, gently. Julie turned off the vibrator and whispered, wait, wait, and snuggled against Sarah. It felt so nice, so warm, yet also so awful.

Julie brought Sarah to orgasm once more; which was great. And unlike guys she's been with, after sex, after the climax, Julie didn't want to run off, like fleeing from a crime scene. She stayed and snuggled in bed. Warm, nice, yet still weirdly sad; Sarah had never felt these things before; the bliss of orgasm followed by this lingering sleepy melancholy, because of the desperation involved. She began to feel more pity for Julie, rather than titillating fear and wonderment. In the cuddle she still felt Julie's heartbeat hammering at various speeds. Julie continued to use the vibrator to get off, pant and scream in her orgasmic pleasure, and then her heart beat would subside and then it would began to race again, and then again the whimpering yelps would begin, building up in frequency and intensity. At first it sort of amused, the *she's going to wear out the battery on that thing,* silliness of it, but that soon wore off to simple mystery and sadness; *what is going on with her, how strange, how sad, how… icky, actually.* Julie had appeared so powerful, so commanding, yet she really was just so weak. Sadly weak.

The way it's supposed to work is, the urge comes, the lust, then it is taken care of, satisfied, and then you're through and are able to function normally throughout your day. Being overly perverted is a hindrance and distraction, Julie had always believed. It's hard to always think clearly, the clarity needed to understand and absorb the complex issues of the day, in politics and news, in order to be a good citizen, smart conversationalist, active participate to culture and life, in the macro and micro ways, if you're a sex addicted, always distracted and fidgety and sweaty with porn, lust, and other sick vices of the flesh, Julie had believed, perhaps influenced some by her religious upbringing, although she never were as strict or convinced about religious morality as her mother and older sister were. But this morning, the sex urge came, she tried to satisfy it, to pacify it, but it wouldn't be satisfied or pacified, like the futileness of trying to fill a canyon with a handful of dust. She was insatiable. At first it was nice. The biggest obstacle, she had guessed, to a female orgasm is that it takes too much time to try and achieve; the guy finishes first and leaves you wanting, or with yourself, you get bored of the effort, it just taking too long. But succumbed, consumed by constant lust, this wasn't a problem for her. It was also kind of annoying (and she assumed this was more of a guy thing, but it had happened to her also sometimes) how sometimes the orgasm ends too abruptly and the pleasing feelings which you had wished to last longer disappear too soon; sustaining the arousal before it blows up and then disintegrates is sometimes better than the explosion, and it's disappointing when the bomb goes off too soon. But with the constant lust this also was no longer a 'problem' for her, and was nice; after the 'blow up' the thing, the urge, the arousal, didn't disintegrate but rather reformed, standing tall and firm all over again, ready to be knocked down; the pleasure and urge just kept kicking in her. Nice but then... not so nice. Annoying. It's impossible to function that way. She wanted to be a well put together, engaged, respected, responsible adult. Not a raging horny party girl, an impulsive, sloppy, selfish slut, a... whatever this rage impulse was turning her into; a monster. She was aware of all this, considered all this, even as she continually worked to self pleasure herself, with the help of Sarah's willing warm body and her vibrator.

And then there was this: when she had woken up the raging lust, blissful and hungry, had blacked out her memory of what had happened the day before. But, like waking from a dream and having the dream gradually melt away by the harsh light of reality, the memory was becoming clearer to her, beginning at about the half hour mark in her bed sex session with Sarah. A memory she wished to forget. White bliss flooding her mind could temporarily block out the memory, but then it'd return, like a gross roach that refuses to be washed down the drain and keeps crawling up the pipes, peeking its ugly antenna waving head out. She tried to wash the memory down the drain again, sexual fantasy and self pleasuring acting as the faucet water in this metaphor. Although she laid next to Sarah, which was nice, and Sarah generously allowed Julie to touch her, Julie still closed her eyes and escaped to sexual fantasies as she massaged her vagina with the vibrator; bulky strong male celebrities, Chris Pratt shirtless in *Guardians of the Galaxy,* Brad Pitt in… anything; fictional literary characters from romance novels she had read recently and as a teen; vampires and troubled alpha dog billionaires with issues only her love could cure; she fantasized over some girls too, which she had never really done before, in such a purely sexual way anyways (admiration and appreciation of beauty is actually most often not 'sexual'; for healthy, normal people anyways; a normal reaction to a striking Monet painting or garden floral display, isn't to want to rip your pants off and grind on it); girls, some celebrities, some models, stripping, at a midnight pool party and all slowly stripping and showing each other their bodies, comparing, admiring, while happy handsome and cute muscular men watched. She even imagined Sarah stripping; thought of how she looked in the bathroom before she got herself completely nude; remembered how she had so seductively taken everything off, and that worked to get her off again in one of her multiple orgasmic spells. She imagined herself stripping in front of a young and eager Brad Pitt who then promised to marry her and build her mansions in Paris, New York and Los Angeles, and that also worked to get her off. But the memory kept popping up, no matter how hard she tried to submerge it and push it away. She shot a girl. Yesterday. While in a jealous rage. With the same gun she had taken under this same bed. Sarah's gun her father had bought for her when she moved out, to protect her from 'scum'. The disturbing thought, the realization of this truth, should quell any lustful passions and sober her. Yet it did not, which made her feel rotten. So she used lust, always teaming at full reserves no matter how quickly she tried to empty it, to continue to try and cause her to blot the memory out. She had once heard that each orgasm kills a million brain cells. Could that be true?

"Get up, put on cloths, put on music, and then strip for me," Julie demanded. "Put your hair in braids, if you can, get a wig. I want bouncy, flirty, playful, fun; laugh, smile, be your youthful spry sexy self; put on a show."

Spent, physically and emotionally exhausted, still feeling strange, Sarah climbed out of bed. She put on a white t-shirt while Julie watched, her eyes wild with lust. She reached for jeans.

"No, a skirt," Julie scolded. "Slip on a cute skirt."

Sarah pulled up her jeans. "Look, Julie," she said, trying to sound tender. "I... this... I don't know. I feel weird about it. It's gotten too weird. I don't think I ever want to see you again. Just... way too awkward... okay?" Sarah picked up her purse and walked out of the room.

Julie realized she was late for work. Duh, of course she wasn't going to go. So they might fire her, so what. She touched herself again.

CHAPTER NINE

Steve Curse: Day Three: Julie Curse, Day Two.

The second day of Julie's jealousy curse she again went to Steve's house, unlocked the door, snuck in, early morning, and went into his room. He was gone already. She had tried to go to work the day before but it hadn't gone well. She was too distracted. She asked her boss for emergency time off. He didn't like the idea, but he liked her. He could tell he wouldn't be able to say no anyways: his choices were to fire her, and if she had continued to act as she had that day, he'd have no other choice or grant her this time off for this 'mysterious illness and personal business' she referred to, quite inarticulately, unlike her usual self. He relented.

Julie had made a pact with herself never to check Steve's internet history. That'd be tacky. She didn't' want to be the type of girl who did that: insecure, doubtful, sneaky, needy. A healthy relationship, she believed, allows for some personal space. Like a good striptease, a little mystique, mystery and intrigue in a relationship can be more enticing and strengthen love, allowing space for wonder and imagination; just showing everything all at once is too much and closes doors where wondering awe could otherwise bounce around and play in. Imagination and mystery are needed to make the things we want to love more lovable than they really are. She didn't want to ever feel she had to know *everything* about Steve, now, as her fiancé, or after, as her husband. Despite it being a minor and easy obligation to keep, she still felt immensely proud of herself for keeping her *no internet search snooping* vow. Wouldn't that be a funny thing to include in their written marriage vows? A dash of levity intermixed with the heavy solemn romantic cheesiness.

However, when she finally fell asleep at 4:00am that first night after having read the cursed book found in the barn, she expected to wake up exhibiting some of the same insane jealousy urges which Steve had demonstrated. She knew, even before the first curse, or "trial" the book had also called it, struck, that the first thing she would do when possessed by jealousy was find a way to sneak into Steve's laptop and check his files and internet history. She hated to admit it to herself, but part of her was kind of glad to have this excuse to do this thing that she had wanted to do yet had vowed not to do, knowing it was wrong.

She checked his laptop the first morning of being jealous. He had wiped it clean. While at work she had spent hours figuring out how to check files and internet search browsing history that had been cleared. She tried her newly gained hacking skills on Steve's computer the next day. She was horrified, outraged and disgusted: Porn, porn, porn, porn, porn, porn. Pages and pages of porn: teens in tights, teen strip, teen in bikinis, teens baking cupcakes nude, on and on. Did he have a 'thing' for teens? That girl, Zelda, might be a teen still. Is he a pedophile, she thought in horror, and more to her horror the thought, 'am I too old for him already? Is my skin not as flush and tight and plush, do I sag where I hadn't before, am I getting wrinkles, am I no longer so fresh faced? They like naivety, those sick boys; they like it when girls are dumb to just how gross guys can be; they like it when girls are dumb in general because it boosts their egos, making them feel smart and capable in comparison. A sickness. The porn sites advertising teens are supposed to only 'use' (and that's the correct word, disgustingly, pitiful, sadly so) girls eighteen and up, otherwise they're illegal and the FBI is on their case to shut them down and throw them in jail. But who knows what all these internet porn peddlers can get away with: their lies, their manipulations, using oversea servers and models where such rules don't apply and who knows what. 'If the police found this material, what Steve viewed, would he be charged' she wondered with worry, yet still again, what worried her greater was what this might portend: he didn't find her desirable anymore, if he ever had at all; he didn't love her. Playboy: thousands of them, all the dumb names of the playmates he searched, endless pictures and videos, all their dumb fake names. Brandi, Brittney, Betty, Ally, Alyssa, Aileen, Leanna, Heather. So many more. All probably gorgeous with gorgeous bodies. Regularly she conceived herself she had no animosity towards nude models. Especially if they were tastefully done, not manipulated or forced. Maybe they just felt confident in their beauty and wanted to make the world a happier place, or whatever, through sharing so much of their beauty. All of it. Posing and frolicking and looking stunning and stupid on beaches and on top of cars and in mansions and in swanky baths and showers and on boats and in studios and lounging on couches and in airplanes and in swimming pools and wherever else. Everywhere else. If they claimed ownership over their bodies and minds, made the decision willingly, no manipulations, needed the money, so what, it's their business; Julie didn't believe in slut shaming any more than she did in fat shaming. Good for these girls; maintaining an attractive body for most takes an obscene amount of work and sacrifice; all the deprivation of deserts and grueling exercise; she knew this firsthand; why not flaunt it if you got it, they should be rewarded for it. Not only pudgy sad and lonely middle aged gross bald loser men whacked off to them; plenty of good people, people like Steve, handsome and ambitions, charming and talented, gregarious, winners, ogled and whacked off to them also.

People like Steve… she wanted to scream and cry at the thought. In her irregular state and mad inner ramblings she loathed nude models; the sluts, the idiots, the harlots, doing the devil's work, enticing good men to turn into base skin worshipers, ruining their lives and their relationships, warping reality, feeding a gross addiction which destroys the soul. Being jealous caused her to raise herself high on her horse; she wasn't fully aware that her thoughts were so condescending and judgmental. *They must be really stupid if they think the only thing of value they have to offer the world are their bodies; those bodies are going to turn ugly soon enough, then what are you, huh?* She searched for her name, 'Julie' thinking it might offer her some solace and comfort if Steve had searched her name, even if it were some other skanky nude model named Julie. She didn't find her name. It burned her up. She's had a few clueless classless morons trying to flirt with her through flattery by giving her the compliment that she could pose for Playboy. As if she'd even want to or need to or was that desperate for money or the sick attention of perverts. Steve had started this porn search at midnight. Of course, that's when the next phase of the curse struck him: lust. So, that would be his excuse. It was hard for her to concentrate, everything fuzzy, details tainted by emotions.

Then she saw it. The smoking gun; the proof he was cheating on her. He had looked up the address of a girl. Zelda. That bitch at the barn, Chad's little sister. The bitch hanging out at the parking lot at Chad's wedding. She was the only one around. She must have left the book there, in the barn. To set off this curse. Her and Steve together, because he wanted an excuse to get with her. Claim he's not to blame, it's the curse's doing. It was so obvious that Zelda wanted him. She said they had made out, remember! Remember that, Julie told herself. They were already lovers? But they wanted a drug, a thing, to make their love even more powerful; their carnal lust; wouldn't it fun, they thought, to devise a scheme in order to hook up with raw lust at a supernatural level and have the excuse that it's not our faults, we were just cursed because of this book? Their perfect little plan. We'll I'm onto you, you bitch, Julie thought. Her nostrils flared, her lips tightened. She threw the laptop against the wall. It shattered. Steve's roommate peaked in and then thought better of trying to engage her. Leave them to their personal business, he thought; they're going through a rough patch. That's not so uncommon for engaged couples; some little trial flares up due to anxieties and uncertainty and cold feet that has to be dealt with; usually just dumb manufactured trivial dramas.

Huffing, Julie marched out of the house and up the street back to her own house. Her roommate Sarah was already gone, otherwise there would have been a confrontation; maybe some blows to the head due to Julie's jealous anger and Sarah's nosiness and Julie needing something from Sarah that Sarah probably didn't want to give her. Sarah had something Julie wanted. Sarah kept a gun under her bed. She kept it in a black box. She kept her vibrator in a pink box in the closet. She didn't care if people knew about her "secret" in the closet. She, naively, assumed that none of her roommates knew about her gun. But they all did. And Julie needed it. More than want: need. Zelda needed to be taken care of.

CHAPTER TEN

Julie Curse: Day Three

In a brief break between furiously masturbating, laying naked on Sarah's bed, literally killing the batteries of Sarah's vibrator, Julie managed to call Candice. "You have to help me," Julie begged. "I'm killing myself here. Where are you?"

"I told you," Candice answered, "I fell out of favor within the Wicca community. They demanded... favors, or tasks I guess you could say, to perform to grant me back into their good graces."

"Why?" Julie asked.

"So they can reveal to me more about the *write your own story* spell, and how specifically, to stop it," Candice shot back with a bit of exasperation in her voice. "We talked about this, remember?"

"Did you fucking tell them we're racing against time here?" Julie shot back. Julie rarely swore. "That our lives are in danger?"

"Yes. You and Steve were supposed to find out who cast the spell, remember? Have you even begun on that?"

"Well..." No way was Julie going to tell Candice that she had shot their one and only 'lead' and suspect, Zelda.

"Just where is Steve?"

as are light and dark; one is defined by the other. Or, using painful sex as a tool to spank away guilt; real bad things people have done which deserve genuine guilt; things like murder.

Anyways, her saying out loud to Candice over the phone, in a totally different context, 'restrain us' had unleashed the stream of erotic ponderous reverie quickly over her, causing her to imagine being bound and tied up in sexual games; the thought aroused her. The arousal overpowered the thought of shot and possibly, probably, dead Zelda; freshly dead, died just the day before; chase that thought away, Julie told herself, that thought doesn't arouse, or, even more troubling, in my lust state, if I lingered on the thought, since everything is arousing me, sick as it is to consider, the thought of killing, being a murder, the power of taking one's life, stomping them out, could also arouse her towards orgasmic climax; horrible thought, horrible reality; think of something else quick, Julie's reverie suggested, and her thoughts swung to thinking about how silly and fun and funny it had been, freaking that cop out, taking his gun and shoving it up her snatch, and then causing him to come crawling to her on all fours, to lick at her crotch where she was toying with his gun; she yipped a little laugh, over the phone with her sister Candice, her lust reserves back at full strength once more, begging to be released or she'd explode; or, more aptly put, begging for the explosion. The reverie and wonder over 'Slave, Master and Bondage' sex spilled out quick, in mere seconds, as she paused, waiting for Candice to talk.

Candice heard Julie's yip and Julie's breath heaving harder. *Gross,* Candice thought. *I am not going to be on the phone with her when she goes through another orgasm. I have got to get off the phone quick.* "I can't torture you or Steve, Julie," she said with dull obviousness.

These orgasms are like hiccups that won't stop, Julie thought. *Wonderful yet horrible all at once.* "There will be a line forming behind me at the homeless shelter to bang me like they were waiting for soup."

"I said not funny Julie," Candice scolded. She had distaste for porn and porn talk beyond the objections of religious morality towards it. Especially the nastier stuff, like gang-bangs. How could guys actually like that demoralizing gross, gag-worthy junk. Gagging is even a common motif in the sex-porn world, Candice knew; the whole oral sex thing, or accepting the grossness of it all thing, gag; a girl has to pretend to like gagging and is expected to even be demur about it; stick the thing in the mouth, gag, in a way that doesn't offend the man, and this is some big trick and turn on or something. Who likes to gag? Gagging is the body's natural reflex towards what repulses it; it should not, under any circumstance, be mixed in with things that are supposed to be pleasurable, Candice thought. Gag-balls and all that nonsense; drool; dampness, in armpits and cracks and body fat, is all just disgusting. Jizz staining sheets and dresses and chins, the sweaty smell of it, just, all so gross, so hellish, ungodly. "I have to go now, I'm in the middle of a thing," Candice said, not lying. The head Wicca of the most powerful local coven had tasked her with finding the bones of some boy who supposedly haunts the side of a highway where he was hit, in order to prove her powers and loyalty were not diminished enough to cause her to be unworthy to learn more of the *story* spell; she wandered a graveyard looking for this boy, while on the phone with Julie. "Believe me; I'm working as hard as I can trying to figure this thing out."

"What are the orgy rituals like in Wicca covens?" Julie asked coyly.

"After I find the name on this grave my Wicca Sisters want me too, I'm coming over with a bucket of lube for you and Steve. It's gross, but I'll do it. Imagine the stares I'll get at the checkout counter. You like KY jelly? Is that what it's called? I've also been working on spell modifiers. They're these daffodil bulbs wrapped in garlic paper and dipped in oil blessed by Wicca high priestess. Swallow those; they should dull some of the urges. I'll work on making more tonight. They're not a cure though."

Julie hadn't heard a word she said. She was imagining young blonde Wicca's dancing around a fire nude in the woods and then being found by some strapping strong young male hunters, who are then engaged in a huge outdoor orgy party.

"But seriously, what are the Wicca orgy rituals like?" she asked.

Candice hung up on her.

After Steve dealt with the Zelda problem he rushed to Julie. They stood looking at each other, wondering what would happen. They knew what would happen, explosive sex, hours and hours, all the rest of the day and into the night, no let up in the thunder, lightening, ground shaking quakes; the electric collisions of all their atoms smashing into each other over and over; his engorged largeness, so big, an abundance of space, to merge into her cute tight absence of space, and in this two flesh becoming one, there creating together the perfect fit, over and over.

They were brand new to each other; their bodies and minds; she had never been with him while so consumed with lust; she had never wanted him, his body, his hardness, inside of her so badly. He had never been so consumed with lust over her. How glad to know that after he climaxed inside of her, like magic he would return to rock hardness within seconds, never done. Neither had to worry about delaying climax, playing distractions to hold off on the climax, thinking of baseball or counting, because after the climax would just come another, and then another, each multiple unceasing orgasms, rapid fire over and over, to overlap and join and come simultaneously just by the laws of averages, both having so many. He wouldn't be able to produce seamen fast enough; her suctioning orifices could not be filled, could not take enough, always wanted more, and he would never empty, would never tire, would continually deliver, with them both in the throes of the lust spell.

She saw him tremble in anticipation. She trembled too. Candice had come over just a half hour before Steve had. She had brought over a mop bucket full of lube and daffodil bulbs. The bucket lay next to Julie. She wouldn't take any of the bulbs; she didn't want her raging lust to be muted (if the bulbs would even d work to quell the passions and afflictions caused by the curse, as Candice claimed). She had thought the trembling, shivering, from sexual anticipations and pleasure, the want inside of the body so strong that it kicks the body from inside, causing it to convulse and spasm and shake, like how Leonardo DiCaprio's Jack character did in the *Titanic* sex scene, was just a myth. But no, it's not, it happens, it was happening to her, shaking as if cold, from want, involuntarily, and it was so maddeningly great, she almost didn't want to get to it just to keep the heart pounding shaking continuing; the anticipation possibly even more satisfying than what was being waited for.

two previous days he had thought the same thing about his semen. How could the body produce so much? Surly it was a sign of supernaturalism to turn the body into this spewing thing with unlimited gunk inside regenerating which needed to be spewed. Just the other day, the last two days, he had produced gallons of semen. And Julie had soaked it in like parched cracked farm dirt greedily absorbing hammering rain from thundershowers. Rather than make her heavier it pumped her with more energy, made her feel lighter, her tits float up, gave her superpowers. Just yesterday it had all been wondrously intoxicating; now the whole thing struck him as obscenely gross.

He thought of what he did to Zelda. To her and with her. To her and with her body. Up in Skykomish, the woodsy mountain river town near Seattle and by Gold Bar. Or, a random patch of forest by the side of the road there. A place where one, in a certain frame of mind, can easily imagine serial killers and the ghosts of serial killer victims dwell. The thought arose like a stench. He vomited at the hint of the thoughts, as if the thoughts could become inner blood and bile he could vomit out, and they would empty out of him and leave him and he'd be forever free of them. If only. He was so horror-struck by what he had done. It shook him. He wondered if he could live with himself, knowing what he had done. How could he. His muscles convulsed and cramped from the abs exercise brought on by all the heaving. It seemed so long ago, yet it was just yesterday. Was it just yesterday? Time and facts seemed so fuzzy, thinking clearly blocked by the emotions and impulses brought on by the curses.

Julie had barged in the door catching Steve and Zelda in mid embrace in bed, both panting. Oh *good, a three way* Steve had thought. *It will give the girls each time to rest between my enjoyments with them. Cool down, not be so soar, and my insatiable appetite will still be fed without hurting anyone. I'm*

glad Julie came; I love her and want her to join in the fun. What
a truly messed up state he was in, he now saw more clearly, to
have his fiancé barge in on him and catch him cheating on her,
mid-fuck, and the first thought and reaction to be, *oh good.* It
happened so fast; the *crack-crack-crack* of the gunfire. Her
hands were shaking, the gunfire had hit all around the bed but
not the bed. Steve's thought had been, *holy shit that's hot.*
Almost being shot had turned him on. What a thrill, what a rush.
From simple, unassuming, Julie. All of his friends had agreed
that she was super hot and he was amazingly lucky to be with
her, but some of his friends confided in him that there wasn't
anything wild or all that interesting about her either. A bit
vanilla. 'But look at her now', Steve had thought; a maniac with
a gun and murderous eyes; wow. So hot. Little girl, look how
she trembles, holding the gun, bad little girl, dangerous little girl,
sexy little girl with a gun. Playing grown up; you almost just
killed us; the rage in you; wow'; was it time for the rage part of
the curse to kick in, he wondered, horny and bewildered. 'No,
the curse was just beginning in her; dumb girl, she read the damn
book'. 'This would be her'---he had strained to think, to do the
math, 'the second day, right? Still jealous; two days of jealousy,
this is her second day of the curse, tomorrow she'll be horny;
how sad that she's not horny now; how eagerly and happily
she'd jump in bed with us, join in the romp, rather than so sexily
firing at us with her little deadly gun. But maybe I can make her
do things she otherwise wouldn't do, with her being jealous;
make her dress up and prance around and demean herself
sexually for me in other ways, in her jealousy. It's not like her to
shoot a gun, she hates guns, loathes the N.R.A. despite her father
being a member, she thinks they're ruining America; I sort of
agree with her I guess, maybe just influenced from breathing the
liberal, soggy weed tainted Seattle air; but look at her, firing
away. Wow, so hot. So had gone Steve's thoughts at the time,

just the day before. She was on her second day of jealousy he was one his first day of lust.

Unlike Steve Zelda wasn't 'turned on' by being fired at. She had freaked out, rightly so. She had leaped out of the bed to run for her life. Julie swiveled as Zelda had darted past her, stupid girl, dank with sweet smelling sweat, flushed all over her body with Steve's love, her body tight and perky, her boobs hardly big enough to jiggle at all as she ran, scare faced and frantic; *my boobs are better than hers,* Julie had thought, holding the gun, crying, her worst nightmare confirmed; Steve's a cheat. Julie had taken sloppy aim while sobbing in totally betrayal to her usual calm and cool collected nature, even during a crisis. She swiveled and fired at Zelda scampering frantic and nude down the hallway and had gotten a lucky hit, striking Zelda's shoulder. "Lucky." Not really lucky. Unlucky. It would have been better, obviously, had she missed. The gun felt heavy and cold in her hands. So cold it burned. She dropped it and it thudded against the hallway rug, just out the door. She fell to her knees, the wondering question ringing so loudly in her it shook her: *what have I just done. Oh god what have I just done. Is she dead? Am I glad? Did she send the book curse on us and if she's dead does that mean the curse is lifted? If it is lifted, then does that mean I'm still so insanely jealous all on my own? Oh god what have I done?* "Why don't you love me anymore?" she had cried out to Steve after shooting Zelda.

Steve ran up to Julie and wrapped his arms around her. "I love you so much I'm going to fix this for you. That's how much I love you. It was a mistake, that's all; just put it out of your mind forever." She felt so nice and creamy, so shaken, stiffened by shock yet softened by sadness; bruised. It, sickly, turned him on; he knew it was sick, to feel turned on, with what had just happened, but still, there it was, the urge, prodding him like a devils pitchfork from the inside; the urge to feel all of her and fill her and be satisfied, sexually, finally, if ever just so briefly, to become unburdened and untroubled, even just briefly, from the overwhelming tickle and sexual urge would be such a release and relief; otherwise he felt he'd explode or go mad or both. He started panting. "Can I?" he had asked, pleaded, begged. "Can I? Please say yes."

It took her aback. Both his request, so soon after what had just happened, and that she was glad he still wanted her. What a relief. Of course she wasn't in the mood. What a disgusting thing to do; how horrible it would make them, together, as a couple, to behave like horny dogs after a girl had just been... it was difficult even to think... shot. But she didn't want to lose him. Whatever he wanted, whatever he needed, she'd give him, because she couldn't lose him. "Yes," she said.

Almost as soon as she said it he was pounding inside her; she hadn't even remembered her panties coming off. They hadn't, he had just stretched them to the side. She had worn a tennis skirt, purposefully knowing he liked it; she thought she looked cute in it; hoped it would remind him what a great pair of winners they were together; they won nearly all of their mixed double tennis matches. It was awful, she hated it, but she'd gladly allow it again; she felt so insecure.

And now, just two day later Steve was in the bathroom, barfing what felt like all his guts and his brains out, trying to expunge the memories of the previous day out of him. Was it just yesterday or two days ago? Julie had shot Zelda two days ago. He had to deal with that problem, driving for so long up in the mountain forests. He had been sloppy; he had called an escort service, paid an obscene amount; had they seen Zelda's body? He didn't want to think of what he had done; what he had to do; trying to take care of such grotesque things while under

her fiancé is inflicted by a cursed book and this is what's making him sweat and convulse? Also, the reflections of shooting at Zelda still flickered in the rearview mirror of her mind; the paramedics aren't the police, but the two seem to travel around together and are buddies; both wear uniforms and use sirens. We don't want the police lurking around us. Thinking of men in uniforms turned her on; made her remember yesterday morning (was it just yesterday morning?) when she had gotten that cop to bang her with his fleshy seed gun; she laughed lost in the mirthful thought for a moment. Yes, the action was sinisterly wicked, yet also so wonderfully strange and funny and had felt so good, just thinking of the tickle of the sensation caused her to laugh. She internally scolded herself for allowing her thoughts to meander in such a way that they'd cause her to laugh while she stood over her possibly dying soon to be husband. It dawned on her for the first time that they had both cheated on each other. She shook her head to snap herself back into the immediacy of the moment. One task: get the bulbs. After he swallowed the bulb, she thought, as a way of self motivation, he'd be less disgusted, and then he'd be able to get a boner, and we can go back to animals lust fucking like we did yesterday, god my body is so soar it feels like I sprinted three marathons; it aches but feels transcendent. The pleasure endorphins zipping and leaping all over her had caused her and Steve to have a mutant like healing factor, like Wolverine from the X-Men, to retaliate against the pains from all the rough marathon sex trysts. *We were like gods,* Julie thought, her mind wandering again, wishing the curse just could have been both of them afflicted with lust for fourteen days. If that had been the curse maybe the promised death after the fourteen days would be worth it. Would the bulbs even work; none of Candice's past spell things and craft projects seemed to work, just another part of her delusions which contributed to her madness she needed to be cured from.

Candice walked out of the bathroom. The mop bucket was in the bedroom. She pulled out the burlap sack in the bucket and out the sack pulled out a slimy onion skin covered daffodil bulb. The thing would be disgusting to try and eat even if one weren't inflicted by a curse which made everything disgusting to you. She'd have to force it down his throat, she decided. It was a matter of life or death. It was up to her to save him. He'd hate it and she'd hate making him do something he hates, but it'd be for his own good, poor boy. And then I'll make him have sex with me, she thought next, wondering what it'd be like to be a dominatrix; how turned on she'd get, and she could get Steve, playing that part. She realized she was rubbing her pussy again. She stopped, told herself to snap back out of it, complete this task; this is a trial. Get Steve to swallow the bulb. It'd help that it was grossly slimy, from the oil she imagined, although strange it hadn't dried; the slipperiness would help it slide down his throat. He'd have to chew it first otherwise he'd coke to death. She walked back into the bathroom, holding two bulbs.

Steve felt some relief that the giant cockroach attack against him had abated. The slimy disgusting creature had oddly zoned in on his crotch. He had had to keep fighting with it to block it and swat it away from chewing off his dick; a man's worse nightmare. He wasn't in a right enough frame of mind to dismiss the attacks as the hallucinations which they were. Hallucination or not, the sights and sensations felt real and affected him as if they were as real and as plausible as if he were being slashed by a knife from a deranged serial killer. He heard a shuffling grow louder towards him. He peeked his eyes open. Standing in the bathroom doorway stood what looked to him like a skeletal zombie women with rotting shriveled flesh. Giant centipedes slithered like snakes in and out of the open gashes in her skin; one slithered out her eye, into her nostril and out her mouth. Stuck to her hand were two giant slugs rolled into balls. The monster hovered towards him like a ghost.

Julie walked towards Steve, still cowering and shivering in the bathroom corner. He looked at her wide eyed as if she were a monster. He peed himself. *I'll have to give you a shower naughty boy,* she thought. *A sexy shower. Then I'll take you. Devour you after you're all washed. Clean you before the sexual killing. And you'll love it.* She stuffed the bulb down his throat. He gagged. Strange, how weak he was. How his fear made him so physically weak. She stuck her finger down his throat to try and push it down. He swallowed. It got stuck in his esophagus. He began to choke. She opened his mouth and blew in it. She found the whole dominating tussle erotic. Her pussy and nipples tingled. She knew it was weird but she couldn't help her body's natural reactions. The bulb was still stuck so she moved around him and propped him up and performed the Heimlich maneuver on him. The bulb shot out. He heaved breathing and dropped to the slippery tile, slickened with his barf and sweat and piss. *What is going on in your head* she wondered. Horrible things were the answer. Unspeakable awful horrible images and sensations. Unspeakably horrific and disgusting things. Things so strange it caused him to seize. Julie walked back to where the bulb had landed after being launched from his mouth. Candice had warned that the bulbs couldn't be cooked or added with other food to make them more palpable. They had to be taken as is. She put the bulb in her mouth. She didn't want to swallow it; she didn't want to tame her raging lust; she loved the feeling of her raging lust. She chewed and mixed the bulb with her saliva. It tasted like rust, dirt and battery acid. She walked back towards Steve. He screamed in terror. "Not again!" he begged. "Just kill me! Kill me! End this!" He then grit his teeth. Poor boy, she thought. I'll rescue you, shower you, nurse you back to health through the power of my sex and beauty and we'll go back to our beautiful blissful endless fucking just like yesterday. I'll make you remember how great that was; how eager you'll be to get back to that, to end this nightmare which is seizing you.

She stood in front of him, pinched his nose, put her palm on his forehead and pressed back. She placed her mouth over his and spit out the chewed soggy bulb into his mouth, like a mother bird feeds her baby birds. She closed his mouth. He swallowed.

She walked back to her room, crawled into bed to wait hopefully for the effects of Candice's curse muting remedy to take effect on Steve. She masturbated bringing herself to orgasm. Her older sister called.

"I'm on my way," Candice said. "I was up all night with the coven. I finally proved my worthiness to them."

"What does that mean?" Julie asked groggily.

"They gave me information on how to counter the *write your own story* spell."

"How long does it take for those bulbs you gave us to take effect?"

"You mean you haven't taken any yet?"

"Well… we didn't really want to or need to, when we were both… super honry."

"What are you now? What is he now?" Candice urgently asked. "Let me see, I wrote it down, what you told me…"

"I'm still on lust. Day two. He just started disgust. I gave him a bulb. Force fed it to him like a bird." Julie giggled. "It sounds gross but it was actually kind of hot. I'm in a mood…"

"I know what mood you're in…" Candice interrupted, irritated.

"It should start working right away," Candice said, sounding perturbed that they hadn't taken any daffodil bulbs yet. "For god's sake, you eat a bulb also," Candice chided. "I'm sure you know you can't think straight while you're preoccupied being *super horny*."

"I mean, if guys feel half of what I feel for even just minutes of every day, then, you know, it starts to make more sense… how they destroyed the world and ruined everything. I mean, poor creatures, they're just dumb with lust, no wonder everything's gone to shit," Julie said playfully.

"It's not like you to swear so much," Candice chided.

"I haven't been myself lately. Understatement of the year. How long are the effects of these bulbs supposed to last?"

"I'm not sure exactly. But I'll concoct some more. The curses have been even more powerful than I thought. When the 'rage' days hit, I fear the both of you might murder people."

"I fed it to him like a mother bird," Julie said, wanting to say something quick to not allow the ringing ugly truths Candice unknowingly unleashed settle deep. "Like a mama bird to her baby chick. It was disgusting but also cute. It turned me on."

"Well… I'm coming. Don't do anything crazy until I get there." Candice hung up.

Julie walked back to check in on Steve in the bathroom. He heard her approach. He tensed in dreaded anticipation of interaction with the hallucinated monster again. Instead of hearing loud insect hissing or banshee and demonic wails he heard the soft voice of Julie. "Steve?" she asked. He opened his eyes and looked at her. He was glad to see her. She was as pretty as ever. She saw him look at her without flinching. She smiled crookedly at him. She swiveled and shuffled her shoulders back and forth. She dropped the silk sheet she had wrapped tight around her body. She fully exposed herself. Her taut plush soft flesh, her generous supple divine feminine shape, the perky soft rounded curves of her chest and hips perfectly a part of her tight and smooth lines; all of her youthful beauty fully exposed. She stood demurely yet confidently in front of him, wearing nothing but her smile.

"Time to clean up Stevie," she said with gentle motherly direction.

He saw her as she was; no putrid hallucination twisting her heavenly beauty into hellish images. Yet he recoiled in repugnance at her nonetheless. He crinkled his nose and looked her up and down with revulsion. He gave her a look which conveyed utter sickness and dismay. He gagged and then took his eyes off her for he could not stand to look at her any longer. He had given her a glance as if he were a nine year old boy catching the shriveled, sagging, wrinkled and hairy body of his plump ninety year old grandmother or grandfather.

His look of putrid distain struck her like an arrow. Her confidence drained. Her shoulders slumped. She wrapped herself back up. She felt as ugly and unappealing as his look conveyed to her that she was. She felt repulsive. *He doesn't love me* she thought. *He can't stand to look at me. And this is different than before, when I know he wasn't in his right mind and needed my rescue. Those eyes didn't recognize me, and he was terrified. These eyes recognized me, I could tell, yet he was still disgusted. He hates me.* She had always thought, a thought she buried deep down even at its birth around the first time that she had met him at the New Years Eve Party, that if he didn't love her she'd rather be dead.

CHAPTER THIRTEEN

Julie sat at the dining room table in her white cotton bathrobe, the daffodil bulb placed in front of her. She looked down at it. She cried softly. How sick was she that she didn't want to take it, she wondered. That she liked feeling full of lust burning her insides. How sad was the stark realization that she loved Steve but if he couldn't fulfill her sexual needs immediately she'd seek it elsewhere. She knew it'd be wrong but she'd do it anyways. It couldn't be helped she told herself; of course it could be helped, all is within her control, her thoughts countered volleying back, no, it couldn't, the urge is too powerful to overcome. Take the bulb to dampen the urge, she told herself; but I don't want to, her other self responded. Her body wanted one thing, her inner morality wanted another, and like a battle between fire and wood, fire always winning, she knew her body would win. It spoke to her on a more immediate visceral physical level. Yet she also wanted to kill herself because of the way that Steve had looked at her. He had looked at her, just a moment ago, like she were a monster he had hated himself for ever having loved and that he could never love again. These strong and contradictory feelings, thoughts, impulses and emotions swirled gently in her.

And yet also, in another stark contradiction, she couldn't deny that a part of her was disappointed in Steve; a part of her newly felt that she hated him. Hated him for being so weak, unable to overcome his internal strife's to just stand up and spring a boner and make love to her, sweetly and strongly like he had what suddenly felt like so long ago, just yesterday. Hated him for making her feel so awful about herself by giving her that look that conveyed to her that, what… that he wanted to kill her, to rid the earth of her evil and ugly existence? But no, I love him, she told herself; love him enough to want to die for him; die and kill for her; when I shot that girl he was fucking it was for him as well as me; it was for both of us. And he loves me; he proved it, by taking the body away and disposing of it, even while he suffered with the curse. I don't want to think of that, she told herself. I don't want to think of anything, I just want to surrender to beauty and be made to feel good. And if I swallow this dumb magic bulb then maybe that won't happen so easily. She cried from the stress of all these strong contradictory feelings simultaneously brewing and swirling in her; a tempest in her. Lyrics and a tune she just made up wafted through her skull: *Fever dreams melt the human psyche/ Who am I really/ A blank glass case to be filled with these curses/ It will result in coffins carried by hearses…* Had she just made those up or was she recalling them, having read them in that awful *If you read this you will die* book. She couldn't recall.

"Hey," she heard the soft yet trembling voice of Steve say. He pulled up a chair and sat by her at the table.

Julie's roommate Alice approached them cautiously and then spoke boldly. "Melisa and Sarah are both mad and weirded out by you guys," she said. "I am too. You like… chased them away while you're doing you're little weird sex and drugs vacation or something. Anyways, some of us have to work. So… I'm leaving."

Both Steve and Julie ignored Alice. She went into the kitchen while being as distant from them as could be physically possible, scooting against the wall, keeping her eye on them. She took a few cereal bars from the cabinet and then quickly left.

"Are you... how are you feeling?" Julie asked. She couldn't make eye contact with him. It felt strange to even be speaking to him. Strange, the day before during the intense physical intimacy, the only talking had been dirty, words to try and turn each other on. That type of stuff as well as fake voices and accents during role plays (her as a princess, him as a British spy, him as a vampire her as a naïve dumb school girl, and so on) and the groans and panting. It had felt like a long time since they actually talked. She found it hard to look at him. Too embarrassing.

It was difficult for Steve to look at Julie as well, although he tried. He was still worried that she'd turn into some ooze monster spitting snot vomit down his throat. "I'm...I think I'm not as bad. It was rough."

Ready to fuck Julie thought. She stuffed the daffodil bulb in her mouth. She gagged on it, chewed it and swallowed it.

"Are those the things Candice brought over? The dandelion bulbs?"

"Daffodil," Julie corrected. "It tastes disgusting."

"Did you..."

"I gave you one. You looked like you could use it. It's supposed to, you know; dull the effects of the curse."

"Thanks," Steve said. "I'm still...I feel like I could barf."

"I'm going to go shower," Julie said, feeling frustrated that Steve was useless as a means of fulfilling any of her burgeoning lust.

Steve gagged involuntarily as she walked away. Julie walked to her room and picked up her Kindle reading app. She knew exactly the passage of the erotic romance novel she'd read while taking a long bath. How nice it'd be to submerge in warm soapy water and escape once again.

A knock came on the door. Steve got up to answer it. He opened the door. He shrieked and jumped back at what he saw; a woman with the head of a praying mantis. He shook his head and rubbed his eyes. The insect head became rubbery and cartoony and then melted. He saw Candice. She carried a burlap sack.

"Are you alright?" she asked. "Can I come in?"

"Come in," Steve said.

She walked in. "You're on day five, aren't you? Of the book curse. Your first day of disgust, isn't it?"

"Has it been five days already?" Steve asked. He meant to say *It's only been five days.* His brain was fried. Time felt like a nebulous thing, where the last five days had both seemed long and short simultaneously. He hadn't been keeping track of time. Five days is a good chunk of time. He quickly did the math. Only nine days left of the curses. This thought came to him as a relief despite the promise of death at the end of the fourteen cursed days.

"And Julie is one day behind you, so she's on lust day two," Candice said, more to herself than to him. "Where is she?"

"Taking a bath," Steve answered.

"You seem jittery. You took a bulb, right? Julie too?"

Steve nodded.

"I brought more. A lot more. I already told Julie, but when rage hits, which is in just two days for you, I'm afraid you'll kill someone, unless the curse's effects are muted."

Steve shook his head, signifying he understood. His dealing with Zelda already felt like events of a fading fever dream, or something he read in some horrific short story by Raymond Carver or Stephen King, rather than something he had actually lived through and participated in. It just wasn't like him to hire high end hookers and pay for them to travel to some woodsy mountain town for fleshy drunken debauchery while the body of a poor girl lay lifeless in a trunk. Even more unlike himself: he had *liked* it. He gagged at the thought. He realized he hadn't gone to work for four days. There had been a lot of messages on his phone from his boss he hadn't checked. He was sure he had been fired. Not that he *loved* the job so much, but still that was a major blow against his overall career ambitions and trajectory. The ladder to success is slick and one slip up can cause a fall back to rung one.

"Oh dear, have some water, take another bulb," Candice said.

Steve shook his head no. The thought of putting anything in his mouth nauseated him. He'd rather shoot his own foot.

"Well, you don't have any access to any guns or anything, or long knives or any other weapons do you?" Candice asked.

Steve shrugged. He had taken the gun that Julie had used to shoot Zelda and put it… he couldn't remember. Was it still in his car? Maybe he buried it with the body. *I'm fucked*, he thought. *We're fucked. There's no way the police aren't going to trace her murder back to us.* At this point, what would the moral thing to do be? Turn himself in? Give a sense of peace and justice to Zelda's family and loved ones? They could try the insanity defense but the 'magic made me crazy which made me do it' excuse probably wouldn't persuade a jury. He was good friends with Zelda's older brother Chad; he just recalled. Poor Chad. Off on his Honeymoon in Hawaii. Or did they go to Disneyworld? Or was that where Julie and I had talked about going; our first conversation was how we were lame Disney freaks after all. She thought I looked like Prince Eric from The Little Mermaid. The whiplash from thinking about Zelda to The Little Mermaid made him dizzy. Zelda really was a cool girl, he thought. There was something special about her. I felt a weird connection with her, similar to my connection with Julie.

"I just made a mental note to remove all knives in both of your kitchens. Your roommates will… simply have to understand. I tried to get good again with my coven as soon as I could. I hope it's not too late," Candice said.

Steve didn't answer. He looked at the floor. He saw swarms of large ants crawl over the tile. They moved their bodies to form letters which spelled out the words, *KILL, MURDERER, DIE.* "I'm hallucinating right? These are hallucinations?"

"Yes," Candice answered. "I've received some answers but I'll wait for Julie to come out of the bath to tell the both of you together. But it is imperative that you find out who set this curse on you. You told me you had some leads? Have you discovered anything?"

Julie stood leaning against a doorway, wrapped in her bathrobe. Her skin looked flushed. "What if the one who set the curse died?" she asked.

"Oh no, that'd be awful. Why would you even suggest such a thing?" Candice asked.

I know you've dabbled in wicked stuff like animal sacrifice and group orgies as part of your spells in the past; don't get all pious on me now Julie thought, feeling a bit envious of her older sister that she had been able to participated in Wicca group orgies while Julie hadn't. "No reason, just curious," Julie chirped. She sauntered towards the table and sat down. "So did your Wicca sisters finally reveal how to end this curse thing?"

"Yes, I think so. At least the dying part, not the other parts."

"Great," Julie said limply.

"Well first of all I've written the days down for you, so we can keep track..." she opened up her burlap sack and took out a notebook.

"Ugh, it smells like onions, dirt and barf, close it up," Julie complained.

"Well... the daffodil bulbs are in there... wrapped in onion skin, dipped in blessed oil..."

Steve sprung up from the table and ran to the bathroom to barf in the toilet again. All bloody bile, no food; how his body had somehow once again conjured up gunk inside to be vomited out, again a miraculous occurrence. He came back to the table, pale and shaky. He flopped back in his seat. Candice showed him the paper she had ripped from her notebook which she had shown Julie.

THE BOOK CURSE:

Day One: Steve: Jealousy day one/ Julie: Nothing.

Day Two: Steve: Jealousy day two/ Julie Jealousy day one.

Day Three: Steve: Lust, day one/ Julie: Jealousy day two.

Day Four: Steve: Lust, day 2/ Julie, Lust day one.

Day Five: Steve, Disgust day one/ Julie, Lust day two.

Day Six: Steve, Disgust day two/ Julie, Disgust day one.

Day Seven: Steve: Rage, day one/ Julie, Disgust, day two.

Day Eight: Steve: Rage, day two/ Julie, Rage, day one.

Day Nine: Steve, Stupidity, day one/ Julie, Rage, day two.

Day Ten: Steve, Stupidity, day two/ Julie, Stupidity, day one.

Day Eleven: Steve: Self Pity, day one/ Julie, Stupidity, day two.

Day Twelve: Steve, Self Pity, day two/ Julie, Self Pity day one.

Day Thirteen: Steve: Depression, day one/ Julie, Self Pity day two.

Day Fourteen: Steve: Depression, day two/ Julie, Depression day one. (Steve dies?)

Day Fifteen: Steve, dead, nothing/ Julie, Depression (death?) day two.

Steve's eyes glanced over the words. He couldn't concentrate on them; they looked like abstract poetry, or math he wasn't interested in exerting any effort in trying to solve. On the "Lust day two/Jealousy day one" part he had thought, bitterly, that's where Zelda was shot; a young beautiful life taken viciously too early. I hadn't really thought much about it; of course I would dispose of the body for Julie, in my lust state, because I love her. It's a man's responsibility to solve problems. Or, that's the traditional role both genders mostly like to believe in, even against their more rational thoughts and politics. Don't worry about anything honey, don't worry your pretty little head, I'll take care of this, everything will be fine. In the "Disgust day one/ Lust day two" part, he thought, that's today. That's right now. While he scanned over the letters on the rest of the page a sense of anger seized him. Who says he has to feel these ways in the coming days? That he's just some puppet others control the strings to, or some empty jar to be filled with whatever vile evil elixir whatever demented cook decides to pour in him? Yet along with this simmering anger was sad resignation, for her knew he was helpless against the curses; he had felt insanely jealous the two days that the book told him that he would be; same for lust, and now, disgust. And so, surly, in two days he'd feel rage, and then stupidity, and then all the other words just as the cursed book dictated. Could death be avoided? Part of him wanted to get death over with, kill himself now, just to take fate back in his own hands and prove the book wrong.

"So how do we... save ourselves?" Julie asked. "Eat a whole bunch of daffodil bulbs?"

"No," Candice answered.

"Some other potion then?"

Candice rolled her eyes. Such a cliché that witches concoct 'potions'. Although there was a glimmer of truth to that Halloween stereotype, but not any more than doctors using herbs and roots for medical treatments. Nature is powerful. We are a part of nature after all, created by nature, subject to it, only able to truly find ourselves in it, Candice believed. "The *Write your own story spell* is too powerful for such an easy solution as merely taking some medicine," she said. "And this certain concoction of it appears to be more powerful than usual. My sisters were… surprised at this spells power. Some had admitted to trying the spell themselves before with weak results."

"Well, lucky us," Julie said sarcastically. "I'm your sister Candice, not your witch friends; I wish you wouldn't call them that."

"Just a religious term signifying commonality and togetherness," Candice said, sounding happy that she was once again let into this *community.*

"So anyways…how do we save ourselves?" Steve asked. It was difficult for him to talk; the room felt like it spun and it felt like every time he opened his mouth he'd vomit. "And *write your own story spell* sounds way too cute still," he added.

"Yes, well. It's as I expected," Candice explained. "Every light causes a shadow and each shadow needs a light. Dark and light. A balance needs to be struck. The spell tips everything towards darkness."

"So we sing a cheery tune and everything will be okay?" Julie asked.

"Hardly," Candice retorted.

"I'm not sure I buy the whole light and dark balance premise," Steve said. "Something wrong can't be atoned by good deeds. It's not like..." he lost his trail of thought; thinking of crime and war made him sick.

"Well... they kind of can, right?" Julie offered optimistically, sounding softer than she had. "Judges often assign community service, a good, as 'punishments' in order to counteract the wrong that had been done with doing something bad. Even if it's forced, a balance is still struck."

Candice paused. "I know I'm... pious, and maybe have been... judgmental of you two."

"Does your Christian conservatism now contradict you being a witch again?" Steve asked curtly.

"They do not contradict, no, not for me," Candice offered. "But as I was saying... you two are victims here. You shouldn't be thinking of counteracting this curse with lightness as penitence for your sins. You had evil thrust on you, you did not choose evil."

"That's true," Julie said.

"I hate religion," Steve groaned, looking like he were about to barf again.

"And no one would be forcing you to accept my proposals," Candice said sounding a little annoyed. "You know, only if you want a chance of surviving."

"Okay, what's the proposal then?" Steve asked. "Or solution, or whatever you call it."

"According to my coven sisters, first of all you get the book. Then you need to counteract the curses with their antonyms; their opposites. Write down your acts of opposites in the book, in the blank pages in the back. Then return the book to the one who cast the spell. That person will then need to end the spell before the end of the fourteenth day."

"And then our lives will be saved?" Julie asked.

"Bullshit," Steve muttered. Despite all that had already happened, all he had felt, been forced to feel, suffering through the days of jealousy, lust, and then, just beginning, disgust, the idea of *spells* and *curses* still felt too outlandish to be real. He still had doubts. Yet he knew there was no other option present in order to provide a possible cure. What would seeking out a doctor accomplish? They'd probably just lock him in a mental institution, the same way they had Candice. 'Mental institution' wasn't the politically correct term to use; when Candice had been sent off he remembered Julie called it something else, the psychotic ward at whatever hospital or whatever, but same thing. An insane asylum.

"Okay, let's brainstorm then," Julie said. She still felt uncomfortably horny; the itch still tickled her; she still wanted to seek out sexual escape and pleasure; she still had a yearning and burning for that distraction and release. Eating the daffodil bulb had calmed the sexual inner swells enough however that she was able, for the first time in what felt like months rather than days, to think and consider things other than her most immediate wants, worries and obsessions (jealousy and lust).

"First is jealousy. What's the opposite of jealousy?"

"I feel like I'm in elementary school," Steve mumbled.

"Don't be so negative! Don't you want to live?" Julie pleaded.

"I'm sorry. I'll play along," Steve groused. He rubbed his temples. "The opposite of jealousy is trust."

"What act can you do, that you'd then write down, that would exhibit that you trust each other?" Candice asked.

"I could… jump from a high place, with Steve below me, knowing that Steve will catch me," Julie offered.

"Yeah, I could do that," Steve said with a shrug.

Candice took out a purple covered spiral notebook, placed it on a table and scribbled on it with black ink. "And what could you do to show that you trust Julie?"

"I could…" his mind drew a blank. "Shoot, I don't know where my phone is." He wanted it to use the internet. Candice took out her iPhone from the burlap sack and scooted it towards Steve on the table. It smelled of dirt and onions. He gagged again. He got up and ran to the bathroom and threw up then walked weakly back to the table.

"You washed your hands right?" Candice asked.

"Yes," Steve mumbled. He picked up the phone and searched *trust exercises* on Google. Most of the suggestions were just dumb group kids camp games. The "fall from some height and have the group catch you" thing, as seen maybe most famously at the end of *Mean Girls*. Julie had already come up with that suggestion. He doubted she'd be able to catch him. She didn't have enough faith or *trust* he supposed. "We could do the blindfold through a maze thing," he limply suggested. It just seemed absurd to him that saving his life from a death curse could be solved, in part, by doing such a silly camp game, where a blindfolded Julie is led through a maze by listening to his directions and vice-versa.

"Oh," Julie squeaked, the thought of being blindfolded and led by Steve's voice arousing her. She stretched her arms up with her shoulders thrust back, hoping to sexually entice Steve. She so badly wanted to be drilled again by his muscular perfect body. She wanted to reach over and feel his firm flat chest and abs. Instead he sat slouched over like a sick boy. It nearly infuriated her.

"Please concentrate," Candice scolded. "That's more trust *building* than trust *proving,* but... maybe it will work." A sly strange smile pursed up on her lips for just a moment.

"Why do we have to do these things? Why can't we just write them down in the book and say we actually did them? Who would know the difference?" Steve asked.

"Nature knows!" Candice snapped. "You can't cheat nature!"

"Nature... watches us?" Steve asked skeptically.

"Yes!" Candice barked. "You cannot subvert or trick nature!"

"Let's move on," Julie offered. "Lust."

"Steve, you need to step up here; I doubt Julie will be much help on this one. What's the antithesis of lust?" Candice asked.

The way Steve currently felt, lust just seemed absurd and gross to him. "Piety?" He suggested. "Opposing superficiality. Boosting the self esteem and self worth of ugly fat people?"

"Let's move on," Candice offered. "The opposite of disgust, or *strong dislike and repulsion,* would be strong like and attraction. Like… smiling after smelling the aroma of flowers on a warm spring day as a breeze wafts by."

"Excuse me, I'm going to go masturbate," Julie said, then stood up and marched away from the table and then sauntered into her room and slammed the door.

"Don't be gone too long!" Candice said.

Steve chuckled. What an absurd thing Julie just said. And gross. He shook his head. Steve and Candice continued brainstorming. Julie came back, flushed, about an hour later. She sat down and joined the conversation over the opposites of the curses and what actions could be done to demonstrate these opposites. Rage: self-control, calmness, glee; stupidity: intelligence, obviously; self-pity: selflessness and charity, give up your sense of entitlement, realize the world owes you nothing so it's dumb to become sad over not having or being more—this one needs more thought, all three agreed; Depression: happiness; and then, of course, the opposite of death is life. Candice scrolled in her notebook quickly as they spoke and threw out ideas of actions they could take to exemplify each adjective. Steve and Julie did so without much zeal, feeling silly about it and being preoccupied with their nagging curses; Julie's lust and Steve being disgusted with everything so much that he had to close his eyes to keep from noticing icky details everywhere, like a stray hair between Candice's eyebrows, and a little spittle of white mucus on her lips which would sometimes pop out like a sudden popped zip, or Julie's voice, a bit higher pitched then usual except when she sounded impatient, then it was lower pitched than normal; why couldn't she just pick a tone and stick with it; it highly annoyed and nauseated him, as well as her new agitating habit of shifting in her seat so much and licking her lips.

"Where's the book?" Candice asked.

"I have no idea. I lost my phone and... my mind is just fuzzy," Steve said, still with his hands over his eyes, his elbow on the table.

Julie shrieked and jumped back, her chair knocking over. She spotted, on the table, near Steve's elbow, the black covered book, the title, *If You Read This You Will Die* face up pointed towards the ceiling. It struck her as being like a massive tarantula which had crawled up the table's leg to unexpectedly appear sitting on the table. How had it got there? Her shriek had caused Steve to open his eyes. He also was surprised by the sudden appearance of the book. He guffawed and scratched his head. Candice hissed at it. Steve looked at her like she was a weirdo. Julie cautiously approached the book and poked it as if it was a dead spider.

CHAPTER FOURTEEN

Julie undressed for her morning shower. She stepped into the tub and turned on the water. She waited for it to heat. She liked it steamy. She thought of fly eyeballs, randomly; the thought just pinged her brain like being hit in the face by a dragonfly while riding a bike. She barfed. Her upchuck splat over her toes. She bent over, fighting dizziness. Along with the sound of the bile splatter and shower spray she thought she heard a knocking from just outside the bathroom door. She tried to dismiss it. She heard it again, a knocking, like knuckles on wood, closer and louder. *It's nothing, just the pipes* she told herself.

She commenced with the shower routine, putting shampoo in her hair, scrubbing. She thought she heard a three note hum. Did I make that, she wondered. It must be in my head. Or, it was nothing. She dismissed it. She heard it again, still soft yet louder; a female humming. She saw a wasp on the window. She shrieked. She calmed herself; the wasp was on the other side of the window. She tapped the window with her fingernail in an attempt to scare the wasp away. The wasp stayed. *Weird* Julie thought.

The plastic shower curtain tore; the bar holding the curtain crashed. Julie's heart stopped. It felt like it froze and imploded from sudden fright. As quick as a lighting flash there appeared in the porcelain tub with her the ghastly visage of a girl, wet and skeletal, her skinny bone white soggy flesh gashed with maggot infested red lesions. Her eyes were skull socket black and angry, her face marred with a scowl. Even with the zombie effect drenched over her Julie recognized the girl as Zelda. Zelda screeched and blood spewed out her mouth and down her chin. She lunched while in a growling scream at Julie. She flopped over Julie heavily in her attack of vengeance despite looking so light and frail. Julie felt like frozen trout slapped against her bare skin as Zelda screeched and flailed away swinging her arms over Julie. Julie barfed and then fainted.

Up from the darkness in her blackout arose a glimmer of a forgotten memory of a dialogue presented to her in a dream. This memory dream was insulated in a bubble, free from the surrounding curse currently inflicting her with disgust. The outlines of the images and the surroundings were fuzzy, the volume from the words muffled, but the emotions and sound were clear enough to be understood. It was after some rare fight between her and Steve. They were outside and it was a sunny blue sky except for one lone black thundercloud hanging low. It was about a month before Chad and Jessie's wedding.

"I'd rather be dead than live without you," Julie said.

"I'll never leave you," he said.

"Do you love me?" she asked.

"Of course I do," he said.

"Say it. I need you to say it."

"I love you."

"Both our parents got divorced," she said.

"We won't," he promised.

"How do you know?" she asked.

She woke up laying in a tub filled with snakes and cockroaches slithering and crawling all over her. The roaches hatched from the snake's skin and leaped. She screeched the loudest scream she had ever released in her life. She ran from the bathroom. She saw Steve. "Help me!" she yelled. He had his eyes closed. "I'm on day two of the disgust curse," he said limply yet with screeching urgency, remorsefully yet with near death panic. "Where's Candice!" Julie scratched. "Where are those damn bulbs!"

Steve cried. "I can't put them in my mouth. I tried… I just couldn't."

Julie ran around the house searching for the burlap sack of daffodil bulbs. The vengeful vesper of Zelda popped out of shadows and behind doors chasing her. "It's a hallucination!" Julie screamed to herself. "Steve, damn it, open your eyes and help me search!"

Steve opened his eyes. "I see her!" he screamed. Blood formed on the walls spelling *murderer.* "I put it in the fridge!" he yelled.

"Why the hell you put it there?" Julie screamed. She ran to the fridge and opened it and saw the sack. She pulled it out.

"It's no use you'll just throw them back up. I tried, just making puddles of vomit everywhere."

"We beat disgusting by using disgusting" Julie yelled. "I can't stand this! There's no other way! When you were sick with disgust I... it has to be this way." She stuffed two bulbs in her mouth and vigorously chewed. She gagged. She ran into Steve smacking against him. He saw Zelda behind Julie and he screamed. With his mouth open Julie barfed in his mouth, the contents of the bulbs spewed down his throat. He reached and grabbed for daffodil bulbs and while flexing his strong abs thrust them in his mouth and chewed. As soon as it slipped down his esophagus he threw it back up, into Julie's open mouth. They continued doing this, barfing in each other's mouths, the contents of the onion covered and slippery oiled daffodil bulbs mixed in with their bile. They slipped on their own vomit, and yet, kneeling on the ground, they continued to try and vomit in each other's mouths. They're hope was that as they did this, enough of the daffodil bulb contents would stay in their stomach's and mix with their bloodstream, to magically counteract the effects of the curse, which in that moment caused them to see the hideous and angry ghost of Zelda, who despite her ghastly appearance, gave an expression of disgust witnessing what Julie and Steve were doing to each other. An expression which suggested sarcastically: *and you think I'm the monster?*

Candice walked through the door, fumbling with two paper bags of groceries. She dropped the bags in shock, from the stomach acid and blood smell and the ghastly sight of Steve and Julie. "I leave for half an hour and looks what happens!" she cried in an exasperated tone, like a mother with toddlers who just witnessed kid vandalism against clean walls.

Candice rushed towards where Steve and Julie lay. She gagged. She ran to the kitchen, filled a pitcher with water, returned to them and dumped the water over their heads. She then went to where she had dropped the grocery bags, found what she was looking for, a bottle of chloroform and a rag, and returned to Steve and Julie. They were both too exhausted to resist her. She placed the chloroform drenched rag over Steve's mouth and then she did the same to Julie. They passed out. With them unconscious Candice stuffed daffodil bulbs down their throats. *What have I done* she thought.

Steve and Julie woke up. They rubbed their heads trying to massage away their headaches. *Come to the table* they heard the voice of Candice say. They obeyed her, wearily lifting themselves and walked towards the dining room table. Candice had cleaned up the vomit and doused air freshener's spray in the air but the vomit smell was still vile and putrid. Steve and Julie still felt nauseous but their hallucinations had ceased. Candice had turned on the TV in the living room adjacent to the dining area to CNN news. Steve overheard Don Lemmon talking about *The Summer of Trump*. "Can you turn that off please?" Steve asked.

Candice walked into the living room, turned off the TV and returned. She dropped the black covered *If you read this you will die* book on the table. It made a startling slap sound. "We need to get to work," she said. "Time is running out."

"I don't want to look at that thing or touch it," Julie stated emphatically.

"You're going to have to," Candice said. "Remember, we talked about this. You're going to have to write in it. If you want to live."

Julie wondered if the effort would be worth it. Maybe it'd be better just to die. No, she threw the thought out; what a horrible thought. She wanted to live; she loved life. She was usually so happy. She had such a bright future with Steve. Cute children, a big house, vacations to Mexico, Paris and Disneyworld; Steve, although not a nerd, other than being a 'Disney Nerd' like her, had expressed acute enthusiasm over the new Star Wars land Disney were building. Wouldn't it be fun to visit it? Visit it with kids one day. And go on a Disney cruise as well; they had talked about that; wouldn't that be fun, out on a big boat? You can't do that if you're dead, Julie told herself. Life *is* worth fighting for. As disgusting as it can sometimes appear, with all the angry insane politicians and class warfare, and real warfare, endless conflicts and death and anger everywhere; there was still beauty in the world, in people, in the future, in little moments, like that Chvrches concert she and Steve had gone to, in music and food and fashion and laughter; in so much.

"Does it matter what color ink?" Steve said, trying a limp attempt at a joke.

"Black," Candice answered. She placed a pen on the table.

"Has this pen been blessed by a Wicca too? Like the daffodil bulbs?"

"The spell will be cast on the book again, after you, and it has to be you, both of you, write in it your living antithesis experiences of the curses," Candice answered. "By the way, any closer to finding out who might have cast the spell?"

"Remember that *this is fucking poetry* guy," Julie asked.

"Right. Trevor. Chad's best man. He talked about writing a book. He considers himself some type of author," Steve said. "He was at the wedding, he had probably gone to the barn. He probably wrote this junk. He was jealous of me you know. Of us."

"He was?" Julie asked.

"He was, or is, infatuated with how hot you were. Holy hell, I just remembered, he said he even based a character in one of his books off of you."

"You just now remember this?" Candice scolded.

Steve shrugged. "My mind has been occupied," he said dryly.

"We'll investigate it tomorrow," Julie suggested.

Steve pawed the book scooting it closer to him. It felt heavier than it looked, or should be, or how he remembered it when he had read it. He tried to open it. The pages were stuck together. He pried them open. He glanced over the words. They looked bigger than before, the ink darker. But as far as he could tell through the glance, they were mostly the same words; dumb junk words trying to loosely rhyme, gibberish without structure, threatening him with these curses and death. How strange such badly written dribble could actually end up killing two formally innocent young people, he thought. He opened to the blank pages in the back. He picked up the pen Candice had given him.

"So what? Write what?" he asked tiredly.

"Write your own story," Candice reiterated.

Steve rolled his eyes. He gagged. "Could you not talk in cheesy cliché's please?" he asked.

"Write a statement of how you will overcome the curse and live. Write authoritatively, against the books premise. State it as fact," Candice said. "That's what my Wicca sisters said. Show no doubt."

"The power of faith... of the mind," Julie mumbled.

"Exactly," Candice said. "The power of the mind is incredibly strong; we see that with placebos and things; the mind can cure itself. In the psyche ward, that's what the nurses and doctors and counselors told me."

Julie scrunched her face up. Candice hadn't talked much about her time in the psyche ward. Julie felt a pang of guilt for being partly responsible in sending her older sister there. She just wanted to help cure her. Make her stop believing in mad and impossible things, causing her to act so irrationally and erratically, like scaring random strangers children on the street by predicting how and when they'd die, and never going on dates and having too much love for her pet cats and retreating from life to enter into this fantasy life she created for herself, as well as other odd and unhealthy behaviors. Candice had actually believed that she could talk to crows. The 'last straw' moment had been when Candice was found yelling and babbling incoherently in a busy intersection during rush hour. Julie had acted out of concern and good-will for Candice, wanting to help her, although Candice hadn't seen it that way at the time.

Steve put the pen to the paper then paused. *This is no time for writer's block,* Candice huffed. *Didn't your high school English teachers tell you don't worry about being 'right' just write?* They did, Steve recalled. Candice was really good at spouting clichés apparently; kind of goes against her avant-garde counter culture witch aesthetic, although she was new again to this whole 'witch ' thing, dabbling back in after her conservative Christian conversion once she had regained her sanity. Now maybe she was going insane all over again, Steve considered. Yet, maybe he was as well, same with Julie. But he knew she was right: he should just start writing. Whatever he wrote couldn't be any worse than what was already written in the book anyways, and besides, duh, why get self conscious over it? This wasn't some work to be entered and judged in some literary competition, this was to save his and Julie's life. So although feeling silly (and disgusted) he began to write, producing:

I have a lot to give and so I will live. Curses be damned, you can't hurt this man. This is all really so silly, I will live, and so will Julie. Screw you dumb book, if you think you can kill me than you mistook. Because you will lose and I will win, and when this book is done is when I will begin; me and Julie. We will counteract things against your spell and we will do them well, and then we will win and we will begin, and we will leave a beautiful life, lived long, and it will all be as great as a really great trance song. I love music.

He stopped. He felt dumb and silly (and disgusted). "Is this good enough?" he asked. He scooted the heavy book to Candice. She read it over. "For now," she said. "Now you Julie, you write your manifestation against the curse."

I will live, and so will Steve, on this we agree. You, you dumb book, will have hold of us no longer, and through these trials our love will be made stronger... She stopped, frozen. A strange déjà vu moment struck her, of some forgotten memory; she couldn't place or focus on exactly what, but something she had just written had given her a disturbing powerful premonition that she had a lost recent memory that had something to do with what she had just written.

Sarah walked through the front door reeking heavily of freshly burned marijuana. She tepidly approached the table where Julie, Steve and Candice sat. She nervously placed her hand on an empty chair and pulled it out. She sat down. She felt a bit like an intruder despite her having equal claim to the table and dining room area as Julie, paying just as much rent. "Mind if I sit here?" she meekly asked, although she had already sat down.

The three others looked at her blankly.

"Look," she said. "I... what happened between Julie and I, I... I've never felt anything like that before. Never felt so wanted. It was... exhilarating. I haven't stopped thinking about it. I guess... what I'm saying is, I want in. I want to be with the both of you. I changed my mind, about leaving here for awhile, being chased away. I want to be with you guys, you know... in every way. ..I know you're going through some freaky stuff but... well, life is short, right? I don't want to be chased away from life. From... love. I want to chase my fears, pursue opportunity, know everything. I'm leaving my boyfriend; I've been staying at his pad and... it's just not working out. Let me in, let me help with whatever plan you've got going." She smiled and then looked up. She had spoken like she had been rehearsing the speech, yet still it came out with nervous herky-jerky unsure delivery. Yet she seemed to feel proud of herself that she had succeeded in delivering her speech. Her heart hammered.

Julie looked at Sarah like she were an alien. The transitions between curses were so extreme that thoughts and feelings even just the day before seemed to be wiped away, or at least have happened years ago and since buried under ever heavier dirt. Even the death of Zelda had become a wilting away memory with lessening sting until her ghost had startled and attacked them.

Steve, with a gurgling burp, spit up about two cups of vomit which splat on the table. Julie followed him with her own burped up two cup upchuck. They wiped their lips as if wiping away fried chicken grease. Sarah sat motionless for a moment, in disbelief. "Um… okay… I'm going to go again," she said demurely. She carefully scooted her chair back, arose, and backed away. She walked back out the door.

"Okay, let's get back to work, shall we?" Candice chirped.

CHAPTER FIFTEEN

It was about a month before Chad and Julie's wedding. Steve and Julie walked along Golden Gardens beach on a sunny blue sky Sunday afternoon. They stopped and watched a shirtless fire spinner. Steve elicited laugher from other watchers as he exaggerated dodging the flames as he approached to place a dollar in the fire spinner's fedora on the sand.

As they walked Julie spotted a thin black cloud randomly streaked low across the blue sky. Weird, she thought and then tried not to think of it. Stray clouds were usually pretty. Ads another little dimension and detail to look and wonder at; makes landscape settings not so boring. Landscape artists are always adding happy little clouds in their skies. That's how Julie usually felt. But she couldn't escape it; that thin black cloud bothered her, her agitation growing the more she thought of it. She tried to remedy this perturbed feeling simply by not thinking about it, but it didn't work, it was stuck in her head. It looked like a turd blemishing something porcelain clean, she thought; a turd smear in a toilet that the water doesn't rinse away; it lingers, stinking. She wanted to wipe it away, wipe the sky clean, rid her agitation. She knew it was an irrational wish, dumb to let a pretty little piece of nature irk her, yet there it was, irking her, against her better instincts. The thing was that, yes, although the dark cloud was created by nature, it still looked, no, it went beyond appearance, the thing *felt* unnatural to her. Like it didn't belong. And yet, while she was consumed with this growing and brewing agitation in her over this stray thin black cloud, she had smiled and pretended to laugh over some joke Steve had made. He was working on some character having to do with his college friend Chad's upcoming wedding. Some joke about how a good marriage is when the partners can contain their assumptions that others they could have married are better looking, more successful, more talented, and would make them happier, to a nagging murmur rather than a roar. He had recently come to joke a lot, with Chad and Jessie's wedding in mind, or inspired by their wedding, or by the lingering dread hidden within him over being engaged ('encaged' he sometimes joked), about weddings and marriage. How people pretend to be greater than they really are in order to attract and impress others; how everyone just lives in a big façade, pushing the ugliness of reality away, in order to trick themselves into happiness. Joking yes, but how much was he mocking and how much was he expressing a real fear, she didn't know. She had pretended to like his marriage jokes more than she really did; underneath the smirks and dismissive laughs lurked troubling questions. Was this how he really felt? Was he really so cynical? Was he himself putting on an act? Who was he really then? Just who did he think she was really, if he assumed she also put on an act, pretended to be more effortlessly *cool* then she really was, pretended to think he was funnier than she really did, pretended to like sports more than she really did just to please him.

They passed a young mother in jogging gear pushing a stroller.

"Ugly baby," Steve muttered.

"Excuse me?" Julie said. She stopped. She thought she caught Steve leering at the young mother's nice ass in the skin tight spandex.

Steve shrugged. "It… was kind of an ugly baby," he stated.

But… at dinner the other day, that couple… you said how beautiful their baby was. You made it smile and laugh, remember?"

"They were clients," Steve said.

"So you *didn't* think that baby was cute?"

Steve shrugged again.

"It looked just like that other baby. I heard you say yourself; you think all babies look the same."

"Why are you so upset?" Steve asked.

"Do you think all babies are ugly?" she asked.

"Don't get hysterical," Steve said, looking around.

Him saying this irked her. She hated his pandering condescending tone. His sexist assumption that anytime she, or any women, were upset, there wasn't a good reason; she was just being irrationally *hysterical* or it was just her hormones, her *time of the month* or something. She knew if she ever challenged him on his subtle sexism he'd deny it, yet still she could just *tell,* the same way she could with her conservative sexist father. Her father's old fashioned *Mad Men* style sexism, if not as overt as the characters on Mad Men, was one of the reasons her mother divorced him. Julie felt tears well behind her eyes.

"Oh god, not here," Steve said scolding again looking around.

It bothered her that he seemed to care more about what others thought than what she was feeling.

"Okay, it was a very cute baby; I was just joking," he said, an obvious lie just thrown out to try and appease her.

"I thought you liked children," Julie said, crying now.

"I do!" Steve said. "A lot! I want to have lots of kids with you, okay? I'll be a great dad; you'll be a great mother, okay?" More words uttered just because he thought she wanted to hear them; no other reason, such as truth, to them. He moved in to hug her. She pushed him away. "Are you kidding me?" he said annoyed.

"People think we're a dull couple you know," Julie said, wiping away a tear. *God, even our fights are dull,* she thought. *He thinks I'm being silly, I think he's being insensitive; it's a big cliché of every young couple fight.*

"We'll fix that, I promise," he said. "We'll do something crazy and unpredictable. Dangerous and daring and fun, okay? Not just one thing, lots of things, okay?"

She nodded her head. She felt strange. That strange thin black cloud still hung up there, like the antithesis of a rainbow. Somehow this little public random tiff was its fault, she thought, not seriously yet still.

"Can I get that hug now? Do you feel better?" he asked.

She stood stiff, arms crossed, her lip pout.

"You really are insanely beautiful," he said. "I'm crazy lucky."

"Is that all?" she asked mumbled through her pout.

He tried really, really hard not to roll his eyes. He thought he succeed; the words actually flashed like warning signs across his brain: do not roll your eyes; smile, be warm, sound sincere when you compliment her intelligence. "And you're even more insanely smart," he said. "Wicked smart. Who else here has graduated from Stanford, huh?" He looked around. "And you're funny, charming, compassionate. You laugh at my dumb jokes even though I know you don't want to sometimes, that takes real skill, don't think I haven't noticed and am not appreciative."

She smiled meekly. He was lathering on his charm.

"There you are," he said, smiling back. He moved in to hug her. She hugged him back. "We're two worlds colliding into one, right?"

Why don't you tell me you love me more she wondered. *Why not, right now; I want to hear it. Why is it so hard for you.*

They both had other social engagements concerning their work that evening and so separated. While away Julie couldn't let go of the nagging suspicion that something was left unfinished, unsaid and unresolved during that little black cloud tiff along the beach. She wasn't sure exactly what though. She loved him so much. He *was* good with children; she witnessed it with her own eyes. Did it matter if it was an act or not? If he really didn't like them? Should it be more soothing or troubling then that he was able to fake his affection for children and others so well? Soothing because it meant that he cared enough to conjure an appearance of joviality, going against his natural grain, which may be internally uncomfortable for him; self sacrificing his own natural instincts in order to put others at ease and charm them. Troubling because he was able to fake so well, like how psychopaths are. Serial killers are all universally charming handsome men after all; monsters in masks.

They met up that night at the corner café along their street, *Sweetly Cursed*. She ordered the turkey on whole wheat with alfalfa and raspberry spread; he got the egg and spinach toasted bagel ham sandwich. They made small talk; he loves the summer but he had a sudden urge for the fall drinks; the caramel apple spices and pumpkin flavored everything. He wasn't sick of summer yet or anything, and once fall did start he said he'd dread all the constant drab gray of the overcast skies which fall and winter in Seattle provide, but just at the moment, wouldn't it be nice if it were fall? It'd mean we'd be even closer to finally being married (a line that she again, suspected, correctly, that he didn't really mean but just threw out because he thought she'd like to hear it; which, on the one hand was irksome because of the dishonesty, yet also nice because of the consideration).

"I'd rather be dead than live without you," Julie stated.

Steve smirked. How maudlin. How melodramatic. How thick. He looked at her. Her soft face glowed with open and earnest sincerity. No muscle twitched the corner of her lips. Her eyes looked to be on the verge of tears. *The purity of a child* he thought. That's what her expression made him think of. How often do you ever sense *that* in an expression, even in children?

"I'll never leave you," he said.

"Do you love me?" she asked. She reached towards his hands. He took hers. He rubbed his thumb over her soft knuckles.

"Of course I do," he said.

"Say it. I need you to say it."

"I love you," he said. It was only the seventh time her uttered the phrase out loud. She kept a tally. She felt like an overwhelmed lost child. She felt like Daisy Buchanan from the Great Gatsby, overwhelmed by the tugs in two directions her love was pulled so she just gives up and pleads to be told what to do, what to feel.

CHAPTER SIXTEEN

Steve: Rage day one: Julie Disgust day two.

Rage doesn't need to rely on rational to exist. There's a common assumption that the angrier someone is at something, the more valid he must be concerning the justifications for his ire. It's the idea of 'he who yells the loudest and whose face becomes the reddest wins the argument' theory. But this is not the case. Rage doesn't usually allow for nuance or open-mindedness or listening. Facts don't matter in quelling rage or changing the raggers mind. Pride is involved; hurt pride, the fear of hurt pride; the idea of being belittled and proven wrong, their whole life philosophy and outlook proven wrong, enrages people. Scapegoating is used; it's their fault; my problems are their fault; all the anger from various life failures and disappointments and injustice, lack of respect, and so on, are funneled and directed on one group of people or one political party or politician: it's all their fault! Certain politicians and radio hosts and others profit from inciting anger and so they encourage it. Calm reason, nuance, empathy and compromise don't fit their needs, don't make them as rich or powerful, and so they are dismissed and not allowed. Rage is needed, they say, and so they build rage in others, a rage which is broad and simple: they are at fault, for every big disaster in the world, and small disaster in your life; kill them.

This is the rambling inner monologue Steve gave himself as he tried to sleep, knowing that, according to the curse, he'd wake up with rage. Anger can sometimes be healthy, in how it motivates the righteous to fight injustice and inequality, to make the world a more fair and humane world. The murkiness comes from the question of what is just and good and what is not; what is most loved and worth protecting, and what is most hated, people's sense of right and wrong. Some of the people who are able to muster the most rage, fueled by hate, are some of the most wrong, Steve believed. History, past and current events show this, he thought. His father got angry a lot; Steve hated that about him. He didn't want to be that way. In his own experience, and through his own thinking, he saw anger and rage as more damaging and unhealthy than healthy. It brings misery and gloom, often times, most times probably, needlessly.

Steve slept on the couch in Julie's living room. He woke up with his teeth grit and his nostrils flared. His jaw felt tight and swollen. He rubbed it. He hadn't been a teeth grinder during sleep before. *It's the first day of rage* he thought. He had woken up before the sunrise and before Julie. He hated that. He knew he wouldn't be able to go back to sleep and that he'd have to deal with boredom. He walked to the bathroom. He brushed his teeth, probably using one of Julie's roommate's toothbrushes but he didn't care. A glass jar of the damned disgusting onion and oil soaked daffodil bulbs sat on the counter. A sticky note was slapped on the jar, with, he guessed, Candice's handwriting imploring to "Take these! As many as you can!" He looked at the mirror; another sticky note. He ripped it off and read it. Candice wrote she had to leave, urgent business with her Coven Wicca sisters. Dumb bitch this is all your fault, Steve thought, no rational or evidence for this claim, yet still felt viscerally. Damn! He thought. He punched the mirror and it shattered. He punched again and again, his knuckles becoming bloody. He had a weird déjà-vu moment; had he punched a mirror before, shattering it, turning his knuckles bloody? Recently, right? Where was this mirror; had it been in my place or her place or somewhere else? Someone, maybe Candice, maybe one of

Julie's roommates, had cleaned up the shattered glass and replaced the mirror; a nice gesture but not one which would quell his hate. He kept pounding the wall with his knuckles, his teeth grit, his nostrils flared.

Julie crept into the bathroom sleepily. She thought the noise which had woken her had been caused by construction. She saw Zelda, her skin covered in blood and maggots, pop up in thin air. Zelda hovered in front of her and screamed. Julie unleashed her own blood curling scream in return and spurn around to run in the opposite direction. She tripped.

Damn she must be hallucinating again, she's on disgust day two, Steve thought; the injustice, the unfairness, that poor pretty Julie should be inflicted with this disease enraged him; he hit the wall harder and screamed. He grabbed a daffodil bulb and squeezed it in his fist and jogged towards Julie. He looked like a giant gooey spider to her and she flinched and hollered in terror again. "It's me, it's me!" Steve yelled. *This is all your fault and your sister's fault* he thought. *You two are crazy; you didn't love me enough, you wanted me to suffer.* He picked her up by the throat and rammed her towards a wall, slamming her against the wall. Even as his blood boiled in anger he still felt shock at what he had done. He long ago pledged that he'd never participate in violence against women. He couldn't deny that he had grabbed her in anger; he normally wouldn't have been strong enough to pick her up around the neck and lift her with one hand and impale her against the wall with such force; the adrenalin from anger gave him this burst of strength. Yes, it was for her own good, but he could not deny that hate streamed through him; hate for her sister Candice, who he blamed for all this although she were the one trying to save their lives, who had given them the curse muting daffodil bulbs and who had sought a way to end this curse; hate at Julie for having such a crazy sister and making such an annoying loud crazy scream at him, although she couldn't help it, it wasn't her fault; still, it had agitated him and annoyed him and angered him and he had released his anger on her with physical force. It jarred him. Yet still, even as these thoughts wormed their way around his skull, he kept his grip tight on her, still pinning her against the wall. He realized she was gasping to breathe. He saw her eyes roll in the back of her head and her body became limp. He released his grip and she fell. *Oh god what have I done,* he thought, *please god I hope she's alive.* His anger grew inward, angry at himself. He wanted to kill himself. He punched his face, bloodying his nose. *Stupid Steve, stupid Steve,* he thought; but no, it's not his fault, it's Candice's fault, or the President's fault, or, someone else's fault; society at large; how could they allow this to happen? Why didn't they ban curses and witches? Maybe they're using witches powers and curses for their own nefarious means; they must be! How else can such idiots stay in power? Greedy idiots. It's all a big conspiracy, he suddenly realized. And it goes all the way to the top. It must! And the world is oblivious! He tightened his fist, the one holding the daffodil bulb, and it crumbled like a dirt clod.

He saw Julie's leg twitch. Thank god, she was still alive. He rushed to her, knelt over her and dropped the powdered daffodil crumbs down her throat. He then rushed back to the bathroom, and saw the carnage he had caused; the busted mirror and the holes in the wall. He took the jar of grimy spell soaked daffodil bulbs and smashed it and then took a bulb and forced himself to chew and swallow. It tasted bad still but it was almost as easy as eating bread compared to the other day when he tried to eat them while he was wracked with the disgust curse. He searched for the chloroform which Candice, the ugly fat bitch, he grumbled in his head, had used against them the other day. It infuriated him that he couldn't find it; where had she hidden it? He ripped cupboards apart and tossed chairs and threw over the recliner in his frustration. Then he found it in the fridge. Duh, he should have checked there before unleashing his temper tantrum, he thought. He filled a rag with the chloroform and placed it over his nose and mouth and passed out, laying next to Julie, to sleep while the bulb worked its magic over his body to dilute the potency of the curse and his rage.

They woke up groggily, around the same time. They looked into each other's eyes. *She looks so beautiful when she wakes up*, Steve thought. *His breath stinks* Julie thought. They sat themselves up.

"How are you feeling?" Steve asked.

"Still a raging headache," Julie answered. "But the hallucinations aren't here, currently. You... stuff a bulb down my throat?"

"I did."

"Thank you. How do you feel?"

"I tore the place up," Steve answered.

"I see that," Julie said, looking around.

"I still feel really, really agitated. Like... I know it's just the curse but..." he tightened his lips and balled his fists.

Julie tightened her own lips and reached over and gently placed her soft hand over his reddening tight forearm. He looked at her. He could tell it was a strain on her part to reach out and touch him, even in this most benign way. He was still gross to her, he knew; reaching to touch him was like reaching out to touch a urine soaked sheet. He appreciated her gesture. "We'll get through this," Julie said. "We'll live. We have to."

"It's Trevor," Steve said. "Remember, at the wedding? The *this is fucking poetry* guy?" Steve's eyes flared, enraged at the thought of him. "He thinks he's some dumb writer. He was there. He must have written the thing and placed it in the barn for us to read. He was jealous of us, I could tell; he thinks he's some great artist or something the bastard."

"Candice did admonish us to follow all leads," Julie offered. "Maybe he knows something."

Steve got up. He called Chad and asked for Trevor's last name; he had known it but had forgotten it and in his anger couldn't concentrate. He got it: Myer. Trevor Myer, a little idiot punk jealous of love and beauty and anything good, little punk, thinks he's a fucking poet little idiot punk Trevor Myer, Steve thought. He used Julie's laptop and Google'd his address. He lived in the newish Marq 21 apartment complexes, about five miles away.

"Should we wait for Candice to come back first? See what she says. Maybe it's best not to… confront him while we… are the way we are," Julie suggested.

"Didn't Candice, *the plump little bitch,* tell us we have to do this on our own? As much as possible? If we want the best chance of reversing the curse?" Steve countered.

"I do need to get out of this house," Julie said. "It reeks of sex and vomit and Sarah's weed. It'll kill me if I stay. *Also the ghost of Zelda lurks here.* Let's walk. It'll help you blow off some steam, *I can sense your rage still simmers,* maybe tire out your anger, and the fresh air will help both of us. Or, not make it any worse than it is now because it can't get any worse; I'm about to vomit again."

"Time is running out, we need to make progress but we'll walk," Steve said in agreement. "We'll pass Westlake park; we can accomplish some of the 'counter' tasks Candice gave us there," Steve said.

They had decided to counteract lust by complimenting ugly people and boosting their self esteem, thus proving that they're not just some superficial carnal monsters. Although, lust isn't necessarily predicated by beauty, and beauty is subjective anyways, and complimenting homely looking people actually probably is in no way the opposite of lust, but they couldn't think of anything better. Was disgust the opposite of lust? Spiritual piety in denial of earthly wants perhaps would be the opposite? Steve had recalled some story of the Buddha, who proved his self control and mastery of the spiritual over the temporal, his power over fleshy temptation and lack of lust by sleeping in a tent with a harem of young nubile naked girls and not touching them or getting a boner at all or anything. During a brainstorming session Steve had brought that up as one possible thing they could do (or something similar; hire a hooker and buy her an ice-cream rather than demand sex from her) to counteract lust. Maybe they'd still do something like that (Julie hire a gigolo and buy him new pants) but in the meantime, complimenting random people and then writing about it in the book couldn't hurt anything at least.

Steve Williams and Julie Goodwin were both young and attractive and had always been. Being blessed with above average beauty brings its own unique perks and challenges. It is a struggle to find the balance between self love yet not too much vanity, yet not being so anti-vain that you come across as fake or dispassionate to others. Yet it's also rude to flaunt too excessively your beauty, except when it's rude to hide the gift of your beauty; a balance needs to be found in that regard as well. The beautiful attract attention, some unwanted. People are inclined to smile more readily and be more helpful towards the beautiful; except when they are stirred with jealousy and resentment. If felt icky to scan the park for ugly people. Even the term 'ugly people' felt insensitive, rude and wrong. Yet scan the park for... people who society might deem not as attractive as others, is what they did. Ironically, their quest to fight against superficiality required them to be grotesquely superficial and judgmental. They made it a rule not to include super old people; people who looked over around thirty nine or so. They discussed it and both decided that people at that age, generally speaking, aren't as affected by either flattery or disparaging remarks about their appearance than younger people are. By that age people probably mostly already gained or lost whatever could be gained or lost from their attractiveness or ugliness. Once the 'good for your age' qualifier must be used in compliments, then both compliments and put downs don't really matter as much, the sting of both losing some potency, Steve and Julie decided.

They saw a plump girl with acne and her too skinny long nosed friend walking their cute pug dog. They hurriedly approached them, in a rush like overeager petition pushers.

"Super cute dog!" Julie gushed, wild eyed.

"Uh... thanks?" the plump girl said.

"You have really nice eyes and I love your hair," Julie said not looking at the girl. The acne grossed her out. She couldn't stand to look at it.

Steve looked at the two comparatively homely young ladies. His scowled intimidated them. He grit his teeth. He couldn't stop thinking of a car that hadn't blinked its turn signal and which would have hit him and Julie had they simply obeyed the rules and law and stepped into the crosswalk without checking for cars first; they didn't need to check for cars, having the right of way; those white painted lines marking the street meant they were supposed to be in a safe zone according to the law, and cars were supposed to stop for them. But people in cars are rushed and selfish and ill-considerate and don't care about people who walk, who aren't in a rush, who aren't polluting the earth with their dirty cars; they don't care about them or the law or rules or life; they'll hit you and just drive off, not caring, smug in their dumb little cars or even dumber 'macho trucks'. Steve steamed at the injustice. "You both have nice eyes," he barked, his mind still reeling from the injustice and calamity of reckless drivers with no care for pedestrians. "Your dog is also cute."

"Freaks," the girls muttered and scampered away.

Other interactions with other park patrons transpired similarly. They left the park and headed towards the apartment complex. They marched up the stairs to Trevor's apartment. Steve hammered on the door with his fist. No answer. He hammered again. Trevor's roommate, who had just woken up from the sound of Steve's knocking, opened the door. "Where's Trevor Myer!" Steve barked. Julie thrust her hand in her Gucci purse, pulled out a slimy bulb, thrust it in her mouth and sucked on it with her eyes squeezed shut and her limp wrists rapidly whipping her hands back and forth, her fingers spread. She then spit the bulb out and blanched.

"Uh… do I know you?" the roommate uttered rubbing his forehead. He was hung over.

"Trevor Myer! We know he lives here! He has some questions that need some answering; some accountability to collect!" Steve yelled red faced. The syntax of Steve's words didn't make sense but anger has a way of jumbling words into inarticulate nonsense during verbal exchanges.

"Dude, calm down," the roommate said, his palms up, totally baffled at how he had woken up hung over and in a clash with some insane angry stranger and his pretty yet mentally slow, perhaps, girlfriend already.

"Where is he!" Steve barked.

"He's at work is my guess. The Barnes and Noble bookstore."

"Which one!"

"Dude... the one at Pacific Place on Pine Street, now leave me alone." Trevor's roommate began to swing the door close.

How dare he Steve thought with indignation. He stopped the door from closing, entered and with his fists balled up smacked the young stranger in his face. Trevor's roommate fell over, landing on his back.

"I'm calling the cops dude!" he yelled still on his back like a stuck turtle. "I'm usually chill but there's a line bro!"

Shit, not the cops, I've gone too far, Steve thought. *I don't need the cops; they'll find out about Zelda, find out I did it; no, I didn't do it, but my... DNA might be on her. It's this damn curse.*

"Let's get out of here," Julie said.

Steve reached down and swiped up the daffodil bulb which Julie had just spewed out her mouth. He put it in his mouth and sucked on it. *I need to get my rage under control* he thought.

"Ugh, here I go again," Julie said holding her stomach. She barfed, trying to avoid her white dress and shoes.

"Let's go to Barnes and Noble," Steve said. "He won't call the cops. He's passed out, drunk."

They marched to the Barnes and Noble store and darted towards the cashier section. He spotted Trevor. He ran towards him. He cut in line. "What do you know about the book!" he yelled.

Trevor guffawed. He looked around him. "Steve and Julie, right? The most attractive, glamorous couple. What can I help you with?"

"And you were going to say dull, weren't you!" Steve barked with his scowl on.

"Um... no?"

"Is there a problem?" a manger asked, creeping up on the three.

"This *fucking poet* just decided to ruin our lives, that's all," Steve said. "He was jealous. You wrote the book! Admit it!"

"I...I... don't know what you're talking about," Trevor, startled, stammered.

"Please excuses us, we're not ourselves," Candice said to the manger while holding her grumbling stomach.

"I mean, yes, I've written lots of books actually, but..." Trevor began.

With that *admission* Steve leaped over the wood divider separating customers from sales associates. He grabbed Trevor and wrapped his fingers tight around his neck and squeezed. The manic anger release felt good, like an emptying out of suppressed and backed up urine felt good; it was similar to sexual release after built up horniness in that way, for Steve. He took ugly satisfaction in the exertion and the violence, causing Trevor's eyes to bulge and his veins to pop; the world is wrong and mad and this is the price to be paid, he thought; I am doing my little part to make the world better and to make me feel well and whole again; this anger needs an outlet and here it is, emptied in justice. He knew his thoughts were crazy nearly the moment they were born, yet still he could not stop strangling, he was sucked in, pulled in, even as he grew increasingly concerned he'd kill Trevor; his animalistic brute urges wanted to kill, must kill, and his lizard brained impulse won out against his calmer inner rational; if he wasn't stopped soon he'd kill Trevor; he wanted to be stopped, he didn't want to be stopped, he wanted to finish the job, as horrible and as counterproductive and non useful as Trevor's death would be. Still, in that moment, made dumb and blind by rage, Trevor represented to Steve all that was wrong in his life, all the curses; his life and the world.

"Stop it you're killing him!" Julie yelled.

The surrounding patrons were stunned frozen from a moment. Some ran, as if they had heard gunshots, others approached the strangulation cautiously out of curiosity, wondering if this performance had something to do with some crime novel book promotion; a skit perhaps, or reenactment of a scene. Finally some man jumped over the divider and tried to pry Steve off of Trevor. Julie also jumped over. She stuffed daffodil bulbs pulled from her purse into Steve's mouth who unclenched his teeth just long enough to accept them. He aggressively angrily chewed and swallowed. Julie and the stranger man succeeded in prying Steve off of Trevor. Steve fell backwards, his hands shaking and his brow damp. *Oh god what have I done,* he thought in horror for the second time that day. *I feel so strange.* He had no idea how long he had been strangling Trevor; too long, in any case, just a few seconds would have been too long. Trevor coughed. He had scratches on his face and red streaks around his neck. *Thank god he doesn't appear too hurt,* Steve thought. He had never understood the type of anger at the world that causes sick people to want to cause mass carnage and suffering. While he choked Trevor he felt a glimmer of that destructive want to cause misery and death on others. The exertion of the strangulation had emptied his rage for just a moment, where his more clear headed and pure conscious of his better self assessed what he had done and what he had felt while he was doing it. The feeling of primal hate he had experienced for the first time in his life, to that murderous degree, shook and scared him even more than the visions of Zelda's ghost had. The grisly and wicked business in disposing of Zelda's body had been a work born from necessity, even a bit of love for Julie, not out of hate. "I...I'm sorry," he uttered.

"Freeze dirt bag!" the store manger yelled, pretending he were in a movie, or already feeling like he were in a movie, the sensation was so surreal, in order to spit out the cliché line.

Steve looked up. The manager pointed a gun at him. *How dare he* Steve thought. All his boiling rage returned to him in a snap. It was as if rage were an evil poltergeist which had left him just to fly around the edges of the bookstore to then ram back into him, fully possessing him again. He snarled. Steve charged at the gunman like a rabid dog. The manager pulled the trigger. Any remaining patrons screamed and fled. The bang of the gun echoed. Steve fell. Julie shouted his name and ran to him, falling over him. "You shot him, he's bleeding!" she yelled. She then barfed over the blood pooling on the side of

Steve's white t-shirt. Steve yelled from the hot sting. He cursed violently and rapidly. Julie waved her hands, fingers spread, as if trying to quickly air dry her fingernail polish. "You shot him, you shot him!" An idea struck her. The book says that Steve will die in fourteen days from the point he finished reading the short badly rhyming manuscript. Steve was on day seven of the curse, halfway through. If Steve dies then that means the book lies. The curses from the book are powerful; she suffered the ill effects of the cursed power the book inflicted on her; she knew its power. She unzipped her Gucci purse and thrust her hand inside. She fished for the book and grabbed it. She hadn't remembered putting the book in her bag, her memory was fuzzy, but she must have. She reached and pulled up Steve's shirt. She saw the gun shot would gurgle out blood like a bubbling geyser in Yellowstone. Maggots squirmed over the wound and his flesh, along with large horseflies. *Just an illusion* she told herself. Her stomach swirled and her dizziness increased. She cracked the spine of the book open, squeezed her eyes closed and thrust the white pages against the wound. "You cannot die yet it is not time, seven more days of curses unkind" she bellowed; a dopey rhyme which sounded like the dopey yet sinister rhymes she had read in *If you read this you will die*. She heard a sizzling hissing sound like cold meat on hot frying pan; green sulfur smelling smoke arose from where the paper pressed against Steve's skin over the side of his rib. The smell made Julie gag and she barfed again; her body miraculously producing bile and blood to be barfed out at supernaturally accelerated rates. Each little or big barf splat did work to ease her nausea just a bit, just for a moment. She opened her eyes and looked at where the bullet hole had been. She gasped. She still saw squirming maggots, but there was no more blood. She felt panicked relief; relief because of the apparent miraculous flesh healing but panic because of the sure manifestation of the books authority. We surely *will* die when the book told us we will. The book just decided to prolong our sufferings.

The stunned manager stiffened with his eyes wide. He thought he may be in a dream and this impression caused him to tighten his grip on his gun to hold onto something real, to grasp onto reality. He realized he clutched the gun tighter and worried doing so would cause him to involuntarily squeeze the trigger. He didn't like guns much anyways; his wife bought the gun for him because of the recent robbery in the area and, he guessed, her wanting him to be manlier. He dropped the gun and shook his head, wondering if he had really seen what he thought he just witnessed.

We have to do something, we have to make progress there's not much time left, Julie thought in a sudden burst of urgency. *I don't know how well we did with the compliment ugly people to counteract the lust curse, thing,* she thought in a burst. She ran up the escalators to the indoor wrap around second floor balcony where the music and moves, children's and teens books and comic book trade paperback, anime, and romance sections were. The second story balcony was about forty feet above the ground floor. *We need to start accomplishing the tasks Candice gave us* Julie thought. *Trust counteracts jealousy.* She climbed on top of the second floor balcony banister, looking down forty feet below at the ground floor. "Catch me Steve, I trust you!" she yelled then leaped, free falling. Steve watched her drop, perplexed, stuck by confusion and disbelief. She smacked the floor below. The manager let out a deep throated gasping yell.

Trevor regained his breath and stood, leaning against the sales counter. The ringing from the gunshot still echoed in his ear when he heard the sound of Julie's limp body slap the floor after the forty foot fall; a sound with an even more disturbing vibration than the pop of the gun. "What the hell is going on!" he bellowed.

The manager pointed at Steve with a shaking arm. "That book… she…. It saved him!" he exclaimed. "Then she… ran up the escalators and jumped down." He narrated what he had just witnessed as a way of processing it, to hear out loud what he was thinking, the words like flinging a saving rope up from the surreal sensation he were sinking in. He at first couldn't register that he had actually shot someone, and then the next two following actions, the magical book healing then the suicide leap, seemed even further beyond belief.

Steve picked up the book by his side. It felt hot like a leather car seat left under the summer sun for hours. He withstood the pain and ran over to Julie's body. He placed the book over her head and quickly uttered: *I place this book over your head so that you may not yet be dead; the book promises death in fourteen days, fourteen days have not yet passed so death go away.* The rhyme just came to him. Trevor had crept closer, despite the strangeness and chaos and danger, propelled by an uncontrollable magnet pull of curiosity. Maybe, he thought, he was witnessing something that would inspire him to write something good for once; or something the literary agents and publishers would express some interest in. He gasped as he saw Julie groan and then sit up, rubbing her head. He looked at the black covered book. *Could it be?* He wondered.

Steve heard a ghostly moan. He jerked his head in the direction of the sound and saw the ghastly ghost of Zelda floating above him. She no longer looked zombiefied however. She looked like herself. She looked pretty. He heard Julie gasp. He looked down at her. He could tell that she too saw the ghost of Zelda. He was perplexed: he had thought Zelda's ghost had just been a hallucination from the 'disgust' phase of the curse.

Now that he was onto the rage phase, the hallucinations should go away. Maybe the hallucinations ware off only residually, he considered. Or maybe ghosts are real.

Zelda floated still and stoic, a long white sheet draped over her shoulders. Glistening tears ran down her soft transparent cheeks. *I wish to live* she whispered.

"I can fix this!" Julie yelled up to the ghost. She sat up on her knees and held the book showing it to the ghost like a preacher holding a bible at his congregation. "I'm sorry I shot you; I was deranged; it's this books fault! But we've seen, the book can make it right too!"

Zelda turned her ghostly gaze onto Steve. She looked at him tenderly with an expression Julie construed as love. *That ghost bitch* Julie thought, although she was still not completely sure if this ghost Zelda were a hallucination or real. *Still, after death, she's trying to steal my man. Maybe it's not such a bad thing she' dead. No, that's horrible, I take it back, my first reaction was right; I want to save her, to help her, the poor girl; I want to take back what I did and never be that way again. Saving her will also save myself; the crime erased, so no threat of police and punishment. I can make this right.*

Zelda vanished.

They've all gone mad Trevor thought. He hadn't seen the ghost. His instincts told him to flee this madness yet his curiosity pulled him even closer. He hadn't known Steve and Julie well, but he knew them well enough to know they weren't usually or normally this insane. They had struck him as a bit vanilla, although an undeniably attractive couple, almost even annoyingly, cloyingly so. He had mused before on using Steve and Julie as inspirations for characters in some new novel attempt (the current one he was working on would finally be 'the one' which would actually get literary agents attention, he was always determined to believe) but had always decided against it; they were both only most interesting, really, for their beauty, and such a main distinguishing character trait can work for the visual mediums of film and television but not for novels. But then they had surprised him. They had emailed him, around two or so weeks before Chad and Jessie's wedding, asking him for a favor, a strange task which had flattered his ego. They knew that he considered himself 'a writer,' although he hadn't actually published anything; not legitimately anyways. They offered him a writing job, to be done in just one day, they needed the book as soon as possible; self publish it, like all his other 'poetic novels', and list it for purchase for just one day, then take it offline. They'd send him a check for fifty dollars, they wrote; more money than he had ever received from any of his other self published works. He would have done it for five dollars. Probably for free, just for the reward of the slight flattery of being asked at all. They were starting out in life, like him, and so didn't have a ton of money, but they were both rich kids from rich kid divorced parent homes, so fifty dollars was probably not much different than five dollars to them; well, that was the case with pretty white rich girl Julie anyways, he was less sure about Steve, although Steve gave off a pretty strong boy of privilege vibe. They gave him a list of adjectives to write about. Just little chapters, just write whatever you want about it, they said (he wasn't sure which of the two had actually typed this email but they both signed their names at the bottom of it). The three strangest aspects of this very strange and beguiling email was that they requested the book to be called *If you read this you will die,* don't list the author's name on the cover or anywhere, and lastly they requested that he not mention it to anyone and that they themselves will act as if they had no idea what he was talking about if they ever brought it up to him. He crept close enough to read the title of the book. His mouth hung open. *If you read this you will die* he read.

"Hey bastard," Steve angrily grumbled at Trevor. "You look like you want to tell us something."

Trevor massaged his throat and gently coughed. His eyes darted towards the exit. He saw the manager flee.

"You try to run I'm going to pick up that gun over there and shoot you," Steve flatly declared. "What do you know about this?" Steve picked up the book and showed it to Trevor.

"I...I... nothing," Trevor stammered.

"Did you place it in the barn at the wedding!"

"No!" Trevor declared. Not a lie.

"Take a closer look!" Steve barked and threw the book hard. It hit Trevor's chest like a fastball. He rubbed where it had hit while he bent down and picked it up. It felt strangely warm and heavy. The cover looked like the cover he had designed; all black, white letters, nothing else. He flipped through and skimmed over some words. He recognized the structure as one he used, and some phrases and sentences as his own; but others were foreign and strange to him, perplexingly so, as if someone had taken his work and bastardized it. He stopped on a random page and decided to concentrate harder on the words rather than skim. He read: *You had a hand but you are not the head or the heart/ In this scheme to either break Steve and Julie together or in death tear them apart/ They may try but they will still lose/ This curse is greater art than a hack like you could produce/ In trying to help them stop theses curses you may try/ But they will still fail and at the right time, shortly, they will die.* Startled that the book seemed to be talking directly to him he flinched at it as if it had transformed into a spider which had writhed, bitten him, and then leaped away.

"You wrote it! You're responsible!" Steve yelled.

"I didn't, I promise, I don't know what this is!" Trevor protested.

"Don't kill him! If he set the spell we need him to reverse it!" Julie implored.

"What spell?" Trevor screamed.

Steve scrambled towards the gun picked it up and pointed it at Trevor.

"Don't shoot him!" Julie screamed. She got dizzy at the gory thought.

"I… You guys sent me an email asking to write a book with that title, with that cover, and I did, but I didn't write the words in it; it's something else."

"You lie!" Steve bellowed, overcome, his face turning red. How he hated liars; how they ruin the world; the despicable, hypocritical, ugly liars, they all deserved to die, he thought; he dealt with liars with his job, dealing with credit fraud and identify theft and online scams, making false promises, preying on the desperate and vulnerable, diet pills that are just nothing, fear mongering political ads convincing old angry people that the world will end unless you give me money, and so on; just endless scams and schemes born from evil liars: Trevor's just like them; a liar. He screamed and pulled the trigger. Trevor flinched and fell, Julie screamed *No!* The gun jammed; it didn't fire. Steve threw the gun at Trevor.

"I'm not lying, you told me not to tell anyone, you said you'd deny it!"

Candice swiftly opened the front doors and marched towards Steve and Julie. She carried a heavy white bag. She approached and poured the contents of the bag, which appeared to be white cooking flour, all over Steve and Julie. "Come on," Candice said, "the police are outside; they won't see you for a minute, we need to leave now!" She firmly ushered Steve and Julie out of the Barnes and Noble and past the police like a perturbed mother pushing her unruly children out of a grocery store. Julie squirmed free of Candice's tight grasp and jolted towards the escalators. She ran up the escalators in about eleven seconds and spun around. She thought, still, we must complete the counter spell tasks and then write of our deeds in the book, like Candice instructed, if we are to be saved. Time is running out; urgency must take hold. I will once again prove that I trust Steve to counteract jealousy. She closed her eyes and bravely leaped over the banister, plunging down. She psyched herself into accomplishing the act, despite the first failure, by pretending that she were fleeing a nausea monster, the thing which caused her insufferable nausea, which was chasing her. She wanted to be free.

"What are you doing, are you insane!?" Candice screeched.

Steve ran and positioned himself underneath Julie right as she landed in his arms. She slid down to her feet, slippery from the white powder Candice had poured over her. Steve squeezed her tightly, partly from anger that she would do such a stupid thing with so little warning, although Julie interpreted the strength in the hug as burning love.

"Now, now, now, we have to leave now, the invisibility spell will ware off in seconds!" Candice hollered.

CHAPTER SEVENTEEN

On Monday night, the day after Steve and Julie fought over Steve's 'ugly baby' comment in the park, they sat and ate together at *Sweetly Cursed.* The corner café usually played good hip music from employee's personal playlists: a lot of new European electronic synth-pop recently. Julie was still bothered by their little fight, which was more of a tiff than a fight actually, but it felt consequential to her. Yes, they had made up, and she had pledged to him, open heartedly, honestly, making herself vulnerable and possibly appear unstable, that she'd rather die than be without him, yet still she felt the issues stemming from their 'ugly baby' tiff had yet to be resolved. It lingered like skunk odor. She had a disturbing dream the night before; she couldn't remember it all exactly, but there was a scene where that strange oddly placed turd shaped cloud she had seen the day before which has so strangely perturbed her, like a smear on a glass that only smudges more as you try to clean it, was prominent. Newborn babies rained down from the cloud and in a panic Julie tried to catch and save all of them while Steve just kicked the bloody soft smashed carcasses away, monstrously.

Steve also felt unresolved issues left over from the previous day. *I'd rather be dead than live without you,* she had said. Her words pricked him and disturbed him; he wrestled with them; they kept him from being able to sleep. He had struggled through work, even more so than the normal Monday blues, from lack of sleep Sunday night and from thinking of that comment. Saying such an irrationally passionate thing seemed so unlike her. How much did he really know her? She's usually even-handed, fair and rational, in conversations, everything from politics to pop culture; so unlike her crazy older sister Candice. Was she really so warm bleeding heart under her cool demeanor? And doesn't saying such a thing, maybe even worse, *believing* such a thing, as rather being dead than being denied the love of some person, a mark of craziness? Maybe she really was as crazy as her sister. No doubt if some girl he disliked, some crazy ex-girlfriend, or even just a girl he was friendly with, had told him that she'd rather die than be without him his response would be to, appropriately, be freaked out and push the girl away, due to her instability and intensity. That's stalker speech. But that it came from Julie, his fiancée, made it different. Initially he had taken it as sweet and romantic. Sexy, even. But so desperate; and there's always a tinge of sadness in any display of desperation.

Another question: did he feel the same way? Both answer's, either yes or no, contained disturbing consequences. He liked himself better with her, he liked his time with her, enjoyed imagining his future with her. They shared a unique sense of humor the outside world didn't always get or appreciate. How awesome and rare to find someone who enjoys yours quirks, who you can make laugh and who makes you laugh. Even though maybe she were faking it sometime? She was smart, the smartest girl he ever dated, and, of course, the prettiest, all in all, girl he ever dated. Sexy as hell, amazing sex, but, he knew, that wasn't reason enough for marriage; sex with the same partner grows staler over time, as time worked its weathering on them; he accepted this, while still hoping against it. There's tens of thousands of jokes, he had discovered, about the differences between hot and constant newlywed sex and 'married a decade or more' infrequent and chore like sex. Even if he somehow woke up a billionaire or/and a professional athlete, he doubted he'd ever find anyone better than Julie; someone who made him as happy, who felt so right. He possessed a healthy ego yet he knew that she could do better than him. One of the best feelings in life is feeling lucky. She made him feel lucky. Yet would life be absolutely unbearable without her? The romantic idea is to believe so, but, really? Forever? ...Maybe. ...Maybe not?

They made small talk at the *Sweetly Cursed* café booth: shared dumb inside jokes, warmed each other up before easing into the more serious conversation which they both wanted.

"I don't want to end up like my parents," Julie said. "Hating each other. It's my greatest fear."

"That will never happen to us," Steve responded. "*Hate?* That's impossible, right?"

"Yes, of course, but... when our parents got married I'm sure they never thought that the day would come where they'd *hate* each other. They also thought that to be impossible."

"I've always been a bit confused by that," Steve said. "To be able to hate and love the same person with such intensity within, I guess, a relatively short amount of time. I mean, either their young naïve selves or dumb bitter old selves must be wrong, in how they judged."

She looked at him. She sipped her cherry-vanilla Dr. Pepper. She usually didn't drink soda. She allowed herself this rare treat. It tasted insanely good. Her mind hummed in pleasure from the taste, temporarily diffusing the dark storm increasingly brewing in her mind. She hated that she felt a tinge of guilt from the pleasurable quick hit of sugar rush. She knew she had to keep a slim figure to compliment Steve's lean muscular build. Otherwise, she feared, she wouldn't be good enough for him. He was so handsome, so charming and outgoing, so smart, young but already with a good solid job at the bank, ambitious and on track for further success, getting his MBA in business (one regret she held of summer ending is that he'd be starting back at school causing her to see him less). Maybe not a 'rock n'roll god bad boy dangerous fantasy' type which so excites, but better than most girls get in reality, by a lot. He could probably have anyone, she mused. "I'll do one hundred sit-ups to atone for this sin," she said, then licked her sugary syrup stained lips.

"Don't worry about that, not at all," he dismissed. "You know I don't care about that."

"I know," she sighed, although she knew that he was lying; he did care. He kept himself in great shape. His eyes always strayed and lingered over other slim attractive women. It didn't really bother her; it's natural to want to observe and appreciate beautiful things. Well, it *did* bother her but she didn't *want* it to bother her, so she allowed herself this inner lie. "Why did your parents breakup?" she asked. "I can't remember if we ever talked about that."

He shrugged.

"I know, I don't like to talk about it either. Why even bring up bad things? Life is too short to dwell on such crap."

"No, it's not that... I honestly, I mean... yes, they yelled in front of us but it just sounded like that *Peanuts* adult trumpet talk, you know, *Waa, wa, waa, wa, wa.* I tuned out. It's not that kids see the world wrongly, necessarily, although they do, with belief in magic and Santa Clause and 'forever friends' and junk, but they see it differently, a different perspective. I honestly thought, like... the way kids do, that parents aren't like, two separate people but like one constant sure entity, you know, a fixed thing, the one parental unit. I should have known better, should have seen it coming, but I guess I was too young, too naïve. I didn't. I don't know why they broke up, still, beyond just the general unhappiness."

"Same with me," Julie confessed. "I mean, my parents went to church together. God was on their side. On our side. So I made myself believe."

"It's a bitter lesson," Steve said. "For the young to learn that the old can be so unhappy. It instills a fear of getting old that maybe never leaves."

"Money and sex, right?" Julie suggested.

Steve shrugged again. He sighed. *Will I make enough money* he wondered fearfully. *For her; for what she deserves. For us. For her to always admire me, enough that she could always love me.* "I think with aging there's this thing that happens to many, not all, not us hopefully, but many, where they're confronted and frustrated with continual disappointments as their illusions of what they dreamed for their lives fade. Potential fades, hope, expectations... And then they take it out on the ones closets to them. I mean, if you're not happy in life then... what's the point? It makes sense that a big life change would be sought after."

"I read a study that most divorcee's regret it. It's worse than being alone," Julie said. "I think my mom was, or is, an undiagnosed depressive. So, do you think depression is an obstacle to a happy marriage?"

She did it again Steve thought. *She did that thing where she utters a mere sentence which is like mental hard candy my brain could suck on for days.* On the surface it's not a tough riddle: of course depression is an obstacle to happiness of any kind. But should a 'happy marriage' be continual bliss or include partners supporting each other through struggles, including depression? Another question stemming from the first question: is it more difficult for a depressed person to love? Can this negatively impact a marriage? He shrugged. "Yes, probably," he answered.

"I'll write it down," Julie said. She took out a pen and purple covered notebook from her bag. Steve smirked. It was so oddly old fashioned yet beguilingly charmingly cute that she wrote in spiral notebooks rather than take notes on various iPhone and iPad writing and note taking apps.

She scrawled and underlined: *Obstacles to a happy marriage.* She wrote *depression* under the title.

"What are you writing?" Steve asked.

She told him.

"Jealousy," she said and wrote down the word.

Other adjectives flew out their mouths: Lust, Steve offered, then immediately felt awkward and embarrassed and braced for a perturbed expression from her. He was relieved to see her non-pulsed, simply writing down the word as eagerly as she did the others: anger/rage, self-pity/selfishness. "Stupidity" he added as a lark but she wrote it down seriously. While she wrote he figured, although broad, general stupidity was an obstacle to a happy marriage: doing and saying stupid things, like having an affair or becoming addicted to booze, drugs or gambling, being insensitive, saying insensitive things, being too dumb to succeed, in business, bad at making money and performing household tasks, could all fall under the *stupidity* umbrella. Being disgusted in each other: she wrote that down as well; a lack of physical attraction, or being so emotionally disgusted with a person, due to conflicting morals, politics or actions, that you can't stand to be in the same room. Like, if one day the partner woke up and decided to be a racist and sexists, or something. She stopped writing, put her pen to her lip and grazed over her list.

"Wouldn't it be nice," she said, "If we could get all the potential trails of our marriage out of the way, all at once. And then afterwards we'd know that nothing could break us. That only eternal bliss awaited us."

Steve smiled, assuming that she was mostly joking. There were so many other adjectives they didn't name that they could have that'd probably be even greater obstacles to a happy functional marriage: money, more specifically lack or misuse of, stress, either from the money situation or any number of things: children. Couples with difficult *problem children* often divorce despite the lies they tell themselves and the world that the child is blameless. Delusion: they had even talked at some length about that but he didn't think she added it to her list. He didn't want to give her any more adjectives. Her list was already long. He looked at her. She was the cutest, he decided, when she was deep in thought. "Can I tell you something?" he asked.

She looked up, chewing on her pen. "Yeah?" she answered tentatively.

"It'd rather be dead then live without you," he declared.

They reached across the table and held each other's hands. Out the speakers chimed a cute voice singing in a Scottish accent along to jubilant pulsating synthesizers about wanting relief and wanting release.

Steve had to know the singer and the song. He used the Shazam app on his iPhone to discover the song was called "Recover" by a band from Scotland. The lead singer was pretty; a girl named Lauren Mayberry in a band called "Chvrches" with the v acting as the u in the spelling. He Google'd them; their tour brought them into Seattle soon. In nine days. "Want to go?" Steve asked, to which Julie happily replied, "of course. Maybe this will be our song."

CHAPTER EIGHTEEN

Candice drove Steve and Julie, covered in white flour, in her aqua-green Ford Escort towards her apartment in Bellevue. They didn't speak. Steve ground his teeth sitting in the backseat, still fuming over various rudeness and injustices from earlier; the inconsiderate driver who would have hit him and Julie if they had entered the crosswalk when they wanted, as was their right, rather than yield to the driver, the dumb Barnes and Noble old manager nerd who actually had the gall to shoot him, the bastard, he deserves to die for it, Steve thought; and Trevor, admitting, basically, to writing the book, or claiming that he and Julie had asked him to write it; the world would be better off without talentless hacks and liars like Trevor polluting it, Steve thought.

Julie, sitting in the passenger side in the front, opened the window and stuck her head out like a dog in a car does, desperate for fresh air, for relief from her nausea. She so badly wanted to forget the gory images she had just witnessed in the bookstore. But she could not forget them. Thinking of them caused her to barf, her puke streaking the side of Candice's car and splat against the windshield of the car behind them who then screeched their tires and honked violently. They heard sirens chasing them from behind and all their hearts beat a bit faster with worry. It was an ambulance; Candice pulled over to the side as the emergency vehicle zoomed past.

Candice reached her apartment complex, parked and got out of the car, as did Steve and Julie. *It's so sad, so wrong, how so many people live like this; live in these dirty little cubby holes,* Julie thought as they walked towards Candice's door. *So, so many people, dirty, lonely, bunched up, like ants crawling over each other. It's so putrid and so sad.* When Candice opened her door a waft of humid garlic odor overcame them. Julie spit up again. She was so sick of doing that, it hurt each time, yet she couldn't stop it.

"Will you stop that?!" Steve yelled red faced. He hit the wall making a dent. "It's gross!"

Julie burst into tears. Steve had never yelled at her before. The only other time she heard him yell was while sports watching. She cried from the terror of being scolded but also from the constant pain of the nausea, the pain of her stomach cramping from all the muscle activity used to magically throw up so much. "You were barfing just as much just yesterday!" she tearfully protested. "Just yesterday!" she said, pleading for empathy.

"The daffodil bulbs haven't been strong enough to dull the power of the curses as much as I hoped," Candice said. "I've been working on a soup; same ingredients but in soup form. It should also be easier to digest."

Steve hit the wall in anger again despite his bloody knuckles. "Why didn't you give us that from the start!" he yelled.

Candice's neighbor opened his door and peaked his head out. "What the hell is going on out here?!"

"Sorry Douglas," Candice said sheepishly and then snapped at Steve and Julie "just get inside, please." She ushered them in.

She had a big pot of steaming stew on her oven. "You're kidding right? An actual witch's brew? Can you get any more cliché?" Steve said.

Julie flopped on the chair by Candice's small dining table and buried her head in her arms and wept.

"Can I have some now?" Steve asked. He felt bad for yelling at his fiancé. He wanted his rage to calm.

Candice got out two bowls and poured the soup made from daffodil bulbs, onions, and blessed Wicca oil, along with some roots, herbs, vinegar and cinnamon, in two bowls and placed them on the table. Steve and Julie ate, mostly in silence until they were done; Julie fighting her disgust at the taste and smell, although grateful that the soup slipped down her throat without her having to chew, Steve muffling his agitation that Candice had forced them to experience those horrible daffodil bulbs when this soup, although bad, was much better; she lied to them, he thought; she told them they had to chew these bulbs whole; she was purposefully trying to punish them; she could have just given them this soup from the start. Anger is the mother of conspiracy theories.

We have to push on with these tasks, Julie thought, tired yet still determined. She reached down to her purse to take out the book but then noticed the book was already on the table. Seeing the book there startled her, but not as much as it should have, not as it did the first time the book popped up unexpectedly. She reached and pawed at the book and scooted it closer to her. She took out a pen, clicked it, and then opened the book up to blank pages in the back. She began to forcibly write, her hand shaky, trying to copy the loose rambling rhyme style of the book, using slashes for stanza breaks, but not concerned with being literary or to try to create anything that her old literature professors would praise.

Lust will not take hold, we are more bold, there can be life saving value even in mold/ Goodness lies in the heart not over skin and where true beauty is not superficial but what lies within/ and so here's a story, where to begin/ Steve and I took a walk in a sunny park, while he was in rage I was disgusted/ we complimented homely people and made a good mark/ and so a aspect of lust was busted./ we have overcome this curse, we gave some good of what we had to give/ and so the beginning of this book lies/ after fourteen days since the time we first read, we will still LIVE!

Now here is another cause of a trial overcome/ the opposite of jealousy is trust and trust we have won/ to prove my trust and love I fell from a great height/ as sure that I'd be saved by my love as surly that day follows night/ And so it was I was not crushed but I was caught/ and so all the previous predictions of our death were for naught/ we have proven trust and gave a goodness which was ours to give/ and so you'll see, the earlier part of this book has lied; see, we will LIVE!

Julie scooted the glossy *If you read this you will die* paperback over to Candice. She took it and read what Julie just wrote. Steve simmered, wondering why she would give it to Candice and not him. He didn't feel as offended as he would have just a moment ago however.. The angry are easily offended; as he felt not *quite* as angry as before he found less to be offended by. The soup must be working. Not that he was cured of the rage curse, but the effects were muted.

"Good," Candice said. "That should do. It's a start."

Steve grit his teeth. *Just a start? This has got to end soon. I can't take this much longer* he thought.

"Now we just need to find who set this curse on you, give her, or him, the revised book, and have her, or him, reverse the *write your own story* spell," Candice said.

Steve slammed his fist against the surface of the table causing a vibration which shook the bowls. "Stop calling it that!" he said. "It's not cute!"

Julie gestured that she wanted the book back. Candice scooted it towards her. Julie opened it and began writing again on the opposite page where she left off.

There is a young girl who recently died/ I saw her tears glitter I saw her ghost cry/ she said 'I want to be alive'/ My shame I could not hide and here is why/ I pulled the trigger that discharged the bullet which took her life/ It is a wrong which I want to make right/ The evil act was done while under a evil spell of jealousy/ I was blinded and could not see/ I am sorry/ But now we write our own story/ What's written in this is what will be/ And so it is written here that this dead girl, Zelda, will

*live, verily/ It will come to pass/ And there will be peace at last/
Unless Zelda is the one who first set the spell of doom/ Then she
is not alive to reverse it and we are all doomed...*

She stopped writing. "What did you write?" Candice
asked. "I can't tell you," Julie answered. "I'll never tell you.
Promise me you will never look at this."

Steve scooted his chair out, walked over to the couch
and flopped on it. He quickly fell asleep. Continual rage was
exhausting.

"Did you put some sleep powder or something in this
soup?" Julie asked.

"No... but that's not a bad idea. Tomorrow you're both
scheduled for rage, right? You should both sleep all day that
day. No good can come of that. Even with all the guns and
knives removed you both might kill each other. Or others."

Julie felt hurt by the accusation. She and Steve loved
each other; no way would they ever want to kill each other.
Although, she considered, unresolved issues had recently been
planted between them. Both had cheated on the other during
their lust phase; if they confronted each other over their cheating
while both enraged maybe it would escalate into double
homicide. She had a déjà vu moment; did she and Steve talk
about love and death before? A serious conversation about how
love can turn into hate too easily, as evidenced by both of their
parents. How strange that is, but not really all that strange; both
love and hate are emotions of passion and sometimes unreason.
They had pledged to love each other forever; eternal love or
death; had that been an actual conversation or just a dream?
Such a shared declaration struck her as too radical and extreme

for them, although deep down she knew she felt that way, had that much passion and dedication, but she kept it buried, knowing it was perhaps *too* zealous and would probably freak Steve out if he knew. But did Steve actually feel the same way as her; had they talked about it, probably at *Sweetly Cursed* late one night? She couldn't recall; how strange she couldn't recall. Wondering over fuzzy memories reminded her of what Trevor had claimed at the Barnes and Noble just an hour and a half or so before. He claimed something that she and Steve had done that she knew could not be true.

"But you said we have to accomplish these tasks and write them in the book even just for a chance to overcome the curse," Julie protested. "We can't do that if we're sleeping; you said that, remember?! Time is running out. Just six more days!"

"You won't be able to overcome the curse if you're both dead already," Candice countered.

Julie decided not to tell her of how the evil book had healed Steve's bullet wound and saved her from the pains, broken bones and ails of smacking the ground after a forty foot free fall. How strange that was; not enough time had passed for her to really consider it. That too, although the memory was only eighty or so minuets previous, seemed as if it could have been a dream. Such strong emotional energy, along with her barf, had been discharged there. Julie feared if she revealed the full power of the book to Candice, Candice might freak out in religious awe and delirium again, maybe worshiping it the way she'd worship found rock crystals back when she was crazy and talked to crows. Then, Julie feared, Candice might steal the book to show her Wicca coven of sisters who she recently was admitted back into the good graces of, so they could study it and worship it or something. The type and power of magic in the book must be rare, even among those familiar with magic, Julie determined. Bringing people back from near death was no joke. She needed her older sister to stay sane and helpful.

"I have to admit, a day of rest sounds nice," Julie admitted. "I'd love to skip a day of rage. I'm already so drained." She turned and looked over at Steve, passed out. For the first time in nearly two days his appearance didn't repulse her. While she was enthralled with lust he had looked like a glowing skinned lightning veined Greek God, then just a day later he appeared as appetizing as a urine soaked moldy red potato. The craggy veins protruding out his temples and neck like tree roots during his berserker phase looked as gross to her as if his entire skin was inside out. Now rested and with her insides warmed by the soup, he looked cute, she decided, lying on the couch like a sleeping little boy tuckered out after a temper tantrum. The poor boy. He was so scary earlier; him with that gun.

"That guy, Trevor, he said something," Julie said. I had a strange hunch that he knew something; I was drawn to him to find out, I can't explain it." Julie took a sip of coffee which Candice had brought over. "He said something strange. He said that Steve and I emailed him and told him..." she rubbed her head, trying to remember. "He said we emailed him a list of adjectives to write about. And he self published a book that looked like *If You Read This You Will Die*. And then he must have taken it off line, unpublished it, since I couldn't find it online anywhere."

Candice rubbed her eyebrow and cocked her head. Her cat purred. It was an orange cat without a tail. It seemed to Julie to have appeared out of nowhere. *Have I seen that cat before* Julie wondered. Candice was always bringing home stray cats. She was slowly, or rapidly, turning into a cat lady; one of those lonely old lady types who devise love by pretending their pet cats care for them because they feed them.

"Strange," Candice said. "Have you checked your sent email folder?"

"Well... I mean, I would know if I sent an email... do you have a computer or laptop?"

"Of course," Candice said, a bit perturbed that Julie would even ask. She got up, went into her room, grabbed her laptop off of her bed and carried it over to the table then opened it and turned it on. Julie swiveled it towards her and logged into her Gmail account. She clicked on "sent mail". She checked back months clicking on anything that looked odd or unfamiliar. Most of the emails were work or parents and other relatives related; most of her online interactions with her friends were done through Twitter, Instagram, Snapchat and Facebook. "I don't see it," Julie said.

"Do you know Steve's email password?"

"Well... yeah," Julie said. She logged into Steve's Gmail. Most of his sent mail was work and school related as well. There was, however, a group email chain involving plans for Chad's bachelor party. She didn't delve deep into that; she recalled that she had already obsessively poured over those emails when she was inflicted with jealousy and felt embarrassed. "No, I don't see any emails to Trevor about anything he mentioned," Julie said.

"How weird," Candice said. "You say you were mystically pulled towards him? You feel he is a piece of the puzzle in discovering who set the curse on you? Do you recall any dreams about him?"

Julie rolled her eyes. "Wait," she said. She remembered while she was afflicted with intense and insane causing jealousy she had taught herself how to uncover wiped internet history and deleted emails. She used this hacking information to search her sent email again. And there, she found it. She recognized Trevor's email address from the bachelor party email chain. She *had* sent him an email after all. How bizarre! But really, mildly bizarre, she figured, compared with all the other bizarre things which had happened since that night in the barn when the cursed *If You Read This You Will Die* book entered their lives. She read:

Hi Trevor.

This is Julie and Steve (acquaintances you may know from the Chad and Jessie social circle).

Anyways, we have a strange request. We know you're a writer and have written many books. Will you write one for us? Don't worry, just a small assignment with some weird stipulations. Write a short 'chapter' on a list of adjectives we'll provide. There shouldn't be 'characters' or 'plot' really, but just a stream of conscious free flow type of thing (I heard you're a fan of Jack Kerouac? I've studied him in a college class; I like him too). And there should be a 'death-challenge' in the chapters too. I'd elaborate more on what that entails and means, but truth is I don't really know for sure; I'm passing on second hand information in some regard. Leave about eighty or so blank pages in the book after the last chapter.

Other stipulations: this must be done in one day. Self publish it and then have it listed for just one day and then take it off. Don't include your name on the cover. Tell no one about this. Don't mention it even to either of us. If you ask us about it we will feign ignorance. Title the book "If you read this you will die". After you self-publish it utter these words: "We write our own story; this is true; I now pass this story onto you."

Here's the list of the adjectives: Jealousy, Lust, Disgust, Rage, Stupidity, Self-Pity, and Depression.

If you agree to this, admittedly strange request we will write you a check for fifty dollars, sent to your address (please provide during reply).

We know this request is a bit strange and cryptic but we'd really appreciate it. A few years down the road I'm sure we'll let you in on what this was all about. (It's funny, really).

Thanks and best regards! Steve and Julie.

Julie was bewildered by what she just read. She didn't remember writing that email. "That doesn't sound like my writing," she said. "Even when I'm drunk. Someone must have hacked into my email and sent this as if they were me."

"That's possible," Candice said.

"We have to go see Trevor again, he didn't tell us everything!" Julie said frantically. "He knows more!"

Candice pawed at the book and pried it open. She started to read over a random page and her eyes slipped over this sentence: *This book is not for you, you dumb stupid witch, get your paws out and don't snitch, Trying to save the dumb golden couple you can try, but you will fail, as surely as green leaves turn crisp and dry and drained of life, in seven days these two will die. Also, by the way, hello and hi.*

"The words appear to change, in parts, depending on who's reading it," Candice said. "A hallucination spell perhaps; a spell which reveals the inner psyche."

"Is that a spell or just taking drugs like LSD or mushrooms?" Julie asked.

"Sometimes spells can cause drug like reactions, with euphoria and healing, without ingesting… it depends. Anyways, I believe Trevor was just a pawn, not a key. The bigger question which needs answering is not what else this Trevor person knows, but what do you know which you forgot. You and Steve."

"But I don't get it, how can part of my memory be erased and I not know it?" Julie asked.

"It can be accomplished by a skilled spell weaver," Candice explained. "Subtlety is key. True memories are replaced with vague false ones; you think you spent a Saturday afternoon gardening, for example, when you were really at the beach. You may discover some loose sand in your kitchen which piques your curiosity but not enough to trigger a full blown trauma questioning perceived reality and time. Little things like that happen all the time; birds appear in strange places, lost keys turn up under hats."

She has such a strange way of talking sometimes, Julie thought. *Scatterbrained.* A pang of guilt pricked her as she considered the possibility that maybe her older sister hadn't been as crazy as everyone once believed, concerning her odd beliefs in magic and spells and other 'silly' things. She hadn't really been in the right mind or mood or condition, or had the time to really consider this before: Candice had been more right about this Wicca stuff than Julie and her parents had allowed. Once Julie really considered this delayed yet new revelation she realized that it should be as shocking as if the local crazy conspiracy theory guy were actually right about whatever crazy conspiracy which he was obsessively preaching about, like 9-11 was an inside job, the moon landing was faked, aliens are among us, or the end of the world is neigh.. Magic, or whatever the Wicca's call their powers, is real! Curses are real!

Candice continued blathering; she were stuck on a soliloquy about this 'memory erase and replace' spell; how beneficial it could be for PTSD victims and war veterans, if only the secrets of the Wicca were widely believed and used, and how there's an eternal debate raging among the various Wicca covens over whether to possibly invite more ridicule and persecution by suggesting this 'cure' be widely used; or even if the spell would retain its power if it were diluted among the masses; and then of course there's the ethical questions involved in wiping away or changing memory. Candice was blathering about how frustrating it was that the Wicca's argued so much and never organized into a powerful consensus, due to trivial little jealousies and drama between various covens and even within the same covens.

"Wait, please stop," Julie said. Candice's whirlwind of words were making her dizzy. Julie peered at her older sister. "It is... so strange. Do you have a way of... unlocking... hidden memories? Not saying there's anything to be unlocked but... if there is."

"Yes," Candice flatly declared.

CHAPTER NINETEEN

Thanks to Candice and the help of a smoke machine to boost the power of her sleeping spell, Steve and Julie mostly slept through their shared day of rage. It was an uncomfortable sleep full of nightmares, grinding teeth, frequent bouts of sudden wakefulness with their sweaty heads pulsating with blistering thoughts of various injustices, both large and slight, worldly and personal, false and true, but at least they had managed not to kill each other or cause too much property damage. But, as Candice had earlier declared, they could not just sleep through every day of their curse; that was a sure path to the death which the curse promised shortly. They had tasks to accomplish.

At sunset the next day, Julie filled with rage, Steve with stupidity, Candice drove them towards a forest by the small woodsy river mountain town near Seattle named Skykomish, by Golden Bar. A few days or weeks before Chad and Jessie's wedding, Candice had known that Julie and Steve went to a concert by a Scottish group named "Churches" (spelled as "Chvurches" for Google search purposes). They were one of Steve and Julie's latest favorite bands. Candice had felt hurt that they hadn't invited her to the concert. Candice played this music for the drive, remembering that Julie had called it 'smooth electronic bliss music which made her happy' and 'the lead singer is a cute elfish girl with a sweet cadence and conviction in her delivery'. Candice played this music for the car ride in order to try and sooth Julie. It didn't sooth her much. It was the first time Julie listened to the album that she didn't enjoy it. It grated he, irritated her like jittery maggots squirming under her flesh, that she wasn't enjoying it; that the awesomeness of the songs didn't work their pleasuring power over her but rather the opposite. She grit her teeth and her left eye twitched. Her head pounded; bad thoughts of politics and internet comments flamed in her. She usually allowed the idiocy of others and the wider world to slide off of her like water over dolphin's backs. Riding in the car to the forest she remembered mounds of dumb and wrong political arguments she had been subjected to that year on big issues such as abortion, taxes, gun control and health care, and little things, like the misuse of *your* and *you're*, as 'you are'. She usually quieted her anal side in order to not let little annoyances really bother her, or to make a big stink over them, but she could not brush such stupidities aside any longer; they gnawed at her. Thousands of dumb arguments she had dismissively brushed off before, from everything to World War II history to Donald Trump's hair jammed in her head, each one screaming, trying to out shout each other. She hated that these thoughts attacked her; there's no beauty or poetry or peace in such thoughts; these aggressive thoughts that clashed against the music which was supposed to temper her rage. Her irritation over the fact that awesome bands like 'Chvrches' and artists like Sky Ferreria would always have less fans and fanfare than some random pop singer puppet propped up by a corporation, or some teen actress who frivolously decides one day that she also wants to be a pop star, who then gets hundreds of millions of YouTube views for some processed pop song she lent her auto-tuned voice for, while real starving artists of passion and pain, guys like Ian of local indie rock band Mayberry, slave away for years for their art and create something really great yet can't get a thousand views for their efforts also blocked her from simply enjoying the music.

Steve had never enjoyed the music more than he did riding in the car up to the mountain forest; it hit the sweet spot for him where the music is faintly familiar enough that he got excited anticipating certain upcoming notes and noises, his 'favorite parts' yet not so familiar that the luster wore off and it became too familiar and stale. A strange smile plastered his face and his eyes were vacant. The music sent him to a blissful state although he had no clue what any of the songs were about. He was totally oblivious to Julie's, sitting next to him, suffering. Normally he'd feel apprehension about returning so close to where he buried Zelda's body, but that concern was freed from his mind as well; his mind was like an open window letting all the pained caged birds fly away and escape into blue open sky.

Seemingly out of nowhere but really the result of a long buildup of pressure, Julie let out screams like a maniac banshee. She slapped and slammed her hands and her head against the car window. Steve giggled. A drip of drool dropped out of the corner of his mouth. Candice stomped on the breaks and pulled over to a stop, causing the tires to screech. "What is going on back there!" she yelled.

"I! Hate! Every! Body! And! Every! Thing!" Julie screeched through hyperventilating and slamming her hands and head against the window. Steve giggled.

Candice frantically dug into her burlap sack and removed daffodil bulbs which she tossed in the backseat. "Eat these!" she implored.

Julie grabbed some bulbs and stuffed them in her mouth and angrily, bitterly chewed, hating the taste and texture yet still swallowing. Steve grabbed a bulb and held it up. "What if I put this up my but," he said and then started giggling. "What if our mouth were our butt holes?" He then sat up to try and slide off his pants, giggling like a stoned teenager.

"Don't you fucking stick your butt hole in my nose!" Julie spit and shoved Steve's rump.

Candice sighed. The Nirvana lyric about Kurt Cobain thinking he's dumb but maybe he's just happy popped in her head, in relation to Steve. "Steve put the thing in your mouth, chew and swallow!" Candice barked.

"Yes mother," Steve said, sitting back and slouching. "But it tastes so gross!" he whined.

"Take your medicine!" Candice barked.

Julie stuffed a bulb into Steve's mouth, grumbling about how stupid he is.

"Pixies," Candice said to herself, remembering the name of the band Steve had said he liked which had influenced Nirvana. She took her iPod, hooked to the car speakers and searched for 'Pixies'. She started the car and merged onto the road again. It hurt her ears and her head but for the sake of Steve and Julie she turned the music up louder, the demonic howl of "Tame!" "Tame!" screamed by the lead singer of The Pixies rattling the windows. She looked at Julie using the rearview mirror; Julie looked calmer than she had. Steve looked just as out of it although he bobbed his head to the beats and clapped his hands off beat. *I want to grow up to be a debaser!* Frank screamed, and in the next song he asked *Is she weird,* then the next quick little song he stated angrily *I've got something against you!* and then the next song was a long melodic trance song about aliens visiting Las Vegas.

"These sisters of yours can really get our lost memory back?" Julie asked, having to yell to be heard.

"Yes!" Candice exclaimed.

"And it had to be a ritual at night in the woods? Under a full moon?"

"Yes," Candice answered again.

"Sounds really stupid!" Julie yelled.

They passed through Gold Bar and then through Skykomish, the brights on the headlights turned on. They almost hit a raccoon on the road; Candice just missed it, swerving. Julie cursed in anger after her head hit the window, despite just moments before her smacking her head against the car window on purpose. A string of cars were parked by the side of the mountain pass highway. Candice parked her car behind an old green Volkswagen bug. "We're here," she said. "We're late... damn it. Our issue was last on their agenda anyways," Candice said.

"Agenda? You make it sound like a business meeting or something," Julie said.

"Hookers," Steve said, then giggled. A faint memory came to him of being up here, near her, and there being hookers with him. It had been a wild fun time, he recalled; fun, except for the dead body part of the experience. "Oh no," he said, recalling that part. He wasn't particularly religious, not like his parents, in their own twisted and hypocritical ways anyways, but he thought with fear at the time, and thought again now, that there was a special punishment in hell awaiting those perverse enough to have a boner while digging a grave for a freshly murdered young women while two coked up giggling hookers watched. Not that the death and gruesomeness of the whole thing had *turned him on* or anything, but while he dug he thought of a lithe girl in a loose fitting white cotton dress twirling, for some reason he couldn't explain, other than being cursed. He wished so badly he could forget that memory; being stupid at the moment caused him to not recall details and names, yet the overview, the dumb cliff notes version, of the event remained in his skull. What had Julie and her older sister told him, he tried to recall; where were they going and what was it for? Something about erasing memory, or our memoires were erased. Something to do with that. He so badly wished he could erase the memoires of that day; of digging the grave while a solid stiff boner poked up against him in his pants, and other more sickening sinful things that happened; forget them and then it'd be like they never had happened, never to gnaw against his conscious, never again to provoke him with fears of hellish justice against his sick crimes.

They got out of the car, turned on flashlights and walked into the creepy darkness of the woods. "I'm scared!" Steve whimpered. "Oh shut up," Julie snapped back. She felt that she still loved him, but in their states, her enraged, him acting like a dumb child, she felt that she loved him just for the meat on his bones. She thought how not all that long ago she'd be sexually stimulated in anticipation of going to this event; this Wicca ritualistic nature séance or whatever; naked ladies dancing and chanting around a fire. Had I really been bi-sexual for a few days, she wondered. Deep down do I also like women? They are pretty, but so are fancy gingerbread houses and glittery unicorn dolls, and she has no desire to orgasm over them.

They walked further into the woods, off trail, snapping through mossy twigs and hopping over giant ferns. "I hope you know where you're going," Steve said. "As do I," Julie said. "Shhh, do you here that?" Candice inquired. A human humming sound serenaded through the trees. "Follow that sound," Candice said. "Um… we're just following you," Steve responded.

They approached a round clearing among the trees by a stream. Ladies stood barefoot around a fire about four feet high, larger than a typical campfire but not bonfire size. Julie counted them: only eleven. All but one appeared haggish to her; old, unkempt, poor looking, like dirty homeless ladies and beggars, despite wearing crudely made and sloppily sewn red dresses. The only one who looked less than forty five was a wild red haired one with skin so pale it looked nearly translucent in the moonlight. *Ugh, such a cliché, red heads are freaks,* Julie thought, annoyed. She recalled that she may have seen that redhead before, hanging around with Candice, like they had been lovers or something. But she wasn't certain. Candice, despite not caring about her looks since her early teens probably, Julie guessed, was much more attractive and younger than these so called 'sisters' of hers; better, really, to put it bluntly, Julie told herself. Why would she want to associate herself with a bunch of old homeless lady campers? She knew her thoughts were a bit pretentious and superficial, *pretty little rich white girl* thoughts, which she normally tried to check herself against, but in her agitated angry state she had no patience or desire to wrestle up any guilt for being a *pretty little spoiled rich white girl* with superficial thoughts of superiority. "I am not yet allowed to wear the official robes of my coven again," Candice explained, meaning, Julie guessed, the ugly red dresses, as if Steve and Julie had been wondering or cared. "I am still in probation."

"Fire, put it out, only Smokey the Bear says you can prevent forest fires!" Steve yelled and he rushed at the fire.

"Steve, no!" Candice hollered.

The ladies in red dresses humming around the fire shrieked. Steve jumped over the fire, kicked dirt at it, then jumped into it again, thinking that the wind he caused by his run would blow the fire out. "The leaping ceremony is not yet!" one of the ladies shrieked.

"I am so sorry sisters! These are the ones I spoke of who are under the 'write your own story' spell, and the 'memory erase and replace' spell!" Candice said. "They are not in complete control of their actions, please forgive him!"

"The names of your spells are so stupid!" Julie yelled at the top of her lungs; a thought she normally would keep to herself, although even if she were not enraged she would have thought it. Such cute sounding names for such seriously sinister things.

The oldest ugliest looking lady broke from the circle and rushed up to Julie. She peered into her eyes. "The law surges in this one!" she exclaimed with wild astonishment. "Her aura is like the strength of a blood moon!"

"What is she talking about?" Julie yelled.

"*Law* is what we sometimes call magic or magic possession; either emanating or soaking in, played or played upon," Candice said, trying to explain.

"Oh, she, and the other one, the fire jumper, have been played upon. Deeply, very deeply," the old lady said.

Steve sill leaped over the fire, thinking the faster he ran towards it before leaping the better chance he'd have of putting it out. He'd then try blowing at it like blowing out birthday candles. Some of the ladies laughed at him, some purposefully cackling in the cliché way cliché witches cackle, just to annoy her, Julie thought. "Stop it, he can't help it, he's stupid, okay!" Julie yelled in admonishing the dumb rude cackling old ladies in ugly dresses.

"She is right sisters!" the old lady, apparently the 'head witch' or whatever the title was, Julie surmised, said. "Did you bring the book?"

Candice pulled out *If You Read This You Will Die* from a satchel slung over her shoulder. Julie hadn't known Candice had the book let alone brought it with her. She felt betrayed. "You bitch!" she yelled. Candice ignored her and showed the book to the old lady, holding it delicately in her upturned palms.

"Agh, it burns it is so bright!" the old lady screeched, shielding her eyes although it was dark.

"Stop your damn play acting!" Julie demanded. "You all could not be more dumbly theatrical!"

"But it burns with darkness!" the old lady screeched.

"That literally makes no sense!" Julie yelled. "That's a contradiction and oxymoron!"

"This fire won't go out!" Steve yelled, huffing. "I think they really are magic!"

Some of the ladies cackled again. They had probably never been so close to a handsome young dumb boy before, Julie guessed.

"Take the object away! It is like bringing us a bomb!" the old lady hollered.

"But... sister, you told me to bring it," Candice said. "You said you would help. Please. My sister and her fiancé need help. They need to remember a forgotten memory, taken from them."

"Very well," the old lady, the 'High Wicca Priestess' or whatever title they used, said. "Gather round sisters, around these two life-force beings. Just as we rehearsed. Come, the night's moonshine does not last forever."

"Ugh!" Julie spat while rolling her eyes. "You're all just a bunch of theater nerd losers who never grew up aren't you!" She then adopted a fake English accent for her next taunt: "Are you all afraid that the evil Lord Voldermort has returned to Hogwarts?"

"Please, don't mind her, the book curse has made her sick," Candice pleaded as the old lady glared at Julie tight lipped.

The old ladies in red dresses corralled Steve and Julie around the fire and circled them, a ring around them, holding hands. They began a unison monotone incantation which sounded like gibberish to Julie.

"What's going on, you guys are scaring me," Steve said cowering nervously.

"Shut up!" Julie yelled.

"They're here to help you!" Candice yelled outside of the circle.

"I hate the dumb made up mumbo-jumbo-fake-Latin-druid-whatever gibberish screenwriters make actresses playing witches say in TV shows and movies!" Julie yelled. "It is so irritating!" She clawed her finger then placed them over her ears and then grunted an angry scream of frustration.

"They're speaking English!" Candice yelled.

Julie listened. She heard: *Memory gone come back in a dream* repeated in a chant. "Why do dumb spells always have to rhyme, it's so stupid!" she yelled, but then immediately realized that what the witches circling around them were saying didn't rhyme and she, in this one instance, was wrong. She looked at Steve. Blank faced, he had joined in the chant: *memory gone come back in a dream.* She shoved him. "Stop it!" she yelled.

"No, don't stop it, Julie, you're being irrational, we're helping you!" Candice called over the chants.

Julie knew her sister was right. She put her knuckles against her own temples and pressed in. Steve was clapping along to the rhythm of the chants. "This is fun," he said, breaking off from chanting along. In his merriment he forgot again, that he had buried Zelda not far from where they stood. "These ladies look nice but they're really mean. I mean, opposite that, they look mean but they're really nice," he said.

Ugh, you're being so stupid, Julie grunted, although she knew he couldn't help it. Poor boy. Then it dawned on her. It became as clear as a sun rise illuminating an open meadow. *She* was the one who was stupid. How could she be so stupid as to not realize it before? Suffering through the curses was not a good enough excuse to let something so obvious slip by. One of these witch bitches was the one responsible for *If You Read This You Will Die.* She shook at the truth of this sudden revelation. She thought the sentence again but slowed it down in her mind, each word landing and sticking like a heavy rock. Of course. The only people who are capable of so called 'spells' or 'magic' or 'curses' are all right here. Therefore one, at least one, maybe more, maybe all of them, must be responsible. Hole-Ee-Shit. Her heart raced.

"Which one of you did it!" Julie screamed. "You?" she said, swiveling towards the youngest looking and prettiest looking, only in comparison, one, the redhead. Girls who looked like this girl were always jealous of me, Julie thought. They always tried to hurt me. Julie grit her teeth, curled her nose and snarled. The girl looked frightened and flinched although she kept hold of the hands of the older ladies at her side. "Or you! Or you!" Julie challenged, swiveling and charging with fists and flexed muscles at various old ladies.

"Keep your formation sisters, do not break the chant, the light is almost in the right place, just a few seconds more," the head Wicca priestess commanded.

"Uhh… what's going on?" Steve uttered dumbly with a chuckle. He suddenly felt like he wanted to cry. He was so confused. He didn't know where he was or where he was going or what all these noises were. He had just enough intelligence to have a comprehension of just how stupid he was, and how bad it was to be stupid, how hard it is to figure life out or get a girl like Julie to admire and love him or do any good in the world or know where to drive to get places, remembering directions, or how to do things; all his knowledge about banks and books and how to fix a sink and computer completely gone, vanished like an alien ship slipping back into the vast swallowing depths of space. His lower lip trembled. "I don't want to be stupid no more," he said.

Julie looked at him, how sad and wrong to see someone once so sure of himself, a capable man, one of the things she found sexiest about him, so strong, reduced and emasculated into a whimpering clueless child. "Who did this to us!" she screeched. "Don't ignore me, which one is responsible!" The ladies continued their chant. Julie huffed. "You were all little high school losers and outcasts just like my sister; you turn to fantasy because you can't handle reality; you play make believe in order to pretend you have any power. You refused to grow up. You're all just a collective of crazy cat ladies! If you can devise love spells then how come all of you are all lonely loveless old widows huh?" Her nostrils flared in anger as she hurled her angry accusations. She really had no idea if these women really were lonely and loveless; she just guessed. Her older sister didn't have a romantic interest since middle school, when those didn't really count. She became too weird, shy, and uninterested to attract boys. In Julie's hatred of these witches she assumed the worst of all of them. All except for the younger wild red head and Candice were raggedy and ugly, even draped in their scarlet gowns; of course none of them had any lovers; none of any quality anyways. Julie picked up a stray rock and picked a lady at random to launch her attack. She smacked the grey frizzy haired witch up the side of the head with the palm sized stone. The others gasped; Candice screamed *Julie, no!* Julie smiled smugly standing over the downed body, standing with an *I told you not to mess with me* posture. The head Wicca priestess swooped into the center, cupped her hand, thrust it in the fire and scooped up ash. Although frail and rickety in appearance she moved like a ninja. She slammed the red ash and embers into Julie's face. Julie fell, screaming in pain. "What is going on?!" Steve yelled helplessly. The old witch scooped up more ash and stuffed it in Steve's face. He fell limp next to Julie.

CHAPTER TWENTY

Julie heard her muffled voice speak out in darkness. She recognized her voice as her own despite it sounding alien to her, the way our voices do when played back to us on recorders. Fuzzy images crystallized. She looked at herself, like a spirit outside her body. She sat at a table in the *Sweetly Cursed* doughnut, sandwich and coffee corner café, with Steve. They were talking about their relationship. She had been upset. She had had a dream about babies falling from the sky which splat on the ground like warm mushy yams; a dream so vivid she had been positive that she would never forget it after waking up from it, she recalled thinking. She remembered a disturbing dark cloud. Steve had called a baby ugly. That had caused a fight. She cried, they made up, but feelings were still sore and raw. Then she confessed that she'd rather be dead than live without him. She expressed worries and fears over things that could derail their marriage; she made a list of the adjectives, lust, disgust, rage, stupidity, self-pity, depression. She saw herself write the adjectives down in a notebook. While watching this scene she thought; *where is that notebook? If I find it then it will prove that this memory actually happened.* She realized that she no longer felt rage. What a relief. Rage exhausted her. The easily angered are the most hate worthy and ugly people, yet also, she realized, they deserve pity. To always feel that way is a torture. She realized once she woke up she'd probably feel rage again, the curse sinking its teeth and chewing her once more. She didn't want to wake up. Realizing that once she woke up she also might feel the pain of the ashes burned on her face also caused her to wonder if it'd be better to lay in this rest longer. She'd float around and look at her past memories, like she were doing now; but the good memories; those feelings that while in them you find yourself thinking, I could feel this way forever; I *want* to feel this way forever; for this moment to never end. At the Chvrches concert with Steve, during and after sex with Steve, her first kiss with a boy named Todd, riding in the back of the high school choir bus after a triumphant concert where she delivered a wicked scat solo in the jazz choir portion to a standing ovation and rave reviews; laughing so hard her stomach hurt with other childhood friends at sleepovers; playing Guitar Hero and Rock Band with some mates at a Stanford bar.

Although outside herself she felt the moods and sensed the inner thoughts of herself as she sat at the café. The scene played out like a movie in how she watched it, but felt like a dream, in how she could discern the inner emotions and conflicts of these 'characters' she witnessed; the 'characters' of her and Steve. In other ways the scene presented itself to her like a narration, reading a book. It was strange how she was watching and feeling something new presented to her from her past; astonishing in the way when one recalls a buried memory of childhood nostalgia by a 'remember when' prompt from another.

That scene faded, dissolving back into fuzziness and then blackness. In the darkness she heard her voice again, along with the voice of her friend Lisa. She saw herself sitting on a park bench under sunny blue skies. She was at the farmers market and street art and crafts fair in Pioneer Square. She witnessed the following scene:

"You want a confession?" Lisa asked Julie. "I'm jealous of you and Steve. What are some of the Oscar Wilde quotes you told me? 'Never love someone who treats you ordinary'. 'Life without love is like a rose garden without sun', 'you love someone not for their looks or their car but because they sing a song only you can hear' and my favorite, 'to love is the realist thing in the world. Most people exist, that is all'."

"It's to live, not to love" Julie corrected. Lisa didn't get the other quotes exactly right either (it was *Never love anyone who treats you ordinary*, not whatever Lisa said) but replacing 'live' with 'love' struck her as egregious enough to deserve the correction, despite hating being labeled a 'know-it-all' and people who are overly anal over grammar and junk, especially during loose conversation.

"Excuse me?" Lisa said.

"Never-mind, I didn't meant to get all 'smarmy-teacher' on you; you got the gist of the quotes right."

"Yes. Anyways, when you told me them; I can't remember what we were talking about that caused you to recite them to me, but when I heard them I thought... those don't describe me, my life, my love-life. Me and Danny. But they fit you and Steve perfectly."

"Steve is doing this character, this bad marriage comedy guy, for Chad and Jessie's upcoming wedding in a few weeks, for some reason," Julie said with a smile. "It's a little annoying but mostly cute. Dumb humor, you know, but I like that stuff. Anyways, as this character, joking he said, "On should always be in love. That is the reason one should never marry." Or no, he didn't say that, that's the exact Oscar Wilde quote actually, but it was so close to it that it impressed me; my fiancé is as clever as Oscar Wilde! But my point is, Wilde actually has lots of tart and sour thoughts about romance, marriage and love as well: 'both men and women are disappointed by marriage; women do it because they are curious and men because they are tired'; 'Marriage ruins a man...'; 'the spoil of every romance is trying to make it last...'".

Lisa guffawed. "Those are awful! He was gay wasn't he?"

"Yes, not that it matters…"

"No, I didn't mean to imply…"

"No, I know you didn't, I didn't mean to suggest you did; but yes, he was in a troubled marriage with a women. Obviously. In Victorian England… sad story, actually, how he was imprisoned for whispers about his homosexuality, then exiled and died too early. But, point being, I'm sure that informed some of his more sour takes on the subject. Not being gay I mean, being in a loveless forced marriage."

"We've sidetracked a bit, although I do love that you're the only person I can talk to about serious literary subjects and authors and stuff. But what I wanted to get at, to ask really, was how do you do it? You and Steve? Even make people who think they are madly in love question their love? It's an impossible question I know, I'm sorry, I guess I'm just fan-girling over you two more than anything; I don't mean to embarrass you."

"Not at all," Julie said.

"You know I can get down sometimes," Lisa said. "A self indulgent sadness, like an author upset over a bad review— this person didn't like your poem, boo-hoo go kill yourself…"

Julie forced a chuckle.

"But still… and I think you, or someone like me, needs someone who points them towards the light, you know, to distract from inner darkness. Danny does that to some extent for sure, but maybe not as much as I need. Not like what it looks like Steve does for you."

"Danny? Really?"

"He doesn't show his inner self much, just like everyone, but he can actually be pretty gloomy. Especially about politics and the environment and stuff."

"Oh," Julie said, a bit taken aback by Lisa's honesty. It's always intriguing to learn of outside perceptions of one's relationships. Yes, Steve made her happy, nearly even close to continual bliss, or as close as one can get while still maintaining a firm grasp on reality. Yet no matter how often movie stars claim that glamour is mostly an illusion, never truly as glamorous on the inside as others on the outside make it out to be, it is only when some other person expresses jealousy over some aspect of your own life that you consider there may be some truth in that cliché. Perhaps partly for vanity reasons, both she and Steve felt compelled to want to make others envious of them, their looks and their love. She did feel lucky to have found Steve though; to feel like she could find no other man on earth who she could love more than Steve, and have him love her back with the same intensity, is a feeling of being lucky, one of the best feelings one can have; a feeling like being high on drugs, one that she knew couldn't last with the same passion, giving truth to some of those dire Oscar Wilde quotes, yet still a feeling perhaps the majority of women, maybe including Lisa, in the world never really experience, however brief, even if they think they have.

"I want someone I feel I would die for and who would die for me," Lisa said. "It's silly I guess, too much to ask or expect really, but that's what you and Steve have."

Danny and Steve approached Julie and Lisa. "Ready to go?" Steve asked.

Julie, watching this scene, saw her and Lisa stand and hook arms with their respective boyfriends and walk down the street. *Why would someone want to erase that memory,* she thought. *Nothing happened; just Lisa and I talking. Maybe that's why it was so forgettable? But why was it shown to me now? Maybe no good reason; maybe it means nothing, just as dreams, even profound seeming ones, don't really 'mean' anything other than brain neurons still snapping while you sleep same as your intestines cause you to fart in your sleep.*

The four walked up Madison Street towards Pike's Place Market. They turned towards a cobblestone ally, past the sign advertising the 'underground Seattle' tour; old Seattle burned on June 6th 1889 and they built new Seattle over it.

"Have you seen this before?" Lisa asked, stopping and pointing at a sign lit up in pink and blue neon which read "Physic boutique and life coach" and an arrow pointing down.

"No," Julie said curiously. "Must be new? I guess?"

"Want to check it out?" Danny asked.

Steve scoffed. "It's a waste of money. I deal with scams all the time for work you know; this stuff, these people are nearly as bad as the bankers."

"I thought you were a banker?" Danny said.

"Exactly," Steve answered. They laughed.

"I hate witch stuff," Julie said.

"I *dare* you to go down there, then!" Lisa teased.

"Well, I do like checking out the décor of shops and places I haven't been before," Julie admitted.

"Scouting for interior decorating ideas?" Lisa offered.

"Something like that," Julie said.

"I don't like the vibe of this either," Steve said. "But since you dared us, I guess we have to."

They walked down the brick stairs. Steve reached and grabbed the long brass handle and opened the heavy door. They walked in. It was a small room, around the size of a modest family living room, cluttered with oriental rugs on the ground, crystals hung on the walls and ceilings, an old red velvet sofa chair and couch, and a few round tables cluttered with clay figurines of idols, candles, lamps, and old looking books. The place smelled of musky mold.

"Hello? Is anyone here?" Steve called.

"What do you think?" Lisa asked.

"The room has a personality; an identity, anyways. Not sure the message its personality is conveying is very welcoming, like a shop should be; the lighting is horrible, no thought in it at all, way too murky and cluttered which is uninviting... but a personality is better than no personality."

"Yeah, not very welcoming at all," Danny said. "And there doesn't seem to even by anyone here. Very strange. Hello?" he called.

Steve had picked up a skinny fairy figurine and was examining it.

"Dude, I dare you to shoplift it," Danny challenged.

Steve chuckled.

"Aren't you guys, like, complaining that people think you're a dull couple, like you're on some TV show or something that cares what people think? Didn't you ask us to dare you to do something that would make you seem more edgy and fun?" Lisa said teasingly.

Steve and Julie exchanged glances and smiled. Maybe we should, Julie thought.

"Agh, what's that!" Danny exclaimed, startled. He gestured towards a sofa chair in the shadows in the corner. What looked like a green blanket was draped over some clutter on the sofa, yet further examination reveled this 'clutter' shape to take the form of a person. There was a hand resting on the arm of the chair.

"Hello?" Steve called. There was no answer.

"Is it real or is it a mannequin?" Julie asked in a hushed tone. They cautiously approached the chair.

"There is trouble here," a voice from the chair spoke.

Julie and Lisa shrieked and jumped back. Steve giggled. "I'm sorry, we weren't really going to steal anything," he declared.

"You two. Leave," the lady said, her arm rising and pointing at Danny and Lisa. "You two, stay," she said pointing at Steve and Julie.

"I'm sorry... who leave and who stays?" Danny asked.

"You and your lady friend leave. The prettier ones stay," the lady said.

"Well that's not rude or anything," Lisa mumbled sarcastically.

"Or, we could all leave," Steve challenged curtly.

Danny slapped him on his shoulder. "Dude, stay. Tell us all about it," he said.

"We'll see you outside. Don't be too long," Lisa said and walked out.

Steve and Julie stood awkwardly.

"Come here," the lady commanded. "Approach."

Steve turned to Julie. "Do you want to?" he asked.

Julie shrugged.

"I know there is trouble brewing in both your souls. Deep questions and concerns about love and future. Come here, let me help you. No charge."

Julie strained a smile, rubbed the back of her neck and looked up at Steve. "We *were* dared," she said. "What would Danny and Lisa say of us if we backed out?"

Steve smirked. "Okay" he said.

"Come kneel in front of me," the lady said.

Julie giggled and Steve shrugged. If we're going to go along with this we may as well go all the way, they figured, no matter how weird it may get. They obeyed her.

"You two are to be married, are you not?"

"Yes," both Steve and Julie answered. It's not such a hard thing to correctly guess a couple may be engaged, Steve rationalized. Especially when noticing the engagement rings.

"Hold out your hands," the lady said. Her head was covered in shadows and a hooded cowl. "Don't be shy."

Steve and Julie obeyed her. She grabbed and yanked their wrists. She rubbed the underside of her soft thumbs over their palms. It tickled. As the lady leaned forward Julie noticed a strand of curled red hair dangle out the shadow caused by the hood. "Tell me your wishes for your marriage," the lady said. "Be sincere."

"Happiness," Julie answered.

"You fear the obstacles that block happiness," the lady said. "You have discussed it. You have even written it down. You have the paper even in your purse now, do you not?"

Steve scoffed.

"I... I do," Julie admitted, somewhat astonished.

"Go and clear and bring a table and bring it near me. Pull up some chairs," the mystic lady commanded.

"Um... okay," Steve said. "We... have friends waiting for us you know, we can't be too long. And this is all free, you say? No gimmicks?"

"Yes, yes, hurry up then," the lady said.

Steve cleared and picked up a table and brought it to her, and then he brought up two chairs next to it which he and Julie then sat on.

"Give me the paper," the women said.

Julie opened up her purse and handed her the paper. Steve was surprised that Julie had it; that she had ripped it out of the notebook and had carried it around with her. The lady took the paper and placed her hands over it, reading the lines as if with her fingers as if she were blind using brail.

"A literary beginning requires a literary spell," the lady said.

Julie smirked and raised an eyebrow. "Spell?" she said. She didn't know what the lady meant.

"You show condensation where you should not," the lady said. "I know you have experiences with witches and magic. You have hurt others with your skepticism and denials. The truth of nature does not like to be mocked."

Steve guffawed. "How do you *know* so much?" he challenged.

"I have powers," the lady answered.

Steve laughed.

"Hold out your palms again," the lady instructed. Steve and Julie obeyed her. As quickly as a lizard's tongue flick the lady's left hand, holding a blade swiped over the palms, drawing a slice of blood.

"Hey, what the hell!" Steve said. His arm was paralyzed, he couldn't pull it away. The lady grabbed Steve and Julie's wrist and slapped then down over the paper, smearing their blood over it. She released their wrists, grabbed the paper and crumbled it up while mumbling what sounded to Steve like Latin words. The paper burst in a flash of flames. The fire quickly went out, replaced by smoke and floating ashes. The lady deeply inhaled. Some of the ashes went towards her face.

She blew and the ashes wafted towards Steve and Julie's mouths. They inhaled; they couldn't help not to for some reason, and swallowed the ashes. It burned but not like it should have; more like swallowing bits of a jalapeno pepper. They both coughed in reaction; both blew out smoke while rubbing their chests. Tears leaked down their faces, from the pain of the heat. Steve wanted to verbally lash out at her, but he couldn't because of his coughing and trying to regain his breath.

"You know a sad and desperate failed writer whose name begins with 'T'. Message him; instruct him to write a book about death and the adjectives you wrote on the page. Tell him not to include his name, and it must be written in one day, quickly. Tell him to self-publish it, but only list it for one day. I will find it and seize it and once this book is in my possession I will complete the spell. Once you have read the book then the spell will be triggered. You write your own life story."

"We'll sue you for everything you have you insane bitch," Steve threatened. "If either of us is hurt…"

"No you won't," the lady said slyly. "You will not even remember this happened. Besides, human laws are merely zapped vapor compared with nature's laws."

Steve sniffed condescendingly.

"Besides, would the lawyers even believe us?" Julie meekly mumbled to Steve with a shrug.

"Magic is not real but people harming others pretending to do magic is," Steve huffed, his lungs still burning.

"So… what is this spell? What happens?" Julie asked.

"Only what you wanted," the lady said. "You will either have overcome all obstacles to your happiness and you two will live in forever marital bliss, or you will die."

"Bull shit," Steve spat. "We're leaving now." He stood up, knocking his chair over. Julie then stood.

CHAPTER TWETNY ONE

Julie woke up with a gasp feeling like she just submerged from water, desperately needing air. She felt her face, fearful that it was burned from the ashes (both the ashes from her dreamlike memory recall, and the ashes which the Wicca priestess had thrown at her face which had instigated the dreamlike memory recall). Her face felt as smooth as it always did. She looked up, wide eyed. The haggish faces of the witches, and Candice, stood over her in a circle peering down. "Where's Steve, is he okay, is he burned?" Julie asked.

"He's still dreaming, recalling the lost memories," the head priestess declared.

"Him being cursed with stupidity causes him to process the recovered memory more slowly," some random witch proclaimed which caused Julie to think *who the hell are you and why do you think you know anything; mind your own business you bitch.*

"What did you see; do you know who cast the book spell on you?"

Julie rubbed her head. She felt embarrassed. "It was... it was foggy. We were so dumb, it was just a lark, we didn't really mean... I mean, we were dared, and we didn't want to be boring, and I guess we had talked about... passionate, personal things... but we're not to blame, are we?"

"No," Candice consoled. "Yet... if you had a hand in instigating it or... asked for it, even partially, even if you thought you were just joking, that would help explain why the spell is so powerful. Did you offer your blood?"

"Yes... how did you know?" Julie asked.

The ladies murmured and nodded amongst themselves like students of medicine observing a new surgery technique.

"Did you see a face?" Candice asked.

Steve groaned.

"No... she wore a hooded cloak. But... I saw a lock of her hair." Her eyes darted towards the pale red headed younger lady. "You," she said incredulously. The red head widened her eyes, gasped and took a step back. Julie jolted up, her rage jumping from five to eleven in a second. Candice braced Julie's shoulders.

"It can't be one of us, despite what you thought earlier, there's many other covens, many rouge individuals, gypsies are a whole other branch and..." Candice said.

"It was her!" Julie screeched, "I know it, that hair, I saw her hair!" she brushed Candice off of her and maneuvered towards the red head.

"I didn't Miss.," the read headed girl pleaded, "I swear, I would never, I do not even yet wield the type of power which could cause such unrest!" she spoke theatrically, a hint of a bad attempt at an English accent in her delivery.

Steve groaned louder sounding like a hungry zombie just waking up.

"Now I know it for sure, that's her voice!" Julie screeched. "I recognize her voice!" It infuriated Julie that this girl had referred to her as 'Miss'.

"It's not me, I beg, I beg, it's not," the red head declared, her theatrics infuriating Julie and cementing her conviction. "Candice, tell your sister that I would never…"

"It could not be Sister Annabelle, she is just a guppy," the head priestess said.

"Steve, get up, grab her!" Julie yelled.

"Huh, what?" Steve grumbled as he rubbed the back of his head.

"The girl is running away, you dumb lug, go get her!" Julie ordered.

Anger born from confusion sprung suddenly in Steve. It hurt that the girl he loved called him dumb. It hurt more that he knew she was right. One moment he was lost in the woods trying to save the forest by putting out a fire, just like Smokey the Bear admonished him to do when he was a child, the next moment he had burning ashes smothered in his face and then was transported to a sunny farmers market street with Julie, Lisa and Danny, and then talking to some weird cloaked gypsy lady, and then he was back in the forest. He grunted. He charged the waifish red headed witch, the one Julie was pointing at, telling him to chase; don't let her get away.

"No, what are you doing, are you guys crazy?" Candice huffed.

"She's running that means she's guilty!" Julie yelled and dashed after her.

"Sisters, we protect our own!" the head mistress yelled and directed her followers to charge at Julie and Steve.

Steve and Julie chased Anna while the witches chased them moaning like banshees. Steve caught up to Ana, scooped her up in a tackle, slung her over his shoulders and kept running, not knowing where he were going, only following Julie through the blackness of the woods. Julie rushed towards the road where they had parked. An arm popped up from the ground and grabbed Steve's ankle. He fell and Ana flung forward, landing with a thump. Julie screamed as if in a battle as she turned to look at the damage behind her. She picked up a rock and slammed Anna's head with it and then she fell over her, just as Anna had tried wobbling to stand. Blood burst from Anna's head and clung to her hair and she again slumped, nose first, back into the dirt. Steve wiggled his leg free of the hold the protruding hand had him in and ran towards Julie. The chasing witches saw the arm wiggling up from the earth and they stopped, startled and horrified by it.

"Zelda, is that you?" Steve called to the arm. "Zelda, I'm so sorry. I've been having dreams about you, I love you!"

Julie dismissed Steve's words to Zelda's arm, if that's what it was, as incoherent babble from a dumb mentally challenged child, otherwise they would have stung. "Come on! Pick the bloody bitch back up and keep running!" Julie implored

Steve. He obeyed her, thinking, *you're the boss and the brains here, I'm just the dumb brawn.* The venom at which she had spit her command had made him want to cry and appease her else she turn her full wrath towards him.

"What sorcery is this sister?" a witch said as they looked at the finger wiggling pale arm protruding up from the earth like a plant.

"Enough games, there's a body buried here, somebody call the police," said another witch.

"They're getting away!" screeched another.

"Call the police about them as well!"

"The police are as useless to us as bat dung and mole snot," another witch said.

"Do not disparage nature's ingredients; bat dung can be very helpful in conjuring certain potions," another witch offered.

"Sisters, can we please stop arguing for just one moment?" another witch implored.

"Ghost, if this arm is your body I implore you to show yourself to us!" the head priestess declared.

"They're getting away! With our Annabelle! They've kidnapped her! Candice has betrayed us again!" one witch yelled.

The arm disappeared. The head priestess ran to it, bent down and dug. Some others joined her. They found nothing. "It was an illusion," she said. "We've been deceived!"

Julie drove Candice's car, Steve sat on the passenger side, Candice and Anna, who was passed out, sat in the back.

"Bitches!" Julie spat. "We've got her. We've got the bitch that did this to us. We're halfway free now. We just need her to reverse the spell after we write in the dumb book our little good deeds or whatever. Then our lives will be saved."

CHAPTER TWENTY TWO

They were both stupid.

They wandered the fancy grocery store isles getting away with things others, older, uglier, wouldn't be able to get away with; singing loudly off-key to the bland ambient jazz music, grabbing yogurt off the shelves, breaking the seals and drinking them messily, staring at others, making faces. Others interpreted this boldness as rude and obnoxious, but also fascinating and 'cool'. They wished they could be as young, as good looking, as in love. They were hated and envied by the other shoppers but no one scolded them or made a fuss. Let the kids have their dumb fun. They're probably on drugs. Stay away children, don't look at them, shield the children's eyes, the mothers in the rows think; it looks like they're having fun now, but that's a deceptive illusion; you should see them when they crash, when they want the next hit, when they're rock bottom without money and hope and feeling like shit thirsting to feel dumb and free and high again.

They snatched brooms from the cleaning isle then went to the produce isle and spilled dozens of oranges on the ground and brushed them towards the front of the store like they were playing some insane game show. "We have to do something, like, really, really, really smart in order to break a curse or else we die," Julie explained to the cashier. "Don't worry my daddy's rich," she added.

"I figured it out. The secret and everything of the world," Steve said to a random young cashier. "The thing that will save the world. The witches showed me. It's nature. The trick to harvesting the energy of the sun and to make gas and solar panels that can produce all the electricity the world needs is in orange peels. What's smarter than fucking saving the entire planet, huh big shot?"

They got in Julie's car, loading up the bags of oranges and drove recklessly, nearly getting in dozens of near fatal accidents as they drove lost and aimlessly, angering those nearly killed or maimed and answering the honks and yells at them with oblivious laughs. They sat on the grassy hill next to Ballard Locks peeling oranges, looking at the sunny blue sky, determined to do something smart to counter their stupidity, as if will and wish alone could transform brain cells and biology.

Julie began to cry. "I can't do it," she said. "It's hurting my fingers. The orange water stings like bees. It's too boring!"

"You've got to be brave and be tough and be smart!" Steve implored. "Think of a way you can do this that won't hurt your fingers."

Julie placed an orange next to her head and grunted in exertion from thinking so hard. She took off her shoes and socks and tried to peel oranges with her toes. "It's no use!" she said with frustration.

"We'll have to think of something else then!" Steve hollered. "We can't give up!"

"What did Candice tell us? Before she had to leave to deal with her dumb witches again or whatever, she told us something."

"I don't remember," Steve admitted.

They sat in silence for a moment, resting from trying to think hard. Julie became obsessed by a lady bug she picked up and was crawling over her hand. "I remember now," she said. "Candy—we used to call her that I just remembered—hey that's something smart, we should write that down. She said, 'you can't be stupid when you're smart'. Or, no, it was the opposite, you can't be... smart when you're stupid."

"That's dumb, that makes no sense," Steve said. "When you're stupid is the best time to be smart! How do you think Einstein came up with the theory of the big bang and shit?"

"Whoa. That's like, seriously profound," Julie said. "I think one of my Stanford professors said something like that once."

"See. It's working! We write that down and our stupid curse will be lifted!" Steve exclaimed.

"Is there a... girl in our closet? Or in our room I mean, on our bed. Red hair. Or did I dream that?"

"I think I had the same dream."

"We must really be in love."

They kissed.

"Wait," Steve said. "You were really, really mad yesterday. Like, scary mad. You wanted to pull out that girls eyes."

"But I didn't," Julie said with a pout. "I don't think I even could. I wasn't in my right mind. This curse supposedly makes me dumb now, or whatever, but I think I was more dumb yesterday."

"Me too. And so was I," Steve said. "Oh, I remember why you were so mad. She wouldn't confess."

"And she's totally at fault, right? That girl was a real B-word."

"But Candice told us not to worry," Steve said. "She bragged that she's way more powerful than that girl. And she'll make her confess and make her reverse the spell."

"Oh good," Julie said with a sigh.

"She said we needed to work on doing…what word did she use… do the opposite of the curses so that we can write them down in the book."

"Did we tie her up?" Steve asked.

"I think Candice put a sleeping spell on her," Julie said. "Like she did to us that one time."

"I had no idea your sister was so freaky," Steve said.

"Neither did I," Julie replied.

They sat lying on their backs on the grassy hill looking up at the sky. *It's so hot,* Julie said. She lifted up her shirt exposing her midriff to the sun. Steve leaned over and walked his two fingers over her exposed flesh. *Bloop, bloop, bloop,* he said with each finger step. Julie tensed and giggled. *That tickles.* Steve's fingers stopped and stood next to Julie's navel. *Oh lookie here, what's this, I found a hole,* Steve said in a carton voice. Julie giggled. *Oh no, it's pulling me in. Help, heellp.* Not able to take the tickling any longer she swiped his hands away while smiling big. After a few pauses Steve said: "I think my little finger traveling friends want to explore those mountains up there. *Where?* Julie said sitting up with a jolt examining the horizons. *I thought the only big mountain around her was Mt. Rain-er?* When she was a child she thought that Mount Rainier was called "Mount Rain-er" because it rained so much in Washington. "I meant your boobs," Steve said. Julie giggled and blushed and said *oh.* She then cupped her breasts while looking down at them and lifted and lowered them in opposite directions while saying *boop, boop, boop.*

Steve gasped. "I just have a brilliant idea!" he exclaimed. He stood up. "We'll kill two birds!"

"We'll kill two birds?" Julie echoed, perplexed but willing to accept the logic of whatever explanation Steve might give.

"No, how's that saying go? Two birds in the stone... A fool... two ideas are better than one stone..." Steve strained to remember.

Julie shrugged and smirked. "I think I used to know that. I don't know."

"Anyways, this smart idea is not being stupid so that... strikes against stupid..." he rubbed his head and grunted.

Julie approached him and rubbed his arm. "It's okay nickname. You're so brave, trying to think so hard."

Steve laughed. "Oh yeah, we call ourselves *nickname* sometimes don't we? Because we couldn't think of any good real nicknames to call each other. Our friends were right; that was pretty stupid and annoying."

"So… your good idea was to have a good idea?" Julie asked.

"No. Yes, that was the first part. The first bird. The second bird is, lust was one of the things. One of the curses, right?"

"Yes… I think so. Although I think I mostly liked that one, if I remember right," Julie said with a sly sideways grin.

"Okay… okay… this is how I know this is a great idea, I have a boner already," Steve said.

Julie laughed. "What is it? Now I'm eager to know."

"Gosh you're so cute. I thought you were cuter as a smart girl but you may be ever cuter as a dumb girl," Steve gushed.

"That's so nice, thank you!" Julie gushed back without sarcasm or irony. She returned the "compliment": "I like you as a dumb boy too. And I usually, like, hate dumb boys so much. So what's your idea?"

"Oh yeah, right. So we slowly strip naked in front of each other and you show me yours and I show you mine. But then we don't have sex. And that will be a… thing-y, an anti-thing-y, against lust!" Steve exclaimed.

"Right here, out in the open?" Julie asked. "Where all the birds and everything can see?"

Steve snapped his fingers and slapped his knee. "That's it! That's where the saying comes from! Two birds looking... stone... no it lost me again."

Julie giggled. "That's okay sweet bear," she said. She took off her shirt. She wore a white cotton bra.

"Oh man, my boner just grew another three inches."

Julie giggled and scrunched her face. "Is that possible? Does it work that way?"

"Want to see?" Steve asked.

Julie swiveled. "Um... well... okay, I guess."

Steve ripped off his long silky basketball shorts. The outline of his boner protruded from his red boxer shorts.

"Oh wow, I think it did grow three inches," Julie stated.

"Your turn, take off your shorts. Please," Steve said while grinning.

She did so. "Wow," Steve said with heavenly reverence staring at her crotch. Julie tugged down at the corner of her panty line at her hip. *Oh man, oh man, oh man, oh man,* Steve said excitedly, nearly drooling.

"You first," Julie teased.

"No fair," Steve said. "Our shirts first."

"I already have my shirt off," Julie said teasingly.

Steve took off his shirt. Julie admired his pecs, abs and arms; firm, muscular, perfect. "Delicious," she said.

"Unleash your boobs. They want to feel the air, they look so good scrunched up against you but they want to fall free and fly like the birds."

Julie giggled. "Even being dumb I know that makes no sense," she teased. She reached back and unhooked her bra and pushed up on her boobs covering her nipples with her palms.

"Oh man, I'm going to explode," Steve said.

Julie giggled. "No, don't, you said you wouldn't, remember? Control yourself. Kill the bird."

Steve slipped off his boxers. "Oh wow, that's so... gross," Julie said with a guffaw, looking at his exposed stiff penis.

"I know, right? I showed you my dog now you show me your little pussy cat. We'll see if they want to play or chase each other."

Julie slipped off her panties. They looked, examining each other; each with a tight and splendid body, both better than the average of human specimen representing their genders.

"So... did we conquer lust yet?" Julie asked.

"My dog really, really, really wants to play with your pussy. It wants to crawl in there and hide out. It's too hot outside; it wants some shade inside that little cave there."

"My pussy really wants to let in your growling dog to shut him up," Julie playfully, nonsensically, bantered back.

Steve barked like a dog then howled like a wolf.

"Did you build that tower just for me?" Julie said acting flattered, looking at his stiff and begging thing as she fanned herself with her hand.

"I did. This is a temple tower dedicated to the eternal power of your blissful beauty goddess," he said, thrusting out and wiggling his hips causing his thing to sway.

"Oh wow," she gushed. "This goddess requires death and sacrifice. I will swallow it."

Steve laughed. "With your mouth or your pussy?"

Julie narrowed her eyes. "Hmmmm… with my pussy."

"We will never be as young again as we are at this very moment," Steve said seriously.

Julie's smile washed off her face. "Oh god that's so scary," she said. "Hold me, I'm scared."

They approached each other and kissed and pawed and grabbed and felt each other. He spun her around and entered her. She leaned back against his weight writhing. They fell and then reengaged and then were done, panting.

"We just totally conquered lust," Steve said.

"How so?" Julie asked.

"My junk is limp again. It won't get up. Remember last time, it wouldn't stay down no matter how many times it exploded and died it would just rise back up like a rocket. Now it's laying there all gross and slimy and just wants to sleep."

"We should probably cover ourselves up," Julie said. "The birds might see us. I think what we did might be illegal?"

Steve laughed. "Awesome," he said.

"I have to pee. Aren't you supposed to pee after sex? I heard that somewhere."

"There's some bushes over there," Steve said. "I'll go pee in the bushes over there, the other way."

Squish, squish, squish, Julie said as she walked over to the bushes as if she were squeezing a volleyball between her knees: *drip, drip, drip,* Steve said as he walked bare butt the other way.

They dressed then drove around aimlessly, lost, stopping every now and then at gas stations and stores to ask for directions. They got pulled over by the police for doing a illegal U-turn. They also ran red lights. Julie called Candice, crying. "We're lost and a police man was mean to me! Help!"

Candice sighed. "I told you not to drive anywhere. I thought I took your keys."

"Oh that's another smart thing we did," Candice overheard Julie say cheerily to Steve. "We found the keys!"

Candice showed up about an hour and a half after Julie called. She led Steve and Julie back to her apartment. Normally Steve and Julie would refuse to hole up for longer than a day in such a small cluttered cat fur layered pad but these weren't normal times. Their minds and will were worn and rattled by the continuing onslaught of the curses. Once back at Candice's place Julie sat at the kitchen table, palmed the book and scooted it near her, opened it and wrote: *The curse said we'd be stupid but we're really smart/ Our smartness tore the dumb allegations apart/ we are smart not stupid human beings/ we've done all sorts of smart things/ we came up with a good idea to squash lust/ we thought up a smart way to prove trust/ we almost solved the problem of climate change/ Isn't that strange! Orange peels!*

Julie dropped her pen, clapped her hands and squealed happily, proud of herself like a newly three year old who successfully used the potty for the first time. "Yay, we did it, we're doing it!" she cheerily boasted.

A moan came from the bedroom.

"Oh my gosh, what's that!" she asked, spooked. She just noticed the fog from the fog machine in the bedroom escaping from the bottom of the closed door and hovering about eight inches off the ground covering her ankles. "And what's with this fog inside? Candice, is it going to rain in here?"

"It's to keep Annabelle asleep so she doesn't escape, remember," Candice said.

"I remember!" Steve bragged, shooting his hand up as if he were in class.

"Oh yeah," Julie said.

"Weren't her dumb witch's friends trying to rescue her?" Steve asked. "And don't they know where you live?"

"I took care of it," Candice answered.

Steve mulled the simple answer over. "Oh," he uttered.

"Wait. So how are we going to get her to reverse the curse? Torture? We talked about this right, I forgot," Julie asked.

"I'll make her. Don't worry," Candice answered.

"Wow," Steve said, shaking his head.

"Wait, why'd she even do this to us? Why'd she hate us?" Julie whined.

"She did it to get at me," Candice flatly declared. "It didn't work."

"Oh," Julie uttered mimicking the same dumb sound as Steve's earlier 'oh'.

A moan and a cough came from the bedroom.

"Wait, so where are we sleeping?" Steve asked.

"On the floor," Candice answered. She went to the kitchen. picked up a knife and then opened the door of the bedroom, walked into the fog, then closed the door. Steve and Julie looked at each other stone faced. Then they erupted into giggles.

CHAPTER TWENTY THREE

Lauren Mayberry, lead singer of the band Chvrches played drums in a punk band as a teen, has a law school degree, speaks French and some German, is also a credited journalist, is a fierce feminist, bashing away misogynists, which cute girls in bands are always subjected to and harassed by, and racists with power, humor and wit, is really funny on social media, appreciates a good humor vine, has great tastes, reads, has a adorable yet powerful singing voice and writes brilliant affecting songs with tender soul touching lyrics, wrapped in the new industrial synth-pop created soundscape, and she's still not yet twenty six. Julie thought this while she looked at Lauren performing on stage, a week or so before Chad and Jessie's wedding. Maybe she doesn't smile as much as she should, maybe not much of a dancer, but she moves well, feels the music, has awesome mic chord whipping skills, is charming up there, raising her hand up mic in fist, bending over to head bang, then cutely and politely yet curtly imploring the jostling crowd to be respectful of each other and don't smash into each other, telling a story of when she went to a concert at sixteen and had to get stitches. Totally girl crush worthy, Julie thought. She wished she could be like her; wished her hair were brunette also; a smarter more substantive look; people have such dumb perceived notions that blondes only just want to have fun on the beach and get banged and giggle all day. She looked at Steve; he was enjoying himself also at the concert; able to dance well in tight spaces without bothering anyone who wasn't lame. An annoying couple by them grinded on each other in obnoxious ways for the first half of the concert, another couple did the stand stiff while he hugs her from behind and they sway unrhythmically every now and then annoying thing, and Julie felt proud that she and Steve were not like either of them. They were mindful not to annoy people with their public displays of affection. Not too much anyways.

The final encore song of the night was "The Mother we Share." Like most of their songs the lyrics are a bit cryptic and more meaning to the song is accomplished with the melding of the lyrics to the melody and singing with conviction and emotion which Laruen does. Julie didn't really know what the song was about exactly but it made her think of one sibling encouraging another sibling who was dealing with troubles. *Our mother raised you to be strong and good, don't worry* type of sentiment. The song made her think of Candice. Candice was shy and socially awkward, never had a lot of friends, or maybe any friends besides the stray redhead every now and then, never had a boyfriend, as far as Julie knew. As a tween and teen Julie resented her older sister for not being "cool" like some of her friends cool older sisters. She was embarrassed by her, frustrated by her; if only Candice would *try*. She could be so pretty and popular, enjoy herself so much more, not seem so sad and lost in her own world sometimes if only she'd *try*. Julie made an effort to live a life opposite from the example her older sister set; to try and be pretty and popular and fun and active and happy. She has mostly succeeded. One of the main sources of sadness in her life stemmed from her empathy for Candice. She wanted so badly for Candice to 'get better'. To not be so weird. Be happy. She loved her older sister. Candice could be so kind. She was kind and considerate, even frustratingly so sometimes, as when Julie tried to confront her. She didn't get mad when Julie stole her black sweater or her toys. Candice had inferred that she wanted to go to the concert with them, but in a passive way. Seeing Lauren up there sing that song to the enthralled crowd singing along and thinking about Candice, made Julie cry.

Steve was one of the enraptured enthusiastic fans singing along, fists in the air, slightly sweaty, slightly beer buzzed to "The Mother We Share". He only noticed Julie was crying after Lauren Mayberry said her final goodnight on stage and the lights turned on. When he saw her tears he rubbed her back and said, "Hey are you alright?" He feared that he may have expressed too much love and enthusiasm towards Lauren and that maybe Julie were jealous. He admitted to himself, bashfully, that in the moment he did sort of think that Lauren was cooler than Julie and that he wished Julie's hair was dark brown like Lauren's. He also felt, as he sometimes irrationally did after a good concert, that he had gone on a wrong track by not trying to be a musician. How would it feel to stand on stage and receive that much hysterical adoration and love for what you have done, how you have made people feel. It must be a rush as good a high as any drug. Or, within that sweet spot, in which Chvrches seemed to be, where there is a large enough eager and enthralled fan base to easily and quickly fill a room of three or four thousand or so, where the newness of it all, screaming fans and everything, hasn't become too stale and same and routine yet, a grind which wears down rather than an updraft which lifts to excitements, and it hasn't become too big where it begins to all feel a bit detached, ever increasingly abstract and esoteric, swallowed by it all in the way where the bigger the fandom and hype swells the smaller and less tangible and less yourself you feel from it; if it happens like that. Sure, every band and musician wishes to be more popular and work towards that goal, for monetary and sustainability reasons, as well as all the other varied and valid reasons people want to be as successful as they can be, while still maintaining their integrity; but just as far as the maximum enjoyment of putting on a show, there's a sweet spot, Steve just then imagined; as if he'd ever know. Being a successful and adored musician able to create art that moves, affects and influences people looked like one of the few really great jobs the earth offers, along with being a successful actor or athlete perhaps. "Successful" is the key qualifier word; most musicians and actors are probably poor and in constant tempest regarding the forces of their dreams swirling desperation as each year that passes without much real progress diminishes their potential, their coolness, their chances of success. Writing of heartbreak while young is powerful and sensible; writing of it when old is just pathetic. But to make good money (if your successful) through art and self expression rather than route dull routine and bureaucracy, sounded ideal and fun to Steve. He and Julie had discussed all this before. But hey, I'm still young; he thought then dismissed the ludicrous thought with a scoffed laugh.

"Yeah, I'm good," Julie answered, brushing her wet cheek. "That was just really great."

"It was," Steve agreed. "It's amazing all that can happen in a year and a half. A year and half ago no one really even knew about them except for maybe five people in Glasgow. And now look at what and where they are. All those people in love with them, with just as many or more in every city they go to in the world."

"It is amazing," Julie admitted. "It's rare, but sometimes sudden bursts can happen in life to dramatically change things suddenly for the better, as compared to the slow trickle of routine and sameness. Like… a comet crash."

"In a year and half we'll be married," Steve observed. "Two worlds crashing into one."

They stopped, the emptying crowd passing around them like water around a rock in a stream. They faced each other, she looking up at him. He wiped her cheek with his thumb. "And what a wonderful world it is," she said.

They kissed.

CHAPTER TWENTY FOUR

On the fourteenth day of the curse Steve woke up from sleeping on the fog coated floor in Candice's apartment struck with a sad and heavy epiphany. Maybe no man is an island but everyone is their own world. And world's don't really collide. That's impossible. He realized that he was profoundly alone. He was completely stuck within himself. And he didn't like himself. His display of charm and confidence was just that; an act. What was he doing with his life? He had entered banking and business with the wish to make a lot of money. That was an early lesson he had absorbed; people respect, admire, and envy the wealthy. The wealthy are exceptional. They have power and influence. They can afford a higher quality of life; finer foods and entertainments and travel. Money to allow for the lifestyle someone like Julie deservers; money to ensure she'd always remain impressed by him. But to what end and at what cost really? So often the very rich are the worst, Steve thought he had discovered, through his work, school and general observation. Sociopaths who care more about accumulating massive ever higher piles of wealth than they do about other people, especially poor people, are some of the most admired within the world of the wealthy banker and business and Wall Street types. Ruthlessness, coldness, are admired; people who run businesses are called 'brave and courageous' for firing people, as if 'he who fires the most poor schmucks or ships the most jobs to India and China where slave labor is basically allowed, is deemed the 'most courageous' and the 'winner'.

Was he on the path to becoming such a monster? Plus it's such a dull and droll profession, as well as being cruel. Shuffling money around, investing, watching your investments, shuffling more money around. Looking at numbers. What is that really? What good does that do the world or your soul really? It's really nothing.

He thought back to the Chvrches concert a week or so before they found *If You Read This You Will Die* in the barn at Chad's wedding. He thought of Lauren Mayberry, the lead singer. Although it had been a fun night, thinking of it now depressed him. It had been so long ago. He hadn't even been, and still wasn't, a Chvrches super fan or anything, already too mature for that intense level of devotion attached to something so esoteric; too much not like a hysterical thirteen year old girl, really. He had too much of his own life to have the desperate need to escape into the fantasy provided by intense fandom, however fun it may be, with all the daydreaming, wondering, collecting and obsessing such devotion either requires or inspires. Yet in this new depression he woke with it was like he had become a negatively obsessed in a sad way type of deranged super fan. He wanted so badly to go back to that night, to be in the same room with them again, with her, with Lauren, and it hurt that he wasn't, that she had moved on and had done so many exciting things since then, while he had stewed and suffered, lost his job, wasted money, partied with hookers, masturbated furiously like a twelve year old boy who just discovered the joys of self pleasuring, buried a body, kidnapped a girl, and so many other stupid and horrible desperate and debasing crimes he didn't want to recall.

It devastated him that Lauren hadn't seemed to have spotted him or smile at him during the concert, as if she had done so it would have given his life meaning but that she hadn't it meant that he was invisible and insignificant and nothing. And then while he walked in the morning dawn a string of other depressing thoughts followed: if Lauren had spotted him, liked him, by the way he danced or looked or some other instant magical attraction, and then after the encore invited him to her hotel room, despite her having a longtime boyfriend, or maybe even being married (he didn't know, although a theme of many of her songs seemed to be the tender yet firm, confusing yet reaching for clarification, feelings stemming from bitterness over strained relationships) he would so eagerly and gladly accept her invitation, despite being engaged to Julie. If she invited him to join her on tour he absolutely would; he would leave Julie for her without a second's hesitation. Then this: joining her on tour would be the only thing in life which would make him happy, as crazy as that is, and that he can't obtain this happiness, to be with her, share in her warmth, her talent, her adventures, her laughter, her conversation, with her charming Scottish accent, then he'd go the deep and dramatic opposite way of happiness; a profound forever painful sadness, stuck in a life of drab grays in contrast to all the colorful and sparkling excitements continually illuminating her world and where she walks. Then this: she'd never pick him; she probably wouldn't even like him in a friendly way. She hates even the mildest and seemingly harmless expressions of objectifying her, which becoming deluded enough to think that you love her, entails. Love the music not my face or body, he imagined she might scold some idiot chanting annoying and stupid things at her. But she *is* the music, isn't she? She was so cool and exciting while he was so lame and dull despite his strained efforts not to be. Coolness can only happen naturally; it can't be obtained by try or effort, other than the effort of mastering some admired talent perhaps; but even then, 'practicing' isn't what's cool, effortless ability is. Then this, maybe the worst thought yet: he loved Julie enough, although not at the moment as much as he loved Lauren, to know that she deserved better than him; him as this strange sad obsessed with some pixie like celebrity girl he could never really know. Julie deserved her own fun rock star billionaire, 'A' list actor or athlete or, to not make the list totally superficial, whatever dude cures cancer or solves the global warming problem or some other type of sexy genius, not a boring financial banker guy, like he was, or what he had been working on becoming.

He had his hands deep in his pockets. He took out his iPhone. He wasn't following Lauren Mayberry on Twitter yet. He corrected that oversight. He viewed her timeline and had his love for her validated. Funny, as part of her onstage makeup presentation she sometimes placed two sparkly tears under her eyes, or one sparkly tear one black tear, yet she seemed so full of happiness and good positive smart energy. There she is wearing Harry Potter glasses in line for the Hogwarts ride at Universal Studios; there she is riding a superhero rollercoaster with her band mates (and boyfriend?) there she is on stage singing into the wind in San Francisco, there she is throwing up a Throw Back Thursday picture of her at her law school graduation a few years ago (god, really? She's so smart). There she is posting another Throw Back Thursday picture of her as a teen in her room playing drums (she's so cool); there she is posting a funny vine of a rude little kid blowing out his older sisters birthday candles (she has such a great sense of humor); there she is singing a duet of "I need my girl" with one of his favorite bands, "The National" at the San Francisco music festival just last week while Steve had been doing who knows what unspeakably horrible things, there she is in the studio and then celebrating the album's release, there she is replying in funny ways to things and linking to super smart articles and other things; she may have watched "Gilmore Girls" season 7 on the plane ride from Scotland to LA. Scrolling through her twitter feed was beautiful yet painful for him, like there was a knick on his screen that caused him to bleed every time he'd thumb swipe. Beautiful because she was beautiful, her face, mind, talent, humor, everything, painful because it was a beauty so far from him, and brought to him through such a small window and heavy filter. *Oh god,* he realized, it just striking him as obvious as a fastball plunking his forehead leaving a dent. *Lauren Mayberry looks like Zelda! Especially her younger pictures.* He mulled this over as he walked towards the wharf area, towards the Space Needle. *Don't I love Julie just as much,* he wondered. *More so; she's real, she's mine.* Maybe depression makes us long for things we know we can never have; maybe depression is like a virus which feeds on sadness so it plays mind tricks on you to cause you to be sad, such as longing for things you can never have, he mused, yet being self aware of this offered no cure but just made it all even impossibly worse somehow.

One of their popular songs is called "Gun." *Hide, hide,* she sings on it. It's easy to find a gun in America, even in a liberal state and liberal city like Washington, Seattle. Kurt Cobain loved guns. He sang about them.

**

Julie woke up with possible names of her and Steve's future children bouncing in her head: Aiden, Audrey, Zack, Zelda... no not Zelda, scratch that name off the list of possibilities; still a good name, underused name, but not for any future daughter of hers. Zoey perhaps? She took waking up with baby names on her brain as a good sign. It meant, she hoped, that the curse was beginning to end, to fade away. She just had another day of extreme self-pity to suffer through, which really didn't seem so bad, or not as bad as the other curses; just a lot of crying, which actually felt sort of good, like medicine. Just a lot of internal monologue and self agonizing over how she hates herself and the world hates her and nobody loves her and the world would be better off without her, she ruins parties she attends, she's a fraud at her job, she's stupid, never as smart as she pretended to be; she's crazy, maybe even more crazy than her older sister, in the big ending ironic twist; she was the one who should have been sent to the psych ward at the hospital, not Candice, oh god I am such a horrible person. And so on, in that vein. She hadn't fully realized it when coming up with the 'marriage ruining' adjectives, but 'self-pity' and 'depression' are entwined twins. They had completed all the 'opposite of the curse' tasks Candice had asked them to and had written of how they did so in *If You Read This You Will Die*, in the looping rhyming nonsense way the text of the book apparently required. Today the witch Anna would reverse the spell, Candice would make her, just as she promised, and they'd live, they wouldn't die, and everything would return to normal, everything would be fine; it all would have been like a horrible two week fever nightmare, a horror movie, now over and behind them, never to be brought up or thought of again. Because of what Julie has written in the book Zelda would return once Anna reversed the spell and it would be just as if she too had only slept for a spell and was now back, her fresh, clean, young and perky, sarcastic self fully reclaimed, the memory of being shot dead erased. Actually, no, Julie considered, this wasn't her second day of self-pity, this was her first day of depression. Right? Considering this she felt in a pretty remarkably good mood from the residual effect of the 'baby names' dream and anticipating, finally, the end of the curse, just as Candice had promised.

She lifted herself up from the thin layer of fog on the floor and scanned the small living room area. Steve had been lying next to her. Now he wasn't. "Steve?" she said meekly. Candice was sleeping on the couch. What day was it, she wondered. Was it Steve's curse death day? No, it was his second day of depression. The death was supposed to come after that, right? Or was it on the fourteenth day the death was supposed to come. *If You Read This You Will Die* had been ambiguous on that point. It wasn't a very clear or well written thing, obviously. Oh god, she thought. She stood up, opened the door to the bathroom, the closet doors, the bedroom where Annabelle laid. "Steve!" she screamed. She opened the front door and ran to the banister surveying the apartment complex parking spaces. "Steve!" she yelled. A random neighbor yelled back at her to shut up. Julie went back into the apartment. "Candice!" Julie yelled. "Wake up! Steve's gone!"

"Huh?" Candice said groggily.

"I thought you said this layer of fog was supposed to keep him asleep. Me too."

"It was," Candice said. "What do you mean he's gone?"

"Today might be his death day!" Julie screeched. "Your car is still here, I think he must have set out on foot. Where's my damn iPhone!"

"It's on the table, next to *If You Read This You Will Die*," Candice said.

Julie raced to the table, picked up her phone and called Steve. She heard his ringtone, a snippet of the song *Good Times* by Chic, a standard cheesy yet great wedding dance song he had put as his ringtone just a few days before Chad and Jessie's wedding. The cheery energetic tune sounded like horror gore to

Julie. Steve didn't have his phone, it was on the floor by the couch, and he wasn't here. "I'm going to go find him, you make Anna reverse the spell, now!" she yelled and marched towards the door.

"Wait!" Candice yelled. "Your body and your blood is needed to reverse the spell!"

"What?"

"One of you has to be here to help reverse the spell. The spell used your blood to cast; it needs your blood to undo."

"Fuck!" Julie yelled. She ran to the kitchen grabbed a knife and started slashing at her wrist.

Candice ran to her and tried to wrestle the knife away. They both screeched *what are you doing* at each other during the chaotic tussle.

"Take my blood then and let me go! I need to find him before he dies! God Candice I told you, I can't live without him!" Tears burst from Julie.

"No, it needs to be at the right time, blood straight from the living pulse," Candice said condescendingly, as if this little spell rule were obvious.

"Damn it Julie, well go wake her up then, make her reverse the curse, now!" Julie yelled while sobbing, obviously no longer in 'a good mood considering she's depressed' but rather feeling defeated and dark yet still frantic.

**

Steve wandered into McDonalds. He sat down at a empty booth. Outkasts "Hey Ya" played out the speakers. He smirked. If any song had the power to demolish a curse of depression, break through any thoughts of suicide and squash that noise, it would be that song, he thought. How can life be not worth living when a song like that exists in it, and will always exist in it? Although, maybe if the dead become spirits, maybe the ghosts are still able to dance. Maybe they're also able to stalk their obsessions and loves. Wouldn't that be nice? He thought this while not in a right frame of mind. Not himself. It's just pure sugar blast of energy; such a good song. It's a song about breakup though, ironically, a song that asks through its ebullient beat, if nothing lasts forever than why should love be any exception. The next song McDonalds played was "In Your Eyes" by Peter Gabriel. Oh god, he thought. This song, oh god. It's so good yet so bad.

The Chvrches Australia show next month sold out in minuets so they added a new one, Steve just read, looking at his Twitter timeline on his phone. He had just added the Chvrches account a minute before. No way my last meal will be McDonalds, he told himself. He couldn't remember what the last thing he ate was. Probably that daffodil-dandelion or whatever soup crap Candice made; a supposed remedy and medicine to diminish the power of the curse. I must have become immune to it, he thought. There's no way he could feel even more depressed than he did. A little ways off, he walked into a Wendy's. Not soon after a gaggle of cool skater type young people gathered in the parking lot. He observed them out the window. Maybe they weren't a "skater tribe" but some other tribe that happened to include some skilled skateboarders. Maybe they were just a few years younger than him, in their early 20's like him, but they looked like they belonged to another generation, like they were kids and he was a geezer; they looked cool, hip, fun; he felt old, stale, over. A model worthy blonde, maybe even hotter than Julie, wore skintight black jeans and exuded a blissful cheery happiness, so in love with her friends and what they were doing, or about to do. Her apparent boyfriend, who she was so blissfully in love with it looked like, was this skinny black boy who looked and dressed like he was the rapper Tyler the Creator. Maybe he *was* Tyler the Creator? He wore a cameo shirt, gold chain, burgundy cap and bright red socks. One of his friends wore a "Gun's N' Roses" hoodie. One had a "Kiss" cap, maybe worn ironically? Other girls were there with them, skating, laughing, smoking the newly legal going on two years pot, some stepping inside to get drinks, Frosties, fries and a baked potato. Steve observed them without trying to be creepy. They didn't notice him. He was as invisible to them and as separate from their world as if he were an eighty year old grandpa. Maybe these are the coolest kids in the world, Steve wondered. Hip and pretty, full of energy. A lanky androgynous boy had been in the bathroom with Steve; he had thought he was a girl but thought, okay, that's cool, cool kids don't need to follow public bathroom codes. Then they jammed themselves in their cars and headed off to whatever adventure awaited them; maybe some forest rave (do those still happen?) or to the beach or to some concert, maybe the secret Tyler the Creator show?

Where were Chvrches now? On a tour bus on the road? Headed where? Salt Lake City. Then Denver. Then Kansas City. Into the mountains and into the boring deep conservative middle of America. The Rocky Mountains then the plains. All the flat land. Endless miles of flat nothing. Further away from him every passing second. In distance and through passing time. Maybe Salt Lake City and Kansas weren't boring; maybe each provided exciting and interesting attractions and people. He didn't know. Enjoyment of a place has more to do with who you're with (and who you are) than where you are, really. Life is what you make it, goes the cliché. Another cliché, almost just as bland and boring and gray: you write your own story. Steve

saw a little Mexican-American boy in a Pope Francis T-shirt
with some message about love written on the back. Love is
embarrassing. He walked out of the Wendy's. There had been
an old lady in there hired to clean tables. She was dressed as
"Wendy" wearing the red pigtails wig and blue doll dress and
big black blotches on her cheeks supposed to be freckles. She
had lain at a booth, eyes closed, and looked dead. She looked
like she may have been pretty when younger. In a normal, better
mood, the quirky image of her would have perhaps made Steve
smile. Instead it, and the added negative symbolism he placed
on it about life, the degradation and unfairness of everything, up
until the end; things getting worse not better through time, the
sadness of wishing to be younger, the façade of everything, just
devastated him. Depression can make you painfully
oversensitive. Little cracks on sidewalks are like fault lines soon
to cause thousands of deaths. It creates a paradox; you feel too
much in the down directions of everything that you wish to feel
nothing at all. So you feel nothing at all and the feeling of
nothing is even worse than feeling the pain. Steve didn't know
that before this day.

**

Candice walked into the bedroom where Anna slept and
closed the door. Julie waited agonizing outside the door. She
heard her older sister muttering strange sounding incantations.
The door creaked open and Julie took a step back. "Hurry,
please," she pleaded. Annabelle stepped out from the fog, her
red hair slicked back, her spine stiff, her eyes glazed and lifeless.
Candice stepped out from behind Anna's shadow.

"Is she awake? She looks like she's sleeping with her eyes open. Did you turn her into a zombie or something?" Julie asked.

Candice lowered her chin, looked up and smiled sinisterly. "No. Like a marionette," Candice bragged. "I control the strings."

Candice's cruel tone took Julie aback. Yet she was determined not to be distracted from her singular purpose: saving Steve, and herself. So many unanswered questions still lingered; why this skinny redheaded pale stranger would want to make her and Steve suffer and die. If she had a vendetta against Candice why didn't she just attack Candice, why involve Candice's family? Although, Julie considered, that's what the most evil, twisted and sadistic villains do; not only destroy the person they hate but destroy that loathed person's loved ones and family first in order to inflict maximum emotional pain. None of those unanswered questions mattered now though, the why's and how's (so many questions about the how's exactly and the larger implications.) All that mattered was ending the curse, save Steve's life as well as her own.

"Well...will it still work?... if she's 'controlled' or whatever?" Julie asked.

Candice ignored the question, all her fiery hatred concentrated on Annabelle. She positioned Anna at the table and had her sit down. Julie scooted *If You Read This You Will Die* towards Annabelle. It was attracted as if by a magnetic pull towards Anna's hands. Candice then went into the kitchen and brought back two long white candles which she placed on either side of Annabelle. She lit the candles and then turned off all the other lights. Candice picked up Anna's limp wrist then plopped Anna's hand over the book. She bent and placed her lips near Anna's ear and whispered. Anna repeated the strange worlds which sounded Latin to Julie. This went on for awhile, an hour or longer. Julie was impatient but the melodic lyrical repetitious words, the flickering candles and some other unseen influence had lulled her into a trance like state, unaware of time, overly relaxed considering the situation.

"Now," Candice declared.

"Huh?" Julie responded. She blinked.

"Snap out of it, your blood. Now is the time," Candice curtly instructed.

"Oh," Julie said. She looked down and realized she had been holding her wrist over where she had previously cut. She stood and walked over towards Anna and the book. She let go of her wrist. The blood had already clotted so did not drip. Candice reached and poked her finger in the wound. "Ouch!" Julie said and flinched. She tightened her lips and held her arm firm over the book. Blood dribbled over the covers in splotches. Candice opened the books pages and blood also defiled and soaked in the white pulp and black ink.

"Okay, that will do," Candice said. She went into the kitchen and used a ladle to scoop up something she had steaming in a pot over the stove. She brought the ladle over to the book and dumped the thick stew over the book. The flames of the candles flickered brighter and hotter. Candice again bent down and intensely whispered in Anna's ears with Anna repeating the strange lyrics, almost sounding like singing. Julie found herself softly mumbling along with the tune.

**

Steve walked until he came upon a pawn store. He entered. "I want a gun," he said. "Loaded."

"Sure young buck," the owner said. "You don't look like a criminal although it looks like you've had a rough night. I'll just need to do a background check."

"I'll pay a thousand extra if you just give it to me now," Steve said.

"A thousand, huh? Well what kind of businessman would I be if I turned down a deal like that?"

Steve walked out of the pawnshop with a loaded glock.

He walked on. It was a loopy thing to think he was in love with some lead singer of a synth-pop band. He wasn't really, he told himself. Where had that even come from? He just woke up with it. Was it sexist for him to feel in love with Lauren and her band? No, he didn't think so, but she, Lauren, might. She wants to be treated just like the guys. No 'marry me!' shouts at her during concerts; she'll strip down whatever fan expresses such sick yearnings, in all forms they come in; that's what Julie told him before the concert; she had done some reading on them to prepare; she liked knowing about the bands she went to go see; said it added to the enjoyment of the experience, gaining a further appreciation through knowing more; Steve hadn't delved so deeply in on them before the concert but he now recalled the things she had told him about the band, like how Julie admired Laurens feminism and toughness, she's not just some 'cute girl'. He remembered all the wonderful things Julie had said of them.

After the show, after she had dried her tears, she had said, "It's rare that electronic music, which I guess they kind of are, can feel as warm as a good hug." Julie did sometimes have a beautiful way with words, Steve thought. She was able to say one sentence which could cause his mind to spin for days, thinking it over. These are my last thoughts, Steve thought. There really are so many great bands out there. Unheralded, underrated; past bands and bands and musicians now; Deerhunter, as just one example; one of his hipster friends who was still into the whole 'indie music' scene more than he was had recently told him about an awesome and exciting new band from Philadelphia called 'Beach Slang'. He really should slack off on this brand new Chvurches obsession, he thought. It wasn't healthy. (This thought struck him even as he contemplated immediate suicide; he was only slightly self aware of the irony). He didn't want to be like a early 20's, sliding quickly into mid-twenties, maybe he already was mid-twenties, six years to thirty already, guy who was like one of those boy band teenage fan-girls, cutting the boy band members names in their arms to try and illicit their attention, sexualizing these boys with gross online comments, actions and suggestions.

One of the three members of Chvrches, Julie had told him, was kind of an older guy who used to write music for TV and movies, along with being in a little struggling indie-rock band like the other two members. And he said the job was soul crushing, just plunking the same note over and over. To most wouldn't that be an awesome ideal job, Steve wondered. If a job like that is soul crushing, what hope do any of us have to save our souls? Lauren had graduate degrees in law and journalism, Steve recalled Julie had told him, a fact he had forgotten until he scrolled through her twitter timeline just a moment ago, yet before the band she was working at some menial labor job doing archives stuff; he couldn't recall exactly what Julie had said, but point being it was something beneath her education and talent;

some boring repetitious thing most of us are forced into doing in exchange for being able to feed and clothe ourselves. Although, then there's the Syrian refuges, for example, coming in waves into Europe who say they'd be grateful for any job at all, no matter how horrible; it'd still be paradise compared to where they were. Maybe Lauren would never be satisfied unless she was a music goddess? Not in a selfish way, but in the same way a lion who was born into a rabbits body would never be satisfied unless it became a lion. Who knows; he really didn't know; he really knew nothing, and as for people, especially celebrities, the more you try and learn the less truth you really actually know. These were his last rambling thoughts, stupid unstructured annoyingly meaningless confused and incoherent thoughts and they didn't matter. He didn't matter. Nothing would be new anymore.

**

Candice huffed and bellowed dramatically into Annabelle's ears. Anna's eyes turned white and blood leaked out of her nostrils and the corners of her mouth. The candles flickered and burst in pulses. A tickling vibration jangled the floor, walls, ceilings and inside Julie's chest. An unnatural wind swirled around the room. "Is it working?" Julie yelled desperately and repeated her question: "is it working?"

**

Steve made his way to the beach along Golden Gardens Park where he had proposed to Julie. He sucked on a watermelon Jolly Rancher snatched from the candy dish his taxi driver left in the backseat. He carried a brown paper lunch sack which held his newly purchased loaded gun. He found a driftwood log to sit on. He watched a young Asian couple, freshly and newly in love it looked like, flying a kite.

'Loving something so much it hurts' sounds intensely romantic but in actually it sucks, Steve thought. He's had a few crazy ex-girlfriends. One was too into him, it scared him, it doesn't take long for flattery from being worshiped to turn into being creeped out. Because you know it's bullshit, Steve thought; few people are really worthy of being worshiped. Those who decide to worship other living humans with any amount of sincerity and earnestness choose to live in delusion; which is understandable, as awful as reality can be, or always is, depending on who you are, but that type of intensity is not sustainable. He wasn't sure, the lyrics without the melody a bit cryptic, but he thought maybe one of Lauren's songs was about ending a relationship with some crazy guy who was too into her. Lana Del Rey, who he also loved, maybe even more than Lauren, had a song like that too, Steve considered. And what had Julie said to him? He had seen it in the memory which had been erased which had been brought back to him by the weird witches in the woods. She had said she'd rather die than be without him. Was that crazy? He didn't know. What did it matter anyways?

I don't love her enough because I don't love myself, he thought, thinking of Julie. *I hate myself.* Depression lies to you. He mustered courage to utter his thoughts out loud, to test and strengthen their truth by pressing them into sound outside his head; statements called out to the universe, collected and stored by time. He moved his lips but his throat was dry. He coughed.

He cleared his throat. He looked at the swaying kite. He whispered *I don't love her. I hate myself.* He clutched the gun feeling the metal through the paper bag, feeling the hard cold contours. He knew that when he took the gun out of the bag in public that he'd have to act quickly else he create a scene; people fleeing in terror perhaps, cops coming. Although maybe not; people can and do dumbly, yet legally, swagger around streets brandishing guns in America; maybe he'd just get annoyed judgmental looks from anti-gun types and maybe some thumbs up from some pro-gun types passing by, or maybe he'd just be continued to be ignored. He didn't know. He couldn't hesitate. If he lost his nerve he'd, perhaps, have to embarrassingly deal with police interventions and local news cameras. About the Seattle police department: why haven't they caught him yet for burying Zelda's body, he wondered, just realizing his dumb luck over it. It's not like he had been careful. Were the police here really that inept? Had Zelda even been reported missing yet or her body discovered? He guessed not. Anyways, he thought, get to it. Pulling a trigger is easy. Don't allow any thought before the pull, he told himself. The decision is already made. I'm already dead. Just a finger twitch to finalize it, easy enough. He scanned the area once more, no children, oddly, since it was summer and they were out of school, same as him. But good, that's a good omen that this was meant to happen. He didn't want his last act alive be to forever traumatize a bunch of children. Of course it was meant to be. It was already written in a book. He took the gun out of the bag and placed the barrel tight against his temple. *Oh god no!* he heard one of the kite flyers screech right before he pulled the trigger.

**

"It is done," Candice declared.

Julie heard a shot in her head. Her heart stopped and her rib cage rattled and she crumpled to the floor, covering her ears. Her hands shook.

"I see by your reaction that the curse has been lifted," Candice said.

"No... I don't think it's that," Julie answered on the floor in a dry throated whisper, her clawed hand clutching her heart. "Oh god," she said wide eyed. "It's Steve. The curse linked us, we both breathed in the same smoke fumes...and now... I don't feel him anymore."

"It's like you wanted," Candice said.

"Excuse me? ...maybe, I don't know, but I... I felt... my head... it's just... it's... it's gone. Or, his is gone. ...He's gone." Her hands and lipped trembled. She was wide eyed, shaken, pale white. "You...you said it would work... you said..."

Candice smiled a tight wicked grin. "It should have worked. You must be mistaken," she said coolly.

Why does she seem so pleased with herself Julie thought. *What's the matter with her?*

The white block of Annabelle's pupils dissipated. She blinked and twitched her fingers. She seemed to be waking from her trance. Candice took a step back while scowling. Julie stood back up and looked at Anna. "Why didn't it work!" she screeched. "Is he dead, is Steve dead?! Why would you do this to us?!" She leaped over the side of the table and grabbed Anna by her collar and shook her. Anna was limp at first but her muscles firmed quickly as she regained herself. She lashed out her arm, her palm up and Julie was hurled backwards, toppling over the table and again flopping towards the ground, by a powerful magnetic like force.

"You bitch," Anna growled. She leaped up and wrapped her hands around Candice's neck, dropping Candice to the kitchen floor, knocking a chair over. She straddled Candice squeezing her neck causing Candice to gurgle and gasp fruitlessly for breath. Julie staggered up and looked at utensils in the kitchen. There was the blood stained knife she had earlier used to slice her wrists. But no, she couldn't stab anyone other than herself. *I'm so ugly, I deserve pain, I deserve to die, I should die next,* she told herself. *This Anna witch should be squeezing the life out of me, not my sister.* She opened the cupboard and pulled out a heavy iron skillet. She limped over to Anna murdering her older sister and stood over her. She mustered all her weakened strength to lift the skillet over her head to prepare for a blow against the top of Anna's skull. Just as she was about to unleash her downward swing Anna jerked her head back and looked at Julie with blazing eyes. She lifted up her palm again and Julie once more flew across the room and crashed against the kitchen sink and onto the floor.

"Why are you doing this to us? To Steve and I?" Julie feebly warbled through her tears. "I don't care anymore, okay? Kill me. End this. You win. Just don't kill my sister."

Anna cackled. She released her grip from Candice's neck. She turned and rose and faced Julie, looking down at her. "You still love your sister? After what she's done?"

"Wh-wh-what has she done?" Julie asked.

"Everything. All this. While she had me in the trance I saw everything. You poor stupid girl. I told you it wasn't me."

"You're lying," Julie meekly said. "I saw you, in recalling the lost memory. I saw your red hair, I recognized your voice. It was you."

"An implanted illusion provided by your dear sister," Anna replied.

"No," Julie whispered.

"I'll show you myself then," Anna said. She ripped the sleeve of her red dress, crumbled it in a ball and then held it over the candle flame. It burst in light and disintegrated into steaming ashes which Anna held in her clasped fist. She brought her fist to her lips and spoke words to it. Then she slowly approached Julie.

"No," Julie begged. "No, not again."

Anna stuffed the ashes into Julie's face and eyes. She screamed in pain.

CHAPTER TWENTY FIVE

Julie saw her older sister as a fifth grader walking home from school. It was fall, nature's last vibrant burst of color before winter's death. Julie sensed her sister feeling and appreciating the beauty of the orange, red and yellow leaves scattered on tree branches and lawns and street, swirling in the crisp air. A gaggle of her peers from school, miniature popular mean girls, followed her, taunting her with this chant: *Crazy Candice has mush for brains/ Crazy Candice is insane/ Crazy Candice is full of farts/ Crazy Candice makes boys barf.* Why were they so cruel to her, Julie wondered. Where was I? I sometimes walked home from school with her back then. I vaguely remember other kids being mean to her. I was embarrassed for her. I was in the second grade then. Still a toddler, basically. Still, I should have... been a better sister. I would get shy and embarrassed when they'd taunt her; I should have yelled at them, threw rocks at them, shown support. Although, Julie considered, while receiving this vision, she had thought that Candice had brought some of her social misery on herself, during high school; selecting to be an outcast, purposefully being weird. Although, of course, no peer bullying or abuse is ever justified, especially in grade school.

Julie looked and saw Candice staring at a murder of crows which had gathered around the carcass of a white rabbit lying in a front yard wilted flower bed garden. Candice's eyes and hands tightened. A swirling wind disrupted the air. "Attack them," Candice said. The husky black ravens cawed and lifted. They circled noisily around the taunting children who froze and looked up bewildered and scared. The crows dived at the children, pecking at their hair as they ran in the opposite direction of Candice screaming. Julie could sense Candice's thoughts: *did I just make that happen?*

Julie next saw Candice as a teen, maybe around age seventeen, standing on the shoreline of the beach. Julie sensed that Candice soaked up the power and beauty of nature in a poignant way. Candice felt the immensity of the ocean in her and she looked up and although it was cloudy and light she removed, in her vision, the clouds and the sunlight and she saw the stars in all their unpolluted glory; the strand of the Milky Way and galaxies and she felt the power of the sky and the ocean swell in her and it tasted sweet to her, it caused her to smile and laugh and she so rarely, Julie recalled, smiled or laughed. Then Julie saw someone who looked like a younger version of Annabelle come stand at the side of Candice. They held hands and felt the beauty and power of nature together. The handholding wasn't romantic but rather more sisterly. Julie felt a pang of jealousy.

Then she saw Anna and Candice both wearing red robes kneeling over dead leaves in the woods in front of who Julie recognized as the head Wicca priestess. "Both of you have become powerful," the old witch said. "I have seen this happen; it is not rare for nature to find favor in the hopes and fortunes of the young. Sadly, perhaps ironically, although natures blesses the young with the most power sometimes, the young are also too dumb and naïve to use the powers effectively. Perhaps this too is nature's wish. However I have decided that only one of you will receive the red jewel necklace. One of you has shown more wisdom and patience in your training. And that one is Annabelle. Be glad for your sister Candice."

"No!" Candice yelled while standing up. "She tricked you, she tricked me, she lied! She said…"

"Enough!" the priestess said cutting her off. "My decision is final. If it is true that she has been cleverer than you, then whose fault is that?"

Julie next witnessed a scene she had been familiar with. Candice blocking traffic in a busy intersection, screaming incoherently. It had been a 'final straw' mental break moment which brought about Candice's admittance into the psychiatric care unit at the hospital. A 'the dam completely broke after multiple little leaks' moment. While witnessing the mad scene Julie sensed that Candice had been troubled by her diminishing powers and that the head priestess favored Annabelle over her. Candice had chased a murder of crows into the street trying to control them, Julie sensed, but in the effort some of the birds internal magnetic compasses had crossed with the electrical currents in Candice's brain. *Poor Candice* Julie thought.

A new scene flashed in Julie's vision. Candice, in a desperate and panicked state, spoke with Annabelle next to the gum wall in Post Ally under Pikes Place Market.

"Help me Anna!" Candice pleaded. "They think I'm crazy. They betrayed me! My biological sister and her boyfriend and my coven sisters both! If I'm sent away to an insane asylum the coven will revoke me! You can't let that happen to me! You know I'm not crazy!"

"Tell me," Anna answered coolly. "Why have all the other Wicca's, or witches, managed to stay out of mental institutions? Because we are smart. We don't flaunt our powers or seek to posses more beyond our means. Myra warned you about that. Your hubris doomed you. Candice, trying to communicate with crows? Really? Do you think you are a goddess?"

"No. I… I've done it before, as a child. I wanted to prove to you… to them… that I was deserving. If only I had the red jewel amulet you have, then the animals, the plants, even the weather…"

"Then what?" Anna said curtly cutting her off. "They'd do your bidding? Is that what you were going to say?"

Candice didn't answer.

"Candice you know nature can't be controlled."

"But…" Candice meekly protested. "That's what we do."

Anna shook her head disappointingly. "If Myra heard you say that. I'm sorry Candice, I love you but… I think it's for the best, for you. Seek the secularist's treatments; immerse yourself further in their remedies and religions. The coven is better without you and you, the world, nature, and the fates are better without us."

"So… you won't help me? "

"No," Anna replied.

"Then I am doomed."

It was the strangest 'break-up' Julie had ever witnessed. Next her vision presented to her montage images of Candice suffering in the hospital. Screaming, being tied down, having hallucinations, sweating and panting as if she were giving birth, sometimes seemingly possessed by demons. Then Julie saw Candice 'pretend' to get better; to admit to past delusions, to pretended to agree with the false diagnosis and accept the treatments for the false diagnosis. Then she was released from the hospital, once again deemed sane, or sane enough to be able to function and no longer be a danger to herself or her community. But it was all a lie, Julie was made to understand, more through feelings and empathy presented to her during the vision, rather than images. Candice held deep resentments which she buried and hid yet still maintained. Julie became aware, for the first time, just how deeply her older sister resented; how she acted so passive-aggressively, in chiding her for having sex outside of marriage for example, when what she really wanted to do was lash out aggressively from a sense of feeling betrayed.

Julie saw Candice standing along the Seattle pier. She saw her sisters eyes narrow and her nostrils flare. A thin dark cloud squeezed into existence by Candice's effort. Next Julie was presented the 'recovered memory' scene she had the last time she had such a vision, while in the woods. The scene where she and Steve entered the basement fortune teller shop and the cloaked lady with the red hair and voice of Annabelle had taken their blood and set into motion the 'write your own story' curse. Everything was the same except for one big difference; the cloaked lady was clearly Candice. *How could I not have known at the time* Julie thought while witnessing once more this scene, and she was answered: *Candice used a spell to mask her true identity. And then when the memory was recovered to you in the woods she implanted the false image to make it appear Annabelle was the one who began the curse against you.* Julie had it confirmed through feeling that this was a sad truth. And another insight: yes, Candice is the guilty one, the one responsible, but so was she. And so was Steve. Perhaps that is why the spell had been so strong.

Julie broke free of the vision, grasping for air. Like she did the last time she awoke from visions received by some witch stuffing ashes in her face, she felt the skin on her cheeks, eyes and nose in worry that there'd be scars. Like before, she didn't feel searing heat pain and her skin felt smooth. She shook, sat up from the floor and scooted away from Candice and Annabelle looking down at her. Julie looked up at them as if they were monsters. Her mind reeled; unanswered questions stuck her like darts; despite her resentment, still, how could Candice be capable of such evil, how could she do this to me, to us; I never really knew her; why'd she try to frame this Annabelle girl; what did she expect to gain by having someone she knew could not reverse the spell try to reverse the spell; did she want Steve to die, does she want me to die; what do I do now? The last question was the clearest to her; the earlier questions were muddled in complexities of human behaviors forever to remain mysterious and unknown; the last question demanded action to try and make a wrong a right, if it could be at all possible. The last question, unlike the others, had a clear answer; I need to try and make this right. I need to save Steve. It can be done. She lifted herself up and knocked the table over. Annabelle and Candice flinched backwards. She reached and palmed the book and slid it to her. Anna and Candice began to bicker and physically tussled with each other again, although both were weakened, Candice from the earlier choking attack, Anna from the excretion of providing Julie the 'clarifying vision' spell. The fighting sounded like muffled trumpets to Julie; she was focused on another task, glad that the other two witches were distracted. She picked a pen off of the floor, opened the book to a blank page in the back and wrote: *My sister Candice will willfully reverse the spell, all will be well, Steve and Zelda are now dead but yet they will both live.* She shut the book and held it. She gathered her strength and then stood up. "Stop!" she yelled.

Annabelle and Candice stopped bickering and turned to face her.

"I don't care," Julie said softly. She held up the book. "Candice... I'm so sorry. I was so wrong. I can never make it up to you. You deserve to hate me. I deserve punishment. You win. But please, I beg, reverse the spell. I don't care; you can deflect blame still, I don't care, we'll never mention this again. But please, just reverse the spell. I don't want to die."

CHAPTER TWENTY SIX

Steve woke up with electricity in his veins and his lips tingling. He gasped taking in what felt like a first breath of life. It tasted full and sweet. He felt light, washed clean, newly revitalized, freshly baptized into a new existence. The curse was gone; he felt it, glad for the relief. But there was more than just this now freedom pulsing through him. Although dead only briefly by earthly time while in the spirit realm profound, timeless and hearty experiences, feelings and enlightenments had gleamed onto him. Moments unworthy of crude earth explanations; moments, sights and sensations which would only be perversely debased, like casting pearls before swine, if an attempt were made to use the alphabet to try and describe. Moments mostly shared with one who, like him, had been brought to death through the same curse and then resurrected, by the permission of the ultimate supreme, by the same spell. This bound them in a shared understanding. "Oh god," he whispered. *I must find her now, as soon as I can* he thought.

He ran and hailed a cab. "To Skykomish," he said. The cab drove towards Skykomish. Steve had him pull over by the side of the forest road in a seemingly random spot. Steve paid, got out and raced through the trees. *Weirdest destination I ever got* thought the cab driver.

Steve raced eagerly, excitedly, leaping over fallen logs and large ferns, dodging tree trunks, barely slowing to marvel at the deer he scared away. There in a tight open clearing by a stream and a large rock bathed in sunlight he saw her. He stopped, caught his breath and then was breathless all over again. In the flesh! There she stood! Glowing and alive again! She faced him and smiled brightly a brilliant smile; every inch of her angelic. He burst into happy tears at the reunion. There she was again no longer spirit but earthly matter; still he recognized her as surely as his own hand. There she was. His queen, his goddess, his best friend, his destined partner, Zelda.

"We made it!" he called triumphantly.

She beamed back at him. She couldn't speak right away. She opened her arms. He ran to her. They embraced. She burst into tears of joy. "My eternal," she declared.

CHAPTER TWENTY SEVEN

**

The following March Steve and Zelda went on a cruise from Miami to Mexico with the band Paramour and special guests in the 2nd annual event with the great title "Parahoy". He liked Paramour; their "Ain't it Fun" song was a joyous self-independent anthem and their "Only Exception" was actually brilliant he thought; perfectly romantic without any schmaltz or insincerity or manipulation; a classic, one of the best rock-love songs, which are really hard to pull off convincingly, ever, as just two of many examples of their impressive catalog. One of the "special guests" on the cruise was Chvruches. They were the co-headliners, or the biggest name after Paramour on the list anyways, along with some other pretty great and respectably exciting bands, as well, Haley from Paramour had informed in the video announcing it, great DJ's and funny comedians. At the concert in Nashville not long after Steve and Julie had seen them in Seattle, Haley and Lauren sang a buoyant version of the song "Bury It" ("Rise Above") together which had been captured and posted on YouTube. Steve was still a fan of Chvrches, and Lauren, but not in any weird and silly unhealthy way which causes sadness from obsession or anything; just in the simple way that enjoyable good things should bring enjoyment and goodness in one's life. Zelda had also become a fan: he introduced them to her. She also liked the other bands on the cruise. They were both justifiably excited for the trip, giddy even as the days counted down until launch. It was a miracle they had been able to get tickets. Or, for normal people it would be. But for those who have died and come back to life by magic, those who have seen and felt what both had seen and felt, secrets they could tell no one except each other, such 'miracles' are attainable. Steve presented Zelda with the cruise tickets Christmas morning. He had slipped them in her Christmas stocking in their lavish Brooklyn pad. Their excitement in anticipating the trip had been validated. Awesome people, fellow fans, friends for life made, memories for life made, silliness happening, beautiful views, romantic moments, excellent concerts and DJ's and comedians, dancing, relaxing; it was all so great.

Steve hugged Zelda as they watched, swayed, and sung along to Haley singing "Only Exception" one night. She sings about how her parents were divorced and broken hearted and as a kid this made her never to want to sing about love because she didn't believe in it. But then she met someone who changed her mind. Someone who made her decided to 'take the risk' despite the potential for hurt. Later that night he stood with Zelda leaning against the railing, looking out at the moonshine sparkle the ocean waves. A pod of dolphins leaped up as if in greeting swimming along with the boat.

"Are you thinking about her?" Zelda asked. She knew the answer. They knew each other's thoughts and feelings.

Steve looked at her. He nodded his head yes.

"You'll always love her, won't you? A part of you."

"It in no way diminishes my love for you. But yes," Steve answered. "I care about her. I'm hopeful that we can one day be friends again."

"Can you see how your life would have turned out? If you had married her; before... everything? Before the curse?"

"Yes," Steve answered. "We would have been happy. Even when tracks lead to unintended destinations to places that are not meant to be, there can still be contentment and happiness attained. For a time anyways. But not fully, not as well as true destiny wants it. When I saw you in the ethereal plane... what we saw together, what we shared... for all that time..."

"Yes," Zelda said. "It was sacred."

"No, after that, no, I could not have been happy with her," Steve answered. "It breaks my heart a little to admit it, since I do love her. But I would not have been able to stop thinking about..."

"Yes, don't say it out loud," Zelda said, placing her hand on his arm. "I know of what you mean. It is too sacred."

"Too beautiful for this earth," Steve said.

Zelda giggled. "That was a great concert though."

Steve smiled at her. "It was," he said in agreement. "I love you so much."

"I love you," she echoed back with deep sincerity.

"I love you too," he echoed once again. "I can't say it enough."

They kissed and there was perfect harmony in the universe smiling down on their pretty little heads.

**

Julie had a tough time dealing with the breakup. She fell into a depression that was nearly as bad as if it were magical curse created. It lasted longer than two days. She had never felt that way before; so defeated, hopeless and lonely. At times throughout her dealing, with the help of friends, professional help, medications, she had thought that she was over it, adjusted, moved on, everything's well, but then the darkness would hit her as blatantly as a bird in the face after having lurked behind like a shadow. She lost her interior designer job and found work as a Starbucks barista. Her father helped to pay her rent. Sometimes she felt like she was on the way to enjoying life as she had before, other times if she had a loaded gun at her hip she'd point it to her temple and pull the trigger just as Steve had.

She played piano as a kid and a bit of the violin. She was a star student in her chamber and jazz choir classes in high school, just as she excelled in all of her classes. Yet, being grounded and level headed she of course never entertained the idea of ever making any money by singing. She enjoyed music but had never really delved deeply into various indie-music scenes, locally or nationally, reading Pitchfork or other such sites much; not caught up on what the most heralded, edgy, hip, and best musical offerings were out there on the fringes. All that noise had been mostly mute to her, not that she was against it or wasn't open, but to really be on top of it all requires a hobbyist time consuming dedication. Steve kept up on that stuff more than she did, both newer stuff and older obscure yet still great stuff; one of his many traits which she thought made him "cooler" than her; him introducing her to new bands and sounds she had previously been unaware of but then quickly come to love because he loved them and the songs made her think of him and how much she loved him was great in its own way. But it also symbolized to her how all great and healthy relationships involve venturing into new discoveries, being taken to new places, a continual expansion as two smaller worlds collide to make one bigger world.

After the breakup and everything that had happened she had somehow fallen into the whole other world of the local indie rock band scene despite, at first, feeling like she didn't fit in, not being a smoker or ever much of a drinker, no tattoos. She and Steve were "Disney nerds" after all. She still was; she still loved the whole wholesome "Disney Princess" aesthetic and memes, thought children's laugher the greatest sound on earth, and constantly yearned to go to Disneyworld and Disneyland again. As a college graduate she was someone who supposedly has already entered the 'real adult world' where youthful delusions of grandeur, such as transforming your little local noisy band into a world touring global force of power and influence, creating ruckuses in Japanese and Amsterdam airports and whatever else, are no longer supposed to have sway in determining life directions. At a certain age, an age which Julie suspected she was at, or about to reach, one is supposed to release the grasp of such fantasies and get a bit more real; survival and optimal functionality in the real world demands that you face reality, as much of a bummer as doing so may be.

Yet she was in desperate need of escape. The loud local indie rock and music scene offered her some escape. The local bands and fans atmosphere was a swirling strange mix of brash fun, desperate hope, willful delusions, tingling exciting anticipations, melancholy shoe gazing, blazing inflated egos, shameless and embarrassing hustling and begging, grimy boy-stink, constraints and freedoms. Sometimes the music was loud, messy, harsh and honestly awful, but she sometimes liked it like that in how it mirrored her misery and life. Other times the music or some moment would reach a level of transcendent beauty that felt like it lifted her above the crude realm of earthly matter into an unearthly bliss. There were the moments she lived for.

Her first fuck since Steve was with Ian, the lead singer, coincidentally, of a band named Mayberry (an old English name he discovered and liked doing a genealogy project). She fucked him because she wanted it and she had enjoyed it but there was also an element of self-abuse derived from a type of self-hatred aspect to it; a sad and angry rebound fuck. She knew Ian slept around a lot and she was being basically like some floozy groupie.

That, however, didn't turn out to be the case. Ian had told other girls they were special and not like the others, but with Julie his claim was true. *There's something different about you* he had told her, and the way he said it made the cliché sound original. *It's like you're an angel who had been dragged through the mud of hell. Your wings have been damaged and ruffled yet you can still fly. You just need to reclaim your confidence.* It was a loopy thing to say; Ian had a way of speaking where she suspected that he were trying out poetic potential lyrics to hear how they sound out loud. Yet his words caused her to think *how did you know?* And *Thank you, that was so sweet; I needed to hear that.*

A few days later Julie and Ian ate together at Sweetly Cursed. After the breakup with Steve Julie had stayed in her house and Steve had moved all the way to Brooklyn (the further the better; good riddance) with Zelda for some mystic bullshit reason involving some magical shared vision they had while they were both dead together engaging in icky spiritual sex for years, each second on earth a year in the spirit realm, or wherever they were, or whatever. It was silly, Julie thought. Silly and dumb. Never mind that they had both been brought back from the dead because of her, basically. Screw them both—she hopes they're happy. She was working on eroding the sarcasm of that wish into sincerity. Sarah remained Julie's roommate and became her local club and indie-music scene buddy. Neither considered the other 'girlfriend' in the romantic way, neither did they self identify as lesbians, but they sometimes kissed, mostly for their own pleasure and not just to titillate or entertain the watching boys in the clubs and venues and bars.

In the corner café where Julie and Steve had spent so much time, had so many stimulating, funny and energizing conversations, where they had discovered some cool music, Ian told Julie that he wanted to try a new musical venture and he wanted her to be the front woman. He said he had become bored with Mayberry; the sound and scene was stale, the crowds and enthusiasm diminishing, it was beginning to feel like lugging a broken van uphill rather than riding a wave. He said he had recently become inspired by new electronic synth-pop sounds and bands like Chvrches, Passion Pitt, Disclosure, and he named some others. He told her that he had splurged and bought a synthesizer, taking a stab that the investment will work out. He asked her what she wanted to name the new band. "How about Sweetly Cursed" she answered.

It turned out that Julie was a gifted songwriter and singer. She tapped into her pain and confusion to create art. She wrote songs of sorrow, anger and also triumph. Not that she had yet felt so triumphant, although it was a victory that she was still alive. She wrote of what she wanted, who she wanted to be, in place of where she actually was, emotionally, for some songs. She wrote partly with vengeance in mind, imagining Steve marveling over her celebrity and success, ruing the day he let such a musical goddess slip away. Or, that was part of it. She also wrote, sung and performed as a method for healing. One poem she wrote which she used as lyrics are as follows:

She sighed saying sadness in sails
Blows me adrift
Waterfalls falls splashes bounces back up creates a mist
She wants to see his silhouette there, whispers it
It's you I miss, it's you I miss
I call bullshit
The horizon lines not so far away still
I rip down the stars points bleed my hands
You can't do all I will
Please stop, don't try to understand
Some get sad, some mad, some glad
I'll claim all three
But gladness stomps madness stomps sadness
I'll never say sorry.

She imagined one day inviting Steve and Zelda to one of her conquering concerts and after her blistering performance, the crowd happy and enthralled in her hands, she'd greet them backstage and they'd share beers and talk and laugh and maybe cry a little bit and everything would be totally fine. That's what she desperately wanted; for everything just to be fine. No more hurt feelings, no remorse, no pain, no more insanity or suffering. They'd thank her for bringing them together; she'd apologize for… well… for shooting Zelda (they'd laugh) and for having made that dumb list of 'marriage buster' adjectives in the first place. She'd tell Steve that she still hates him (they'd laugh) but a part of her will still always love him. She just can't let a love that was that huge, that full, just empty and disappear so easily, even with the trick of transforming a big chunk of that love into hate (laugh; just kidding; not really; but really though). But seriously, a love that powerful just can't completely fade during a lifetime. But she's moved on. She's doing well (understatement; laugh). She's fine, she'd tell them. Honestly, I'm fine. Everything's fine.

"Sweetly Cursed" blazed on the local music scene like a earthquake. They were good. Great, actually. Despite different tastes, types of genres and the subjective nature of personal enjoyments and art, it was still almost instantly obvious that "Sweetly Cursed," Julie more specifically, were special, just as Ian had known. They had something. Word spread quickly. The internet promotions helped as, of course, did Julie's beauty. They soon packed the biggest mid-size venues in Seattle, Portland and Vancouver. On stage Julie felt like she escaped into a different world. She loved it. She found comfort in the escape like a mermaid returning to water. She danced, scowled, laughed, jumped, sweat and cried up there. And the crowd loved it. They loved her.

She stood over the crowd gripping the microphone. She had a powerful aura in her stage performance; an aura which exuded even in promo pictures; an aura difficult to describe, but an other worldliness about her, like she's traveled to other planets and knows things others don't know, or that she'd been touched by something supernatural. "Our last gig got a bad review!" she shouted out in stage banter. This was a lie. Still the crowd booed and Julie laughed at their reaction. "But they just don't get it. This is fucking poetry man!" The crowd laughed and cheered lustily. She basked in their adoration, thinking in the back of her mind *how the hell did this happen. All of it. You just can't always predict the turns life will take you*

*on. I always thought you could; I was so careful, so intricate in
my planning, in working to attain my goals; a happy wife with
good friends, a good fulfilling job, cute adorable kids, yearly
trips to Disneyworld and Paris. But I guess life can have a way
of knocking you over and saying, nope, instead you'll be a rock
goddess on a stage singing sad songs to electronic beats to a
adoring crowd. I never would have guessed this. Yet weirdly it
still feels right. It feels like it was meant to be.* "This song is
called Back to Blue" she called out. The crowd screamed in
appreciative anticipation. Julie sang and most of the crowd sang
along:

*They said the pages foretold my destiny
I read you must suffer to never be lonely
Then three sins crawled up to posses me
Rage, lust and jealousy
I reveled in it but I broke through, always thinking of you*

*They said play or die
They said run and hide
I admit, I cried, I cried, I cried
But look at me now, like a jet I fly
All to get away from you
And to turn the red sky back to blue*

*They said my story's already written
They said I've been smitten by all I'll be smitten
But then three sins crawled up to posses me
Disgust, depression and stupidity
I reveled in it but I broke through all for you*

Let the pages from my story burn
Let lessons learned be learned
Now throw the cursed book far away
With new pen and blank page I start another day
Character, plot, conflict, verse
All to conclude in climax with coffins in hearse
But I threw that story away
I bleed life into a new day
Still I wonder who can love me now?

Steve died
He didn't want me
He came back to life
He still didn't want me
But I'll survive anyway.

**

Candice and Julie's relationship was demolished, obviously. This ending was nearly just as devastating to Julie as the death of her and Steve's relationship. It factored nearly just as much into Julie's initial malaise of shocked sadness after all that happened.

Candice struggled with the ruptured relationship with Julie as well. Yes, she had wanted to exact some revenge against Julie for always being so skeptical, for not being supportive, and mainly for committing her to the mental hospital. But she had wanted to do so in a way where she wouldn't be blamed or suffer repercussions. Her 'plan' wasn't expertly thought out, but she possessed the power and will. There actually was a modicum of truth, more than she ever admitted to herself, in the accusation that she didn't always think clearly or rationally. She wouldn't have minded if Steve had died (or stayed dead) but it had never been her intention to permanently harm Julie. She believed that despite Julie's love obsession with Steve, Steve wasn't right for her anyways. The astrology did not have Steve's and Julie's names entwined together in the stars. Part of her believed that while extracting some revenge against Julie, Steve, Annabelle and the Coven, she'd actually be doing both Steve and Julie a favor by breaking them up, either through stress or Steve's death.

Julie's emerging musical success and exciting potential was won by her own merits and talents. But, as with most successes, especially within sports and the arts, after the first requirement of being excellent is met, good fortune, or luck, are a major contributing factor. There are tons of examples of works of art, in all felids, that under other more providential circumstances would be, could be, much more admired, seen and praised than they end up being; conversely some works of lesser quality become huge. Despite all the study, no one really knows exactly why that is; why things catch on while other things don't. In regards to Julie's musical luck Candice, unbeknownst to Julie, had been a benefit. Candice had cast a "success spell" over Julie; a powerful spell that exerts a great coast against the caster; were it not so witches would rule the world rather than remain hidden. Nature demands a balance. Matter, even spiritual matter from which fortunes and fates dwell, cannot be conjured or created from nothing. Candice's "success spell" over Julie had drained all of Candice's Wicca juice dry. Misfortune befell her, although she was already so downcast, never knowing a boyfriend, never with any friends, never with much of her own money (her father didn't lend to her like he did Julie; he had always loved Julie more than her) that she had hardly noticed much of a difference in her daily life. She did notice, acutely, painfully, the un-tethering between her and nature which she had once derived so much delicious strength and joy and superiority from. The winds, sun rays and cosmos didn't coarse through her pulsating veins with any more force than it did any other human. Crows no longer responded to her whispers.

She walked along the Seattle pier on a cold drab grey rainy winter day. An old lady draped in orange scarves and crystal trinkets badgered strolling tourists under umbrellas asking to tell their fortunes in exchange for a dollar or two. One sunny, despite the rain, attractive young couple decided to take the bait. Candice observed them.

"Hmmm… let's see here, give me your hands," the old fortune teller said. The young couple showed their palms and the old lady examined them. Before the old lady could grant them her predictions, something fortune cookie flattering and life affirming picked from stock, Candice barged in. "Whatever she says is not true," Candice said. "You cause your own fate. You write your own story. Any other information is false."

The End

Thanks for reading. If you like, please leave a rating and review on Amazon and Goodreads and wherever else and tell a friend. I also have a bunch of other books including:

Mortimer the Vampire and Drake the Dragon

Dance and Basketball Love

Amber's Summer

Cassandra's Comet

Alice Pranks

Alice's Summer Road Trip

Pink Frost

Sarah's War Journal

Delano in Hollyhook

And a bunch of others, all for 99 cents on Amazon Kindle, as well as paperback. Feel free to email me at cameronglenn224@gmail.com

51190417R00162

Made in the USA
Charleston, SC
12 January 2016